Praise for *Lost Luggage*

2018 Macavity Award nominee for Best First Novel
2018 Lefty Award nominee for Best Debut Mystery

"Thomas makes a rollicking debut with this comic mystery featuring an unconventional protagonist who proves to have the skills of MacGyver. With its sexy overtones, this fun, character-driven novel will appeal to Janet Evanovich fans."

—*Library Journal* (starred review)

"A breath of fresh air in a world gone mad . . . has my vote for one of the best new characters in mystery/crime."

—Kathy Boone Reel, *The Reading Room*

"Thank heavens! I've been waiting for years to find a successor to Janet Evanovich, and I've finally found one."

—Cathy G. Cole for Kittling Books

"Ms. Thomas has an absolutely lunatic talent for plot and one of the funniest first-person voices I've read in years . . . what kept coming to my mind as I read this were comedy films from the 30s—for me, the golden age of American film humor."

—Timothy Hallinan, Lefty winner and Edgar and Macavity Award-nominated author of the Junior Bender and Poke Rafferty novels

"Thomas packs a whole franchise's worth of adventures into her heroine's debut . . ."

—*Kirkus Reviews*

"Laugh-out-loud funny and enchantingly ridiculous . . . highly entertaining . . ."

—Jessica Howard, *Shelf Awareness*

Praise for *Drowned Under*

2020 Anthony Award nominee for Best Paperback Original
2020 Lefty Nominee for Best Humorous Mystery

"The passenger list in Wendall Thomas's *Drowned Under* is a cavalcade of randy former nuns, gigolos, stowaways, near-extinct marsupials . . . and one brilliantly sexy disaster of a globetrotting travel agent named Cyd Redondo. Thanks to her wildly creative mind, the fruits of which produce frequent affronts to her dignity, Cyd is easily one of my favorite amateur sleuths in fiction today. Thomas's writing flows effortlessly, and her plotting is complex but perfectly tied together. This is a remarkable novel in what is shaping up to be an exciting and hilarious series. Don't miss *Drowned Under* or its predecessor, *Lost Luggage*. You'll love Cyd, perhaps the funniest heroine out there. Highest recommendation."
—James W. Ziskin, Anthony, Barry, and Macavity Award-winning author of the Ellie Stone Mysteries

"Bravo. Cyd Redondo, Redondo Travel, is at it again. What a wonderful sequel to *Lost Luggage*. With her clever mind, tart comebacks, and Balenciaga tote bag, Cyd is a fearsome force. I love her pluck, the way she digs her way out of trouble, and her willingness to do everything she can— even die—for her clientele. What a heroine for the modern age. Do not miss this!"
—Daryl Wood Gerber, Agatha Award-winning national bestselling author of the Cookbook Nook and French Bistro Mysteries

"*Drowned Under* is laugh-out-loud funny. With its finely tuned timing and zany, emotional protagonist, this novel puts Thomas in a class with Carl Hiassen and Janet Evanovitch."
—Nancy Tingley, Lefty-nominated author of the Jenna Murphy Mysteries

"Fans of Janet Evanovich's Stephanie Plum will cotton to Cyd."
—*Publishers Weekly*

Books by Wendall Thomas

Cyd Redondo Mysteries

Lost Luggage
Drowned Under
Fogged Off

Fogged Off

A Cyd Redondo Mystery

Wendall Thomas

For Grady Thomas, my dad and my compass.
I would give anything to be able to travel to where you are.

Acknowledgments

First and always, I'm grateful to James Bartlett, who dropped whatever he was doing to read pages, let me talk through a story problem, tell me whether the Tube was capitalized, or laugh at my jokes. His love, support, patience, good humor, and regular delivery of wildflowers during the writing of this novel was monumental. There is no better husband to be had.

I also have a sister for the ages. I could not have finished the book without Kim Thomas Stout's belief, counsel, imagination, good sense, and lightning-fast turnaround. Thank you, Belina.

This novel also would not have been possible without the kindness of Emily Richard and Edward Petherbridge. Thank you for taking me to Kenwood and to Gordon's, and for giving me a home away from home in West Hampstead for so many years.

Thank you Daryl Wood Gerber, Rochelle Staab, Nancy Cole Silverman, Howard Michael Gould, Nancy Tingley, Smith Richardson, Gabriel Valjan, and Patty Smiley for crucial notes and support and to Paige Shelton, Jim Ziskin, and Catriona McPherson for the early reads. I will never forget your generosity during a time when everything was a struggle for everyone.

I am eternally grateful to Bill Harris at Beyond the Page for being my dream editor and publisher. Your particular combination of professionalism and enthusiasm has been positively inspiring and I am so happy the series will live on with you.

Thanks, as always, to the readers, book sellers, bloggers, and reviewers who have been so kind to Cyd and her purse.

Finally, in many ways this book is an ode to libraries and museums, so sincere thanks to all the wonderful, heroic librarians, curators, scholars, artists, architects, and taxidermists who have created and protected the spaces where I have learned so much and been so happy.

Chapter One

January 2007

"Jack the Ripper had it made."

"Cyd! If you're going to babble, babble en route." Debbie Pinkowski slapped a twenty on the deli counter, grabbed our Italian heroes, and shoved me out the door.

"I'm not endorsing spree killers or anything. It's just, you know, no surveillance." I could hear Debbie's eye-roll over the click of my kitten heels. "Seriously. The man, if it was a man, sliced up five women, in public, walked home drenched in blood and entrails, and is still getting away with it, hundreds of years later. I have one drink, one drink, with Sally Jessup's cousin—in Queens, for God's sake—and it winds up in the *Bay Ridge Sentinel*. Now I'm a pariah. Again."

"He's off-limits. Everybody knows that."

"He's off-limits for sex or marriage. Not bourbon."

"Bourbon leads to marriage."

"I am living, breathing, 150 percent proof that that's not true."

I checked my watch. It was street cleaning day. We sped up. Debbie and I had race-walked in synch since the first day of kindergarten, when we both sprinted for the thirty-foot rectory wall to escape Sister Ignatius Clara Clegg's lead-filled ruler. We bonded over matching broken ankles and had been avoiding punishments and parking tickets together ever since.

We turned onto 77th Street. It was still lopsided. I might be lucky. Bay Ridge Brooklyn's "alternate side parking" meant when the city cleaned one side of the street, everyone double-parked on the other, making the whole neighborhood list to one side. This inevitably led to "neighborly altercations"—i.e., assaults—in the hours when half the neighborhood was blocked in. The instant the time was up, if you hadn't moved, they'd hit you up with a huge ticket—like the one on the windshield of my emerald green 1965 Ford Galaxie 500.

One of my New Year's resolutions had been to swear less. Well, that didn't last. As the youngest—and only girl—in a family of ten macho, overprotective cousins, I tended to swear a lot, especially when the object was the Department of Parking Services. I use the word *services* loosely.

"See? This is what I'm talking about. How can I be the only person with a ticket? It's Big Brousin everywhere I go. I can't sneeze without a client dropping by with Benadryl." Bay Ridge still felt like a small town, made smaller by the fact that I either was related to, had gone to school with, or dated about seventy percent of the population and booked the other thirty percent for their Golden Retirement Getaway. "How can everyone know I ate a whole box of Wheat Thins in one sitting last week? Is someone going through my recycling on an hourly basis?"

"You ate a box of Wheat Thins in an hour?"

"So?" I glared at her, then at the ticket, tempted to tear it up. But if I did, there'd be no chance my brousin Frank, newly restored to Detective status, could fix it for me. I rammed it into my red vintage Balenciaga bag and considered relocating to Iceland, which was thirty percent off at the moment on Lufthansa.

I unlocked the door for Debbie. We were due at an underground poker game I needed to win and no one in my family needed to know about. I checked the rearview mirror every six seconds for familiar vehicles and tuned my scanner for the 68th Precinct's radar. We were almost through Fort Hamilton when my new cell phone rang. Debbie held it up to my ear.

"Cyd Redondo, Redondo Travel."

Debbie commandeered the wheel while I repeated a few "Rights" and "Okays," and finally, "Thank you, bye." She sighed as I took the wheel back and started the fifteen-point turn the acre-wide Galaxie required.

"What is it this time? The Gottis leave their CPAP at Euro Disney?"

"Nope. Body."

Chapter Two

"A body. Right."

"Shep Helnikov. Heart attack. Isn't that awful? He keeled over in his bedsit in London."

"Bedsit? Who are you, Tiny Tim?"

"Sorry, I've been bingeing *Prime Suspect*. Anyway, he was there for his yearly trip and I guess his heart or something else vital gave out. I'm his emergency contact. I need to handle the paperwork and make some calls."

"What's the hurry? He's not going anywhere."

I finished my turn back toward the neighborhood. "That's not the point. He's a client."

"If you go by the office, we both know what's going to happen." I chose not to look at her, for obvious reasons. "So what do you actually have to do? Ship him back? Who pays for that?"

"I always get my clients full repatriation insurance."

"Does that come with auto?"

"I'm serious. It's not like the British government has a special slush fund to transport aging lotharios who ignore their cholesterol back home."

"Shep Helnikov? A lothario? Seriously?"

"Well, according to him and, well, Sister Ellery."

"No."

I shrugged. "She called it a blip."

"Well, if anyone knows about blips, it's you and Sister Ellery."

"Really? What about Nathan O'Connor?"

"More of a bleep than a blip, to be honest."

"Ha."

"Well, can you at least drop me at Food World? I'm out of Babybels."

I swerved into the Food World parking lot, which was crammed, as per usual, since Wednesday was "stale bread on sale" day. I asked Debbie to snag me some baguettes.

"They'll be weapons by the time you get them."

"Croutons in progress. Aunt Helen will love me."

"No, she'll just tolerate you. You can always come stay with me, you know."

Debbie had lost her parents when she was fifteen and moved to Coney Island to live with her grandmother, who'd passed two years ago. Debbie kept the walk-up and the furniture, which smelled like gravy and home.

I understood. I could totally see myself hanging on to Uncle Leon's Barcalounger and Gary, his bison head, or Aunt Helen's Dutch ovens and sherry glasses, not to mention my mother's collection of trendy gardening tools. After all, I still drove my late father's car and kept his compass in my purse at all times.

"I'll keep it in mind." I wouldn't, but I loved her for asking.

She air-pecked me so as not to waste our shared supply of Wet & Wild's discontinued Responsible Raisin—no animals were killed making this lipstick—and opened the car door, then froze.

"Duck!" She squatted down below window level and jerked me to the seat.

"What?"

"It's Pam Owens."

"They let her out?"

"I think she's working at the craft store on day release. Incoming, ten o'clock."

I looked left. "Oh God." Pam Owens was Chip Jessup's former fiancée and headed for the driver's side.

"Traitor! Slut! Slut traitor!"

The entire parking lot turned to watch Pam, in a flowered smock and an unplanned ombré color job, bang on my driver's-side window, then climb on the hood.

"It was business!" I said, grateful the Galaxie was built like a battleship.

"Yes! Whore business!"

A gray-haired man in a golf shirt and khakis arrived, grabbed Pam by her waist, and pulled her down.

"You have customers waiting, Pam. We don't want to have to let you go."

She burst into tears, then leaned back toward my window. "How did he look? Was he wearing that pink shirt I gave him?"

The man touched her arm. "Pam? Register."

She gave me a double middle finger salute and headed back toward the shopping center.

I rolled my window down. "Sorry, Jerry. It was just a drink, honest."

"You should be ashamed of yourself." He shook his head and walked away.

Well, anyone who hadn't witnessed this scene would hear about it at the Third Avenue Businessperson's Association meeting, where Jerry, owner of Artsy Fartsy, was a member-at-large.

Debbie pushed off the seat to standing position.

"Thanks for sticking up for me," I said.

"You did fine. Let the governments handle the Shep stuff, you've got enough on your plate." Several cars honked at me as I pulled out of the lot.

I swung into the parking spot behind Redondo Travel. Due to a recent break-in, we had double dead bolts, which froze up if it went below forty degrees. In the old Bay Ridge, no one locked anything. If something got taken, everyone knew who did it, or knew exactly what the stranger looked like. Nonresidents were subjected to stares worthy of a police lineup.

Maybe the old Bay Ridge was over. After I WD-40'd the lock open and entered, I hung my coat on the rack, flipped on the lights, and headed to the front of the office and my desk/sanctuary. Redondo Travel was started by my great-grandfather, Guido Redondo. My Uncle Ray had run it until a few months ago, when he'd had to make an unexpected change of residence, and, at least for the next eighteen months, or ten for good behavior, it was all mine.

At least I didn't feel like a complete fraud anymore. For my first sixteen years as a travel agent, I'd never actually been farther than New Jersey. It hadn't been from lack of trying. I'd booked dozens of holidays for myself, from Winnetka to Bora Bora, but every time, something would conveniently come up with the business or the family, or my mother would lay on the guilt about leaving her "drowning in Redondos," and I'd be forced to cancel. I'd tried to overcompensate with research but now, with two international trips under my belt, at least all of my knowledge wasn't theoretical. I could look my clients straight in their cataracts and say Business Class was worth it and Global Entry wasn't.

I lit the Maui Breeze travel candle on my desk and observed a moment of silence for Shep Helnikov. When you specialized in senior citizens, losing clients was part of the job, but that didn't make it any easier. Besides, Shep had only been sixty.

I could still see him standing over my desk, shoving his wedge of jet-black bangs off his forehead with his palm and a jerk of his head. I don't know if he always stood up because he was an adjunct professor and permanently in lecture mode, or because of his sciatica, which flared up regularly and required an aisle seat. He would loom over my desk, his leather-elbowed jacket gaping over his embroidered waistcoat and school tie—he had either gone to Yale or raided a thrift store in New Haven—and make me squeal with disgusting details about toads in the hole and back-alley prostitution. It was heady stuff for a sixteen-year-old.

Shep was the reason I'd had Jack the Ripper on my mind. He was an expert on the legendary psychopath and I arranged his trips to London every winter to teach Homicide History at a London university and lead Jack the Ripper tours in the East End. I had his bestseller, *Jacked!*, by my bed and had started it several times. He'd been researching the sequel, *All Jacked Up*, when he died.

I had to stop thinking about him or I would just cry. I could do him the most good by calling our insurance carrier and getting the paperwork for the repatriation in motion. If memory served, he'd only been in London for two weeks. I always did his bookings a year ahead, as we got the best prices that way.

I pulled up his file and froze. It had been opened on December twenty-third. While I was in Australia. The user had been my hapless brousin, Jimmy. I got a horrible feeling.

Chapter Three

Why were my horrible feelings always right?

The booking had been changed—by Jimmy—with four days added, including a two-day getaway to Paris on the Eurostar.

Jimmy was my Uncle Ray's youngest son, for anyone who considered forty-three young. At thirty-two myself, I hoped it was. He'd been banished by the family to suburban Fresno to avoid questioning on charges I hesitate to mention, but had snuck back briefly over the holidays. He'd obviously been in the office while I was away.

Although I hate to speak ill of family, Jimmy, despite his Redondo heritage, was possibly the worst travel agent on earth. He was rude to clients, never double-checked or followed up on anything, and could barely manage a seat assignment without losing his attention span. He had once put a visa application in for a hamster, as the hamster's name, Rusty, was the only thing he remembered from a client's call.

I jumped to Shep's insurance contract. I was psychotic about travel insurance and included the full package in any travel estimate I gave my clients, especially when they were going overseas. Since a majority of them were over sixty-five, I always took out the maximum for medical, medical airlift, and repatriation, to ensure their return would be covered, dead or alive. Without coverage, costs in these situations could run anywhere from ten thousand to half a million dollars. I had five red arrows pointing to it on every reservation file I created. I guess in Jimmy's case, I needed six.

Like most insurance policies, there were a zillion exclusions. It was crucial to follow all the rules to the letter, especially the one about immediately alerting them to any changes in dates or destinations. Jimmy hadn't.

Which meant, since the trip was already in progress when Shep died, the policy was void, including the repatriation fee, which by itself could run upwards of thirty grand. Not only was Helnikov's return to the U.S. not covered, but because of an arcane rider, if a travel agent had booked the package, they were responsible for covering said return. They meaning me.

I called my insurance broker at Wander Safe, my go-to travel insurance company, hoping they would take pity on me. But my contact was on maternity leave and her replacement wouldn't budge. I think we can all agree, corporations are only good neighbors when legally forced to be.

I was already panicked about meeting the monthly bills—hence the poker game I'd been heading to—and now we'd be on the hook for thousands more. Was body retrieval a write-off? I'd have to ask Abe, my accountant. Possibly from jail.

I couldn't face the calls I had to make and was just about to head into my supply closet, which included a kickboxing bag, when the office door opened.

"See you're in the paper today, Miss Big Stuff." Sister Ellery Malcomb, my former eighth-grade teacher, dressed as usual in an alarming shade of orange, with her white hair spiky on top and flattened on the sides—imagine Ziggy Stardust with arthritis—flopped into the chair across from my desk and opened a newspaper. "'Sightings,' no less."

"Sightings" was the "Page Six" of the *Bay Ridge Sentinel*, without the wit. Or the celebrities. Written by former cheerleader and now bored Amway wife Janine Jablonsky, it was the epitome of sleazy innuendo.

Sister Ellery put on her reading glasses. "'Seen in Queens, a certain Bay Ridge travel agent and a former Bay Ridge football star cozying up over cocktails. Are wedding bells finally on the horizon for someone so close to her sell-by date?' That Janine Jablonsky is a real hag. Plus she could never spell."

Janine spent most of her time lurking around the parking lots of Bay Ridge, Fort Hamilton, and Red Hook, looking for cars that weren't where they were supposed to be. What she'd been doing in Queens, I had no idea.

"So, Chip Jessup, huh?"

"No. It was work."

She rolled her eyes.

"Seriously. He called me. I'd heard Peggy Newsome left his family stranded in Tonga during a cyclone. I thought I might be able to swing the whole clan over to us. They have cousins galore, who do three big vacations a year. They would be a great acquisition."

"Acquisition is an interesting word."

"Nothing happened!" I realized that Peggy Newsome, my travel agent nemesis, was probably the one who gave Janine the "sighting." It would be just like her to turn her mistake into my walk of shame.

"Well, anyway, I'd stay away from Chadwick's for a week or two if I were you." Sister Ellery grinned at me, then noticed the candle and crossed herself. "Who died?"

I told her about Shep Helnikov. And how Redondo Travel could be over for good.

"Oh ye of little faith. A solution will arrive."

She winked at me as she headed out the door and back upstairs to the apartment I was supposed to have inherited. Long story. I sat down and looked at the clock. It was too late in London to call the U.S. Embassy.

Knowing what had happened to Shep magnified my baseline client guilt about a thousand-fold, so I did a spot check. I booked a lot of winter holidays to Europe. If you avoided ski resorts, it was much cheaper for hardy seniors on a budget who'd already had their hips replaced. I had two couples on a Paris, the City of Museums tour (baguettes, Gauloises, and the *Mona Lisa*, optional), one couple celebrating their silver anniversary being "bundled" outside Copenhagen, and two life partners checking out the Gaudi buildings and low-cholesterol tapas in Barcelona. They'd all arrived and were listed as alive.

The bell on the door went again. "Don't tell me, I've made *Newsweek*."

"Have you? How very surprising."

Chapter Four

This charming remark came from a puffy man in a Brooks Brothers suit too crisp to be secondhand. I would have taken him for a banker, except for the eternal male mistake—the bow tie. Still, that often signified aged prep school graduates who had money for upscale travel.

"Cyd Redondo, Redondo Travel." I rose and held out my hand.

He gave it a cursory shake, unworthy of Harvard.

"Ah, Miss Redondo. I'm Dean Dean McAfferty. Brooklyn College. I'm here about Adjunct Professor Shephard Helnikov. I was his department head. And colleague, of course."

"I'm sorry, do you know that he's . . ."

"That he's dead. Yes, of course. Pity. Tragic loss. That's why I'm here."

He sat, crossing his bulbous legs and revealing polka-dot socks that echoed the plum in his bow tie. Dear lord.

"What can I do for you, Mr. McAfferty?"

"Dean McAfferty, please. I'm here on behalf of the college. We'd like you to fly to London and accompany Helnikov's remains and belongings back to Brooklyn."

"Dean McAfferty, dealing with the repatriation requires an executor or next of kin."

"Or the executor's designated representative," the dean said.

"Are you the executor?"

"No." He pulled out a slip of paper. "Your uncle, Mr. Leon Spartacus Redondo, is."

My jaw dropped to my underwire. "His middle name is Spartacus?"

"In poor taste, I agree, but apparently, yes. I assume then you're not a close family?"

My total shock kept me from responding to his insults with a knuckle sandwich. Wow. How had my Aunt Helen not let this slip after too much prosecco? The missed opportunities of the times I could have screamed "I am Spartacus!" almost made me weep.

"Miss Redondo?"

"Ms. Redondo, please. I still don't understand. Why don't you ask him to designate you and go yourself?"

"I'm much too busy."

"Right, and you think I can just drop everything here and jump on a plane for you?"

"Well, you'd be compensated, of course, in addition to your plane ticket and hotel. You aren't living in the Dark Ages, you do have a cell phone, correct? We would also cover any fees involved in getting the body back."

I let that hang there for a minute.

"When do I leave?"

Chapter Five

I had opened the first stage of negotiation—show willing.

If growing up in Bay Ridge had taught me anything, it was how to barter. And one of the crucial tenets of bartering—especially over something you absolutely needed—was to ask for huge things in return and act as if you were ready to walk away. It took nerves of steel, but that was the benefit of growing up with ten tough older brousins. I had contact balls, if nothing else.

By the time I was finished with Dean Dean, I had used his credit card (having him call ahead to verify purchase) for a business class return ticket, a four-night hotel reservation (he limited the budget, but I had vouchers I'd been saving for a decade), reservations for transport to and from both airports, as well as enough petty cash in pounds to handle my per diem. I'd walked him down Fourth Avenue to Northwood Bank for this, so I'd have a witness I'd known since first grade, Herbie Ryan.

I tried to get the repatriation money in advance too, but he insisted it was impractical—he would wire that fee directly to the appropriate parties. I did make him sign a letter accepting responsibility, however, also notarized by Herbie.

Since I had all his financial information and was the travel agent on record, I could screw with it all once he was gone. He required a few guarantees in return, which is part of bartering.

"So you'll call the estate agent and have her secure his belongings until you get there?"

"Absolutely. But I have to warn you, legally, the U.S. Consular Service is responsible for retrieving them. They may have already."

"That fast?"

"It probably depends on how many Americans died in London this week."

"Well, let's hope it's a large number," he said. "I will want you to give me a complete list of his paperwork before you return, to be sure all his research materials are intact."

"Of course."

"And, then accompany the body back yourself and deliver it directly to me."

"Are you sure you don't want to do a cremation? Most of my clients' families do, as it's less complicated in terms of Customs and health regulations. And less expensive."

"Absolutely not. The faculty wants a proper viewing." He reached into his wallet and pulled out a worn business card that read "Heep International" with an address at Heathrow. "Mortuary services. They're extremely professional. You can use my name."

"The embassy has their own preferred services, I may not have a choice."

"They should be on the approved list. Get the paperwork signed. Good day."

"You're welcome," I snarled at the swinging door. There was something very strange about all this, and if I hadn't been afraid of losing the business, I might have taken more time to think about it. As it was, I had a lot to arrange.

I didn't want to jinx it until Uncle Leon had signed the documents I'd downloaded from the State Department. First I emailed my real estate contact, Shelagh Gulhogan, who'd helped me find Shep's flat, and told her to keep it locked until I got there. Then I grabbed the paperwork and prepared myself for the icy walk back to 77th Street and my family home, where I'd lived since my annulment from Barry Manzoni. He'd remarried the appalling Angela Hepler and I still got my laundry done for free.

In my opinion, T. S. Eliot notwithstanding, January is the cruelest month. Christmas is over. Everyone is bloated. Unrealistic resolutions hang over your head. If it's not snowing, gray-black snice is melting on everything. There are sales, but all the decent stuff is gone. Everyone's in their post-Christmas belt-tightening, so people aren't spending on luxury vacations. And everyone is either sick, getting over being sick, or worried about getting sick.

I was going to have to ignore all that and figure out a way to tell Uncle Leon, I mean Spartacus, about Shep, if I could keep him still long enough. Since he'd retired as Head Taxidermist for the Museum of Natural History, it seemed harder and harder for him to stay in one place for more than thirty seconds. He was a nomad in the house, wandering from one room to another, occasionally watching nature shows on PBS, but incapable of sitting through the ten minutes of promos before the next show. Come to think of it, no one can sit through those, but still. As I spotted our hedges, I wondered what was up with him.

Of course, the Simpsons still had their holiday decorations up. It normally took a hurricane warning for them to come down. At least a falling pine tree had taken out the twenty-five-foot inflatable snowman. He lay like a filthy white sinkhole in the yard beside our house. I gave him a kick with my Stuart Weiztmans before I headed up the driveway.

Our three-story house was, as usual, ablaze. It was a red brick affair on a long narrow lot, featuring two fir trees surrounded by the topiary that had been my mom's hobby during menopause. It had a bricked-in sun room on the left side and a bay window on the right, separated by a heavy oak door that had withstood a lot of slamming. I heaved it open and almost hit Uncle Leon, who was coming down the front stairs.

He was wearing his standard attire, the kind of tight, sixties-mod suits favored by the Beatles, but tonight he'd added an ascot and looked hyper dapper, even for him.

"I'm going to London," he said.

"You know about Shep?"

"Of course I do. I'm his executor."

"I'm so, so sorry."

He patted my arm. "Yeah. He was just a kid. Will you fix me up?"

"About that," I said. "Want a drink before dinner?"

He pulled me into the den and sloshed us shots of Jack Daniel's.

"Pretend it's vodka," Uncle Leon said. "To Shep."

"To Shep, he will be missed." We shot our bourbons and were quiet for a minute.

"How long 'til dinner?"

"I imagine we'll get the usual run-up."

I told him about my day. He leaned toward me, hands on his bony knees.

"I'm not signing it."

Chapter Six

"What do you mean, you're not signing it? I thought I laid it out. It's the only way to save the business."

"I heard that part. I'm retired, I'm not a nitwit."

"Then why?"

"Because if I do, you won't take me with you."

"Why do you want to come with me?"

He shrugged. "The road's my middle name."

Actually, I thought, it's not. Out loud, I just sighed. Granted, he was the most well-traveled of the Redondos. He'd started his career studying with many of the greatest taxidermists of the twentieth century, in London, Florence, Paris, Venice, and at the Field Museum in Chicago. But since I'd been a kid, he'd never been anywhere. My aunt complained the driveway was too far.

"Aunt Helen will have a cow."

"I've handled her for fifty years. She won't say a word."

"She doesn't have to say anything to be lethal." Aunt Helen had strategically missed me with a couple of pieces of great-grandmother's china many times over the years, when I got in after curfew or snitched on one of my brousins.

"I thought you might say you needed me along."

"Oh brother. And what about Mom? This is going to require a MoMA private tour and four dozen macaroons, at the very least."

"We don't have time for all that," Uncle Leon said. "Give me a minute." He got up. I couldn't believe he was just going to tell her, with no buildup and no gift. Was he insane?

The yelling started before I was out of the chair. In our family, that could mean that the mozzarella wasn't melted properly, but this didn't sound food-related. I went into the hall and leaned my ear against the kitchen door.

"So this is what you've been doing with the long-distance phone calls, on and off, on and off, all day? You're going to see her, aren't you?" Who was her?

"It wasn't her. And that was five years before we even met! Anyway, she's been married for fifty years."

"Happily? Well?"

"I'm not in a position to know that, since I haven't spoken to her for fifty years!"

Oh my God, what were they talking about?

"Then what's with the phone calls?"

"London stuff. I'm Shep's executor. I have to go. Plus, it will help Cyd out of a jam Jimmy got her into. Again."

"Harrumph." My aunt was the only person in the world who could actually say a recognizable harrumph, get away with it, and maintain the impact it had in print.

"Well, you're very quiet, Miss Bridget," Aunt Helen said, slamming the oven door. My mother, Mary Bridget Colleary Redondo, was usually quiet, which was what Aunt Helen—who liked lots of room in a conversation for her pronouncements—preferred.

"I hate to be rude, but I was still an embryo when this happened." I almost slid down the wall. My mother had said embryo. I didn't know any Redondos even knew that word. I waited for crockery to fly.

Instead, Uncle Leon laughed. "Well, that makes me feel old as hell."

"You're as old as you feel, you leathery bastard," Aunt Helen said. These were all words that I had never, ever heard from the adults in our house.

"Let him go," Mom said.

"So suddenly you have an opinion?"

"He's a grown man. You've been married for fifty years yourself. If you can't trust that, you can't trust anything." This from a woman who'd lost her only husband—my dad—after just five years of marriage and who still wore her ring. It was jealousy speaking, but she'd earned it.

I figured this might be my cue. I pushed open the door, to find my mother protecting the china cupboard with both arms wide, while Aunt Helen brandished a ladle, spitting capers. At least it wasn't marinara. Uncle Leon looked over and winked at me. Sometimes I really wished I had his cool.

"If you would have let me finish," he said, "I would have told you that in exchange for letting me go, Cyd has planned a trip for the two of you, all expenses paid."

The hell I had. Dammit.

Aunt Helen pointed the ladle my way. "You're in on this? I should have known."

"Hey," my mom said, "if Cyd's involved, there's no way it's not on the up-and-up."

"That's not what I heard. Chip Jessup? Really?"

I wondered what Aunt Helen might look like with a few capers stuck to her significant eyebrows, then contained myself.

"Perhaps you might recall that I am currently supporting all of you through my work as a travel professional. A travel professional who arranges the travel my clients request, however cockeyed it might be."

"Cockeyed. I thought so."

"Aunt Helen!"

She shrugged. More capers flew. Uncle Leon tried to sneak a piece of focaccia. Aunt Helen hit his hand with the ladle, without even blinking.

Uncle Leon gestured to me. "Cyd?"

"Fine. By choosing door number two, you've won a weekend in Boston—the Pops, Faneuil Hall, Durgin Park, lobster bibs, upgrade at the Copley Plaza." I was riffing off one of my standard weekend packages, as it was an easy train ride from Brooklyn and I had a driver I loved at the other end who looked after my clients. For handling Aunt Helen, I'd have to tip him extra. I calculated the cost in my head and realized it would only be possible on my emergency emergency credit card, but it was family.

Aunt Helen put down her ladle. Uncle Leon took her in his arms and swung her into a movie kiss. As my aunt's osteoporosis had pretty much turned her into a human comma, this bent her the wrong way. My mother and I grabbed each other's hands, afraid she might break.

But no one knew her flexibility like Uncle Leon, who leaned her back just enough. When he let her up, she folded back into herself like a fruit bat.

"What do you think, doll?"

She shrugged. "One condition." We all waited. Her conditions tended to turn yes into no. "Cyd goes with you."

"Done!" my uncle said and winked at me.

"Can you make me a plate? I have to go back to work." I glared at Uncle Leon.

"What, you can't spend five minutes with your family?"

Chapter Seven

An hour and a half later, chicken piccata-ed into a coma, I headed back to the office. Who did that, on a Wednesday night? I had to figure out how to get Uncle Leon onto all my reservations, set up a trip for Mom and Aunt Helen, check on all my clients, make sure I had their itineraries and contact info on my phone, and talk to the Consular Services office in London. I made an espresso and sat down at my computer.

Two hours later, everything I could do online was done. Now it was time to educate myself in all the details of repatriation that Wander Safe had shielded me from. Given the number of forms that had to be filed, they didn't charge enough. By the time I finished it was almost midnight. Still too early to call London. I was settling myself for a power nap on the floor when the phone rang.

"Cyd Redondo, Redondo Travel."

"Andrew Heep of Heep International."

"Hello. Can I help you?"

"I am calling to liaise with you regarding the body of a Shephard Helnikov. We've already contacted the Home Office. We should have the body by the time you arrive."

"I beg your pardon." That was quick—not only quick, but illegal. "Since Mr. Helnikov was not covered for the repatriation, as the executor I'll need to register the death and get all the certificates before you take charge of the body."

There was a long silence. "Dean McAfferty said everything was arranged."

"It will be. I'll be at the U.S. Embassy by Friday afternoon. If you give me your information, I'll be able to pass it on to them, as our mortuary of choice."

He obliged, but the more I heard his voice, the less I liked it. I hung up.

"You decent?"

I jumped. Sister Ellery was never that quiet. At anything.

"Yes, and busy."

"But not the right kind of busy. I hoped Chip Jessup might be here."

"Right." I caught her up on the situation.

"Who's going to cover the office? Eddie's back at the docks, right?"

"Right. Damn. I forgot. Maybe I'll just close it. We're only going to be gone for a few days."

"I can do it."

She looked so hopeful in her leopard-print footed pajamas, what could I say? After all, she had managed a classroom of twenty holy terrors every day for thirty years; she could probably manage this. Of course, that meant I had to train her.

By the time we were done, it was finally business hours in London, so her first task as my assistant was to arrange an appointment at the embassy, and one with my real estate contact.

By that time, it was five a.m. and I was about to pass out. I hated leaving the office in anyone else's hands, but anything was better than Jimmy. And Sister Ellery would keep him away. He was terrified of her.

I got back to 77th Street and dragged out my trusty twenty-inch carry-on. I would need casual and business/grief wear. I folded my sequined little black dress, a black pencil skirt, my navy Donna Karan peplum jacket, chiffon, silk, and cashmere tops and scarves, five sets of La Perla lingerie—just to be optimistic—one pair each of kitten heels, stilettos, and black knee-high boots, all patent leather in case it rained the whole time. Tights went into my set of flat nesting Tupperware, so they wouldn't snag. There wasn't a weight limit for carry-on on British Airways, but I still didn't want a dislocated shoulder, so I'd wear the boots and my black Bendel's winter coat on the plane.

I was just grabbing my always-packed cosmetics ziplock when Aunt Helen lurched her way up to the attic. I hadn't noticed her meddling in my room lately and strangely, I missed it. I had spent so much energy hiding things from my family, it felt strange not to have to do it anymore. I gestured to my fabric-covered rocking chair, a present from my Uncle Ray.

"Hi," I said, not sure why she was here.

"Your uncle is not as well as he likes to pretend," she said. "That's why I want you with him. Also, of course, to make sure he keeps out of trouble with the ladies."

"What ladies?"

"Are you blind? Your uncle has always been a ladies' man. Seriously, why do you think he wears those ridiculous suits?"

"But isn't he a bit past it now?"

"Well, nobody's 'past it,' missy, until they're in the ground. You have clients his age, you should know better. It's just that it's more likely you'll fracture or pull something."

"Stop! Got it." I wasn't ready to imagine Aunt Helen and Uncle Leon playing geriatric sex Twister.

"No, you haven't got it. He's being extra cagey this time. Extra cagey. So this is not a vacation for you. I'm holding you completely responsible for him."

"Look, I will keep an eye on him, but he's not going to want to run around all these government offices with me, so I can't be with him every minute. It's not fair to ask me to."

She harrumphed out of the rocking chair. "Your diaphragm is still in that push-up bra, you know," she said and headed downstairs.

Chapter Eight

By the time I'd gotten my carry-on downstairs, Uncle Leon already stood in the asphalt driveway. He looked particularly sharp, in a forest green suit with stovetop trousers, pointy, perfectly shined, cardamom shoes, a skinny tie with burgundy and brown swirls. Beside him was the largest suitcase I had ever seen. Plus a garment bag. In a travel agent family, that was like an Orthodox Jew bringing home a hog to slaughter for Christmas.

"You've got to be kidding me. What is that?"

"I need it."

"You need some underwear, an extra shirt, and maybe another tie. That's it."

"I have some things that need to be checked. Metal things."

"Metal things, my ass." I tried to pick the suitcase up. "Cripes! What's in there? Cannon balls?" I dropped it back on the ground. He glared. "Okay, but you're paying the additional weight fee."

"Of course."

It was unspoken that he would borrow the money from me. It was lucky I had my emergency emergency money buried half in my bra and half in my Balenciaga.

An hour later I looked with palpable lust at the "no luggage" line, while we waited for twenty minutes to arrive at the British Airways counter.

"Hi, Jessica. Cyd Redondo, Redondo Travel." I held out our passports and paperwork, then held in my stomach muscles to prevent a hernia while I heaved Uncle Leon's bag onto the scale. 175 pounds. He could have fit me, my luggage, and all the shoes I left at home in there. The clerk's eyebrows rose. Here we go, I thought.

Uncle Leon straightened his tie and leaned in. "Is that Lovely perfume I smell, Jessica?"

The clerk blushed. "It's probably corny, but Sarah Jessica Parker is my idol. You know, 'cause we have the same name. I had to have her signature scent, right?"

"Well, it suits you."

She slapped the label on the heaviest suitcase in America, handed me the matching numbers for pickup, and smiled. "Have a fantastic trip. Hope to see you again, Mr. Redondo."

Uncle Leon winked at her. Over the squeaking wheels of my carry-on, he whispered, "There's more than one way to skin a cat, Cyd, and I should know." Aunt Helen was right. I had my work cut out for me.

I had hoped for some quality uncle/niece time on the plane, maybe a few stories I hadn't heard about my dad, or about the whole Spartacus thing, but after we had the complimentary champagne and dinner, he passed out for the duration.

I sighed, gestured for another two airline bottles of Jack Daniel's and Cuervo Silver, tucked one each in my bag, and checked the film list. I'd already seen *Little Miss Sunshine* (the family had seemed a bit too together and communicative for my taste), and I had no desire to traumatize myself with *Snakes on a Plane*. I was already thinking about dead bodies in the hold, since my conversation yesterday with Ginger at Air Trays Galore.

Air trays were not something most people knew about, or wanted to. They were the containers required by airlines and Customs for flying caskets, bodies, and cremains from one destination to another. Apparently they were priced by how leakproof they were, which is not something anybody wanted to think about either. They were plain rectangular boxes with straps, made from various materials from cardboard to lead. The ones the military used even had a name—Zieglers. They also made air trays especially for animals. Sadly, I'd arranged a few domestic "flights" in the past for people and pets, and had gotten to know Ginger.

She'd sent me my favorite piece of promotional swag, ever. It was a high-quality mousepad, featuring the image of a coffin with wings, accompanied by the Grim Reaper—scythe included—in an electric blue cloak and the motto *Give them wings to their Final Destination*. Too bad I could never let my clients see it.

Ginger had been effervescent as usual. "Cyd! Lovely to hear from you. How can I help you in your grief?"

"I have a body in the UK."

"Condolences. Mainly because they have a lot of regulations. Won't your insurance company handle it?"

I told her the sad story, which of course made her laugh.

"Thanks a lot," I said. "Do you ever deal with Heep International?"

She hesitated. "We have."

"And you don't like them?"

"They were, um, pushy. They overstepped, maybe, is the word."

"They've been requested by the client."

"That's too bad. They're known to take a few shortcuts with the UK rules. They don't call them Heep on the Cheap for nothing, is all I'm saying, so watch yourself."

"I will."

This made me even more anxious about the trip, which was feeling fishier by the minute. Why would Dean Dean want a specific mortuary? How many dead professors from Brooklyn were transported a year?

I banished visions of floating air trays by finishing Shep's *Jacked!* I had just formed my own theory on the Ripper murders when we started our descent and Uncle Leon jerked awake.

We breezed through Customs and the Arrival Hall, where I bought us both pay-as-you-go English phones and put twenty pounds on each, so we could reach each other if my U.S. phone gave me any trouble. Or the roaming charges started adding up. Then I led us out to the drivers' queue.

A man in a black wool coat with perfect hair held up a sign reading *Mr. Redondo.* Uncle Leon waved at him and moved that way, revealing a much shorter man in a red jacket with the sign *Miss Redondo*.

I did a double take. The tall driver was already putting Uncle Leon's behemoth case in the trunk of a town car.

The other man came toward me. "Hello, madam, are you Cyd Redondo?"

I held out my hand. "Yes. Nice to meet you, can you hold on just a second?" I gestured to Uncle Leon, who jogged over and kissed me on the cheek.

"Be seeing you, toots."

Chapter Nine

"What? Wait, what? Where are you going?"

"I'm sorted out. That's all you need to know."

"That is absolutely not all I need to know! I have a room reserved for you. In Ernest Hemingway's favorite hotel." I was flabbergasted.

"Sorry, but this is work." I just stared at him. "When I found out I was coming, I got in touch with some old friends. Turns out they could use my help. So I figured I'd stay with them to get to spend more time. After all, I live with you, day in day out."

"Thanks a lot. And help with what? Like health help? Taxidermy help? Or twenty-five on six in the fourth kind of help?"

"It's not racing season."

"Well, you would know."

He just grinned. "Don't worry, all aboveboard. Very above. You're not missing anything, they're not your sort."

"I beg your pardon. What is my sort?"

"Apparently those in the medical profession, or medical adjacent."

"Hey! My personal life is none of your business."

"And mine is none of yours, missy."

"I'm not a missy anymore. I'm a Ms." I touched him on his scrawny arm. "I promised Aunt Helen I'd make sure you're okay."

"I don't need a babysitter. She knows that more than anyone."

I guess he saw something in my face. I think it might have been terror.

"Don't worry. I can handle her. Now look, I know it's hard for you to understand, but this is important to me and, well, I probably won't be back this way again, you know, before the end."

I punched his shoulder. "Cut it out!"

"You cut it out. I'll be fine. I have your damn phone, don't I?"

"No, no, wait. You have to come with me to the embassy to sign the paperwork."

He reached into his tight coat and pulled out several folded sheets. I glanced at them and, in fact, they were the right documents. He had signed and initialed them all, authorizing me to make the arrangements. As they smelled vaguely of orange hand lotion and disinfectant, he must have done it in the airline bathroom. He looked at me.

"Anything else?"

"Don't lose that phone. Seriously. And call me once you get to where you're going so I know you didn't disappear en route."

"You're a good one, Squid. I'll call."

I was completely torn. I knew I shouldn't let him go, to avoid blowback from Aunt Helen or worse, but I didn't want to emasculate or "senior shame" him. My clients complained all the time about being treated like children when they'd survived the Depression, WWII, Vietnam, bell bottoms, and Nixon. Uncle Leon had been around the world multiple times. I was the one who needed him, really. I hugged him as hard as I thought his spine could handle.

My heart still skipped a beat as I watched him walk away. I had lost too many people I cared about lately. He was spry, but breakable. I remembered what Aunt Helen had said about him being cagey and I wondered exactly who these old friends might be. Well, I would find a way to figure that out, but first, I needed to drop off my bag and get to the embassy. And cancel Uncle Leon's room.

Hotels hated last-minute cancellations—that's why they always charged you. And I didn't want to damage my relationship with the hotel of my dreams—the Savoy—the most famous and probably the most expensive hotel in London.

I had booked just enough clients there to earn points and, with the coupon I'd won as Brooklyn Travel Agent of the Millennium and Dean Dean's budget, I had scored two of their smaller rooms. There was a rumor the hotel was closing for renovations at the end of the year. Doubtless they would ruin it. I wanted the old Savoy anyway, the place Marilyn Monroe stayed while she shot *The Prince and the Showgirl* or where Duran Duran made their videos. And their concierges were supposed to be the most connected and discreet in the city. I reached Reservations, asked for Polly, and explained.

"No problem, Cyd. I've canceled one room, upgraded you to a better one, and won't charge you a penny."

"I owe you, I'm on my way."

When the car pulled up to the famous entrance, with *Savoy* in lights over the taxi rank and the gorgeous façade behind it, I couldn't breathe. The Plaza Hotel was one thing, but this was something else altogether. I'd be staying in a hotel built with profits from light opera and sleeping above a ballroom that had actually been turned into a lake with gondoliers for one party. It featured views of the Thames and it was Barbra Streisand's favorite. Come on, for a girl from Brooklyn, it didn't get any better than this.

I would have happily stayed in one of the elevators, and when I saw my room, complete with four-poster bed and Molten Brown cosmetics, I thanked whatever travel gods were looking out for me. I cast a jet-lagged eye on my watch, now on GMT. I only had an hour before my appointment at the embassy. I called down to the front desk for a cab, got out as many small bills as I thought I would need for tips, and put them in my most accessible coat pocket.

I reserved ten pounds for the concierge, Kent. After he called me madam and gave me the royal treatment into my cab, I gave him twenty. Tipping always pays off.

The black cab felt bigger than my bedroom at home. I sat on the flat red seat, which seemed a million miles away from my cabbie, who turned around and smiled.

"U.S. Embassy, Grosvenor Square, ma'am?"

"Yes, please."

"That's never good."

"No, it's not. I'm Cyd Redondo, Redondo Travel."

"Ronnie. Cabs are us."

I laughed. "Nice to meet you, Ronnie. In your expert opinion, any chance we can get there in half an hour?"

He snorted. "Just." He took a left into what felt like oncoming traffic to me and headed what I thought was east. To my delight, he kept a running commentary on the traffic, the landmarks—Hyde Park, Speaker's Corner, Park Lane, the whole works. By the time we arrived at the famous square, I'd already promised to book a Disneyland excursion for him and his wife. I took his number and, even though I knew tipping was different here, gave him a huge one.

He handed half of it back. "Don't show off."

"Did I make a mistake with the concierge?"

"Kent plays the horses, he won't mind."

"I'll set your trip up as soon as I'm back in the office."

"What are you doing at the embassy, anyway?"

"Collecting a body."

Chapter Ten

I looked at the building in front of me and squared my shoulders. This was not the first time I'd been to an American embassy in a foreign country. The last time hadn't gone so well. This time I hoped I wouldn't need to hide inside a stinking cargo truck and sacrifice a beloved pair of Stuart Weitzmans to escape the ambassador.

I didn't have extra shoes on me, but just in case, I did have travel vouchers for upgrades on five airlines, a fat roll of British pounds, a newly developed bullshit detector, and if all that failed, an ear-splitting personal alarm I'd smuggled through Customs in my bra. Good thing I have a slow, steady heartbeat. Most of the time.

The bottom line was, given my last experience, I didn't have complete faith in the whole embassy system. At least today I should be dealing with an underling. Underlings were my people. I was filled with instant sympathy for them here, since they worked in a huge building that screamed Khrushchev via the Watergate Hotel or some Lego project from occupational therapy. Here I was in a gorgeous, historic square, with ancient, beautiful buildings on three sides and a "modern" monstrosity on the fourth. Leave it to Americans to ruin Europe.

I sighed, nodded to the Eisenhower statue in front, pulled down my hem, and walked into the "must have seemed modern, now seemed sad" building. After passing through a metal detector, signing in, and having my passport checked by two security guards, I asked for the Department of Consular Affairs, which handled most tourist issues, including sudden death.

"And what may I tell them it is concerning, madam?" A particularly squat security guard—at five foot two, I had at least an inch on him—stood in my way.

"I'm here to obtain a Report of a Death, a death certificate, and to arrange final transport for an American citizen." As the official version provoked no response, I took out a tissue and embarked on a fraudulent sniffle, which succeeded in moving him out of my way.

I was allowed to proceed to the elevator, which I rode to the fifth floor with a couple of bureaucrats. It seemed the staff here dressed at least one designer up from the Men's Wearhouse attire I had encountered in most U.S. State Department offices. I was glad I'd freshened up and worn my DKNY pencil skirt (85% off Century Twenty-One after Christmas sale), white chiffon blouse (camisole attached) under my peplum jacket. That was as bureaucratic as I got.

The hallway was straight out of every Kevin Costner/Matt Damon/ Will Smith CIA movie ever made. I finally found the right office for the Deputy Deputy Director of Consular Affairs.

I knocked a few times. Since the door was partially open, I eased in. Past the empty reception desk was an office with papers scattered across every surface and a Harvard crimson and black scarf hanging off the head of a longhorn steer head on the wall. In my taxidermist-adjacent opinion, it needed a touch-up. The room smelled like curry, shoe polish, and vodka.

"Hello? Is anyone here?"

I heard a moan. After a few seconds, a red cowlick shot up above the glass-topped desk, followed by an almost perfectly round, Howdy Doody-sized head, which took one look at me, ducked back down for a few seconds, then popped back up and unfolded to his full six-foot height. He looked like he had spent about fifteen years at an Ivy League school, drinking his way through most of them, with the perpetual adolescent aura that preppie-dom brings, until you got close enough to see the bags under his eyes. He was probably thirty. I gave him my most professional smile and held out my hand.

"Cyd Redondo, Redondo Travel. I'm very sorry to disturb you, but I'm here about Shepard Helnikov. He died on Tuesday?"

He wiped his hand on his tie and shook mine.

"Hey there. Harley Blankenship. The Fourth." Even without the longhorn, I would have pegged him as a Texan—he sounded like a watered-down LBJ. He grinned. "Long night. Sorry, what was it you said you needed?"

"Shepard Helnikov. I'm here to get the remains back to New York."

He came around the desk, moved a document box from a chair, and gestured to it, then sat down himself, looking more than a little green. He reached for a half-full water glass.

I reached into my Balenciaga's first aid kit pocket. "I don't mean to be presumptuous, but would you like an Alka-Seltzer with that vodka?"

He laughed. "Oh God yes. This is actually water, the vodka was last night. I always thought being a Delt meant I could drink anybody under the table, but these Brits are serious." He popped the Alka-Seltzer dry. That's how bad it was.

"I wouldn't underestimate yourself."

He shrugged, drank a little water, and burped. "Now, where are my manners? Very sorry about your loss. Was he a relative?"

"A client and family friend."

"Well, I'm new here. And to be honest, I haven't dealt with a death abroad yet."

"I'm not surprised. I'm always telling my clients how safe England is. Thirty-two million Americans came here last year and only five didn't come back."

He asked me to repeat that, then wrote it down. "Good to know. They like statistics around here, it's one way to get ahead. Okay, let me see how I'm supposed to handle it."

He opened a binder the size of the Ukraine, booted up his ancient desktop, and started clicking. This didn't seem good. He looked up as he scrolled. "So where're you from?"

"Brooklyn. Bay Ridge."

"Last stop on the R train! Brooklyn girls are the best. Hey, any chance you know Chip Jessup? I think he's from there."

Seriously, could any more people mention fricking Chip Jessup? What was he, the new Kevin Bacon? "Yeah. Actually I had a drink, a platonic drink, with him last week. How do you know him?"

"Poli sci course. Junior year. And a couple of spring breaks. What's he doing?"

"Wall Street lawyer."

"Figures." He was still scrolling. "Well, next time you see him, tell him Gnarly said hi."

He did a final click. "Could I see your paperwork?" He took it, flipped through it, and frowned. "Let me check something." He started to look through the papers and back at his computer. "My gal knows a lot, let's get her in here." He picked up the phone. "Delores, could you come here a minute? Thank you, ma'am." He gestured with the phone. "She's been here forever."

"So, you've just started? Where were you working before?"

"It's my first job."

"Ever?"

"Pretty much. After college I did the whole Europe and Asia thing and then some internships."

"And now you're basically an ambassador?"

"Résumé builder. My uncle has some relationships."

"Yeah, I know what that's like."

"They've got me mostly working on pet quarantines. People are psychotic about their pets. No offense."

"None taken."

"I mean, our family had three golden retrievers like everyone else, but there are limits. People will leave their children in a Heathrow bathroom, or their husband will go missing for three days, no problem, but if their pet isn't ready the instant the quarantine is over, they're on the phone to Uncle Charlie."

"Uncle Charlie?"

"Sorry. The Consular General."

Delores entered. She was wearing some extremely cute navy blue patent leather shoes with curved Louis XIV heels. She looked at me expectantly. "Yes?"

"Cyd Redondo, Redondo Travel. May I ask where you got those shoes?"

"LK Bennett. January sale." A sister. We smiled.

Harley stood up. "Miss, or Ms. Redondo is here about a body, this is her paperwork."

Delores took it. She had either taken a speed reading class or had done this a lot.

"Let's see. Right, right, oh. This needs an Apostille."

"An apostwhat?"

"Yeah, what's that?" Harley looked confused.

"An Apostille. A document that verifies notarization. This isn't notarized."

"Oh. Of course, I should have known. Is there somewhere we might go nearby?"

She laughed. "It's not like home, where every stationery store and most people's aunts have a seal. UK notaries are public officials or lawyers. The kind of people who"—she looked at the clock—"do half days on Friday."

Shit, I was a notary. But my seal didn't always travel with me, especially when there was a weight limit. "Is there no one in-house who could do this for us?"

"There'll be someone at the building across the way on Monday morning. Shall I make you an appointment?"

"That would be terrific, Delores. Just for the record, is the paperwork correct?"

"Yes, it seems fine. Just needs the seal and the attachment."

"Well, since it's just a formality, could I get copies of the death certificate and pick up Mr. Helnikov's belongings?"

"Sure," Harley said.

Delores sighed. "Sir, perhaps you've forgotten, we can't do anything until the executorship has been formally transferred."

I turned to her. "Don't I have to register the death in five days? And don't I need the certificate for that?"

"Yes, you do. We have the certificate, we just can't give it to you. I think you'll be fine doing it all Monday."

"What about his belongings?"

Harley shrugged. "They're not here."

"What do you mean they're not here?"

"Ever since England lost the Ashes, we can't get anyone to return our calls. And if they do, they just want to rub Sacha Baron Cohen's Golden Globe in our faces. It's been brutal. So, no one's had time to get to his place and retrieve the items."

"No one, meaning you?" Delores gave him a stern look.

"It's above my pay grade," Harley said. I imagined a lot of things were.

"Oh, that's too bad," I said, meaning the opposite. I could get there first and secure whatever it was Dean Dean was so anxious to get back.

I gave Harley Blankenship the Fourth my U.S. and English phone numbers, and told them I'd be back on Monday with either my uncle or an Apostille. By the time I'd exited the building, I was already on the phone with my real estate contact, Shelagh Gulhogan. She said she'd meet me at Shep's flat in Bloomsbury with a key in half an hour.

Chapter Eleven

I sprung for another cab to the flat. Not having to overtip helped, but it still wasn't cheap. Dean Dean had sent two texts while I was in the embassy and I needed to have some news for him, especially since it looked like I might have to extend our stay, and my per diem. I called, then texted Uncle Leon. No answer. At least I had the weekend to get through to him.

I kept my eyes glued to the window as the driver took me down shopping mecca Oxford Street. I didn't have time to stop, but at least I could see Selfridges from the outside.

I pulled out my Streetwise London. I instructed tourists never to do this on the street—it was like a mugging beacon—but the cabbie already knew I was a tourist. I loved the Streetwise maps, as they were laminated and you could actually fold them back up without swearing.

We turned what looked like east and now there were more Burger Kings and McDonald's, cell phone stores and discount shoes. Discount shoes. I put a red dot on my map. It was amazing to see the places I'd discussed and booked and dreamed about. After Atlantic City and Orlando, London was the most requested destination for my senior clientele. It was the easiest international flight from New York (except for Iceland), there was no language barrier, and the whole country ran on the concept of concessions—i.e., discounts—for anyone over sixty. I had booked hundreds of trips here and part of me felt like I was coming home.

We crossed Tottenham Court Road, where people erupted out of the subway entrance, which I reminded myself to call the Underground or the Tube. Past the stop, the street was full of small brick buildings that had probably been there when Dickens was around, but now mostly featured prix fixe pizza menus. Finally the cab pulled into Red Lion Square and there it was, three sides of British-looking houses, built around a garden. It was a bit scragglier than the real estate photos, but isn't everything?

I mini-tipped the cabbie and got out, looking for the address and the four-story brick building with bright navy blue trim Shep had been so fond of.

He had wanted a place that was near the British Library and the British Museum, with a square where he could sit and think. I understood that. It was why I drove to the cruise parking lot in Red Hook. He was so happy when I found this place the first time. Now he'd been a valued tenant every

January through March for fifteen years. It was one of the jobs I'd done well and knew it.

I looked up at the thick glass windows, rimmed by that hopeful blue, and wanted to cry. For Shep and for me. I was finally in London, but only because he was dead. There were moments I really wondered how well this whole travel agent thing was going, when all my travel so far had been because something bad had happened. Had my family been right? Was it dangerous to leave the Redondo perimeter, not just for me, but for others? I wondered where the hell my uncle had gone and I wished he were here with me. I had just murdered a travel tissue and pulled out my mini travel mirror/eyeliner brush, when I heard the thunk of wide heels.

"Cyd?"

I turned to see a roundish freckled woman in her early forties, about my height, with hair that must have been a rosy red at one time and now was shot with gray, making it more of a sienna. She wore an open navy blue wool overcoat, and a pink-striped shirt under a slightly-too-tight gray suit and what the English call court shoes. Believe me, I wouldn't wear them to court, or anywhere else, since their bulky square heels were death to the short-legged like me.

Her smile, and the key in her hand, made up for the dowdy shoes. I grinned in relief and moved forward. "Shelagh? Cyd Redondo, Redondo Travel. So nice to finally meet you."

Shelagh had not only helped me arrange Shep's flat for all these years, she'd helped me out with a series of rentals and hotel suggestions that included tub handles, wheelchair ramps, and oatmeal, along with the blood sausage, on the menu. She understood what seniors needed and I felt I could trust her with my most valued clients. Any travel agent worth their salt held on to those kinds of relationships.

Shelagh shook my hand. "I was so sorry to hear about Shep. Such a lovely man."

"Yes, it's still sinking in."

"I understand. It's always heartbreaking to lose a repeat client. I brought the extra keys from the office. You probably want a bit of time alone. It's on the third floor—fourth for you Americans." She shook her head. "It's such a shame. He'd booked it for the whole month."

Her Irish lilt belied her practical sentiments, so I let it go. Everyone saw the world through their unique filter—waiters and waitresses felt murderous over an unfilled ketchup bottle, traffic cops equated 45 in a 35 with a homicide, and travel agents saw an expired credit card as the ultimate betrayal.

"I took the keys. "It's paid for, though, right?"

"Right. Through the end of the month. You won't apply for a refund?"

I shook my head. "I wouldn't do that to you. Besides, if I have to stay longer, I may need it. Look, has the embassy been in touch?"

"They just called, the nerve, on a Friday afternoon. I told them I would let them in on Monday. The man actually sounded relieved."

"Texas accent?"

"Is that the Holly Hunter one?"

"Kind of."

"Then yes. Look, I have to run, but maybe we could have a drink. Later tonight or tomorrow? Where are you staying and for how long?"

"The Savoy."

"Oh, fancy. U2 stays there."

"If I didn't hate Bono, that might mean something."

"Oh, blasphemy," Shelagh said. "Truly? You can't be part Irish and hate Bono."

"We will agree to disagree."

I explained about the notary. She said her boyfriend was a barrister and might be able to help. At least I had one ally here, in the midst of all this sadness and paperwork.

I gave her my new English number so she wouldn't have to make an international call, and she clomped off. I said a quick prayer for Shep, then unlocked the front door and moved into the entryway.

To say it was dark and narrow would be generous. There was some illumination from the triangular fanlight above the front door, but the one tiny bulb on the ceiling must have been on a timer. The hall, which led down to what I assumed were two apartments, was barely wider than the flight of uneven, uncarpeted wooden stairs directly in front of me, with only room for a small side table littered with mail. Just to be responsible, I checked for Shep's, found a few pieces, tucked them in my purse, and headed up to the fourth floor.

The building smelled like the 1800s. And bacon.

For a moment, I thought fondly of my bacon-loving Tasmanian sidekick, Howard the thylacine, who'd hidden out from smugglers in my purse. I wished he were here with me. Or someone was. I stopped and tried Uncle Leon one more time. No luck.

I put the key in the lock. It seemed jammed. I almost dislocated my wrist turning it, but the door finally gave way. To a high-pitched scream.

Chapter Twelve

I heard a crash inside. I eased the door closed again and reached into my Balenciaga. I couldn't bring my pepper spray or taser on the flight, so I'd have to rely on my trusty roll of quarters first, my roundhouse kick second, and if those failed, my 130-decibel personal alarm.

My purse itself was heavy enough to be a decent weapon, but it had been through some rough times lately and I didn't really want it back in the infirmary at Bay Ridge Leather. I was only going to be more jet-lagged the longer I waited, so I took a deep breath, quarters raised, weight shifted on my left leg, and shoved the door open.

The knob hit the back wall with a bang, startling the quarters out of my hand. I stood still for a second, and when it seemed no one had been hiding behind the door, I stepped into another narrow entryway—narrow apparently being a recurring feature of British domestic architecture.

It was quiet, but I could sense, and smell, someone here. On top of the reek of pipe tobacco, damp tweed, slightly soured milk, and Shep's preferred cologne, Acqua di Parma, there was a forward note of Tommy Hilfiger's Tommy. Which told me a lot. As did the pink scarf with pilling pom-poms thrown on the top of the men's overcoats on the antique coat rack to my right. These items also probably went with the faint panting coming from the end of the hall.

"Hello? Hello? This is Cyd Redondo, Redondo Travel." No answer.

I moved forward into what we called in Brooklyn a railroad apartment, a long central hallway with rooms off the side. I crept to the door of the first room on the right, which had a bay window overlooking the square. It would have been cozy and inviting if it didn't have books and papers thrown all over the floor—not Shep's style.

To my left was a smallish kitchen, neat and mostly clean, with an electric teakettle, a tin of Fortnum & Mason's tea, some Ritz Crackers, and a bowl of apples. There was a brown teapot and a couple of mugs on the drying rack and one half-drunk and now fermenting cup of pale tea, which was probably the source of the *eau de* sour milk. The neatness in here reinforced my feeling of violation in the sitting room. Dammit.

Why did this kind of emergency always have to happen when I was jet-lagged? I closed the front door loudly and remained just inside the kitchen door, completely still for at least two minutes. Then, I heard footsteps. I came around the corner with my best roundhouse kick and nailed my target. My sensei, Bob, would have been proud.

I looked down to find worn red Doc Martens below a tapestry skirt, a medieval barmaid bodice—unripped—and goldilocks hair under a worn red beret. The intruder looked up at me and screamed. Twice. It sounded professional. Like a Jamie Lee Curtis in *Halloween* scream. She shifted into a more dramatic, flayed pose too, then moaned.

When I didn't respond, she opened her eyes. "Don't hurt me."

"I'm only going to hurt you if you make that movie scream again."

"Too much? I was hoping for Julie Christie in *Don't Look Now*."

"Not even close. Who are you and why are you in Shep's apartment?"

She pointed her finger at me. "Who are you? And why are you in Shep's apartment?"

"I'm the one with the key." I held it up. "I'm calling 911. I mean 999."

"Don't call, please." She started to try to get up.

I lowered a heel on her bodiced rib cage. "Seriously, explain why you broke in."

"I'm his girlfriend. I have a key too. May I?" She reached into her pocket and pulled out a key attached to a 3-D Shakespeare's head.

"You're Hilary from Teaneck? He didn't tell me you were English." Or jailbait.

"Who is Hilary? I'm Jemima. Comstock. From Islington. What is a teaneck? And who are you? His therapist?"

"His travel agent. And believe me, when he has a plus-one, I know about it."

I guess Sister Ellery had been right about Shep and I hadn't known him as well as I thought I did. And now I never would. This, of course, made me feel like crying. And punching the blonde. "So, what are you doing here, Jemima? That's your name?"

"I came to try to find his author photo, to use for the memorial service. May I rise now?"

I lifted my shoe and regretted it, as she unfolded like a praying mantis with a good ten inches on me.

She tossed her hair back and adjusted her beret, which I guess I'd kicked sideways. Then she shifted her bodice and sniffed. This woman was what we in Brooklyn call highly full of shit. I didn't buy a thing she was saying or doing, certainly not the Renaissance Faire curls, as I'd spotted the straight, dark roots during the beret readjustment.

"So, if you're here legitimately, why didn't you answer when I called out? I clearly identified myself."

"I would hardly consider that clearly." Her speaking voice sounded like every PBS mystery series actress rolled into one.

"Well, I'm here as Shep's executor to collect his belongings, and I need to know whether you're the one who threw all this stuff around." I gestured to the sitting room.

"No. It was like that when I got here. That's why I hid. I was afraid whoever had done that might be back." This was semi-believable, but she'd faked her moans, so she wasn't above faking an alibi. She put her hand to her forehead. "Can we have a cup of tea?"

"Only if tea means coffee. I assume as girlfriend you know your way around the kitchen?" I followed her there, where she took out a couple of turquoise mugs with the Lewis chessmen on them, put on the electric kettle, then got down a box of Tetley and a grimy tin of Nescafé.

Instant coffee. My heart sank. Since when did Shep, Bay Ridge born and bred, drink instant coffee? "Let me in there," I said, opening the freezer. Yes. A bag of espresso beans. If I had to chew them into a grind myself, they were going down. By the time I'd found a grinder and a silver Italian coffeepot, her tea was ready.

We sat down. Her beret stayed put, clearly part of her schtick. I wondered if she took it off during sex. I knew I was being unkind, but I felt pretty unkind.

"So, what are you doing here, again?"

"Looking for photos, as I said before. The other London's Afoot! guides and I are going to have a little ceremony tomorrow morning and I wanted to see if I could get a photo blown up for that. Our Secret Pubs of London expert has a darkroom." She reached into her bag and pulled out a crumpled sheet that read "Celebrate Shep Helnikov's Life—From Hell!"

She saw my face and laughed. "It's a reference to the famous Ripper letter. He was obsessed with it."

I remembered that from *Jacked!*, but not what it said. I hoped the book had an index.

I poured and shot a grateful gulp of espresso. "Did you disturb any of his papers?"

"Not more than they were already disturbed."

"Is that his research on the floor?"

She raised her teacup and sipped. Like all of her gestures, the sip belonged in a Noël Coward play. "Some of it. I know he often leaves things in his office, or in the BL."

"BL?"

"British Library."

"Oh. Right. Anywhere else?"

"He might leave a bag at the tour office if he were coming back to bring the night's earnings. You might check there."

"Thanks. So, how long had you been seeing each other?"

"On and off for two years. When he was here. I didn't know there was a Hilary, but we did have an open relationship."

She leaned forward and held out her cup. "Tell me thou lovest elsewhere, but in my sight." She did a version of a bow with her head. Just what I needed. Sonnets.

"Right. So how did you meet?"

"I'm a guide as well. I do the Sunday and Thursday Theatre District tours. And I alternate on the Swinging Sixties walks. It leaves me open for auditions."

"So, you're an actress?"

"Actor."

"Of course. Look, do you know anyone who might have had reason to break in? Anyone else with a key?"

"No. He'd been getting letters though. He said they were unsettling."

"Unsettling as in threatening? Did he say who they were from?"

"I'd guess another Ripperologist."

"You didn't find them when you were looking for photos, did you?"

She shook her head.

"Anything else you can tell me?"

"I don't think so."

"Well, I'm glad we had a chance to meet." I rose, hoping she would take the hint.

"Oh, are you leaving already?"

"No. I'm staying. As I explained, I'm responsible for his belongings. I need to collect what's here."

"I'd be happy to help."

"That's very kind of you, but unnecessary."

"Would you like another coffee before you start?"

Yes, I would, but not from a low-rent Helena Bonham Carter. "No, thank you."

I finally got her near the door. "Thanks for the information. It was nice to meet you."

"Don't you want to come to Shep's service? I'm sure he would want you there."

I took the flier. "Thanks. Yes, I would. My uncle is here and knew Shep well, may I bring him?"

"Of course. We welcome anyone who wants to celebrate his life. We'll all be doing readings. Bring anything you think will honor him."

Oh God. As she moved toward the door, she seemed to be holding her lumpy green cloth bag particularly close under her arm. Could I require a bag check at the exit? I let her go, with reservations, bundling her off down the tiny lift I hadn't noticed on the way up. "See you there."

I watched for her out the front window. She stood on the stoop for a long time, and finally walked off towards Holborn, still clutching the green bag.

Once she'd left, I locked the door and made myself another double espresso. I thought about calling the police, but they might make the flat a crime scene and I needed to go through everything first. I started in the office.

Most of the papers on the floor were from articles on trace DNA and forensic handwriting analysis. I put them in order and stacked them on his desk.

The lack of a computer concerned me, but it could be at his work office. Maybe if he was getting threats, he felt it was safer there. I started on the drawers. There were some lovely pens, boxes of ink cartridges, a stapler and paper clips, but no diary or calendar, no folders, no flash drives. Just a few clear plastic bags with the British Library logo on them, full of what looked like xeroxes of Victorian newspapers with gory illustrations.

I lifted a framed photo of Shep in his academic robes and another obviously taken when he was leading a Jack the Ripper tour—wearing a top hat with the Tower Bridge in the background. I was tearing up, so I headed to the bedroom and made it worse.

Chapter Thirteen

Lying on the double bed was one of Shep's blue and white Yale scarves. I could still see him throwing it over his shoulder as he left Redondo Travel, just before he turned to give me a wink at the door. I had to admit I'd had a crush on Shep, and having met Jemima, was a little insulted he'd never asked me out. Of course, multiple people in my family would have done him permanent injury if he'd even thought about it.

I looked around. Dean Dean hadn't been specific—he'd just said "Bring everything." It wouldn't hurt to call him, though. It was four p.m. here, and eleven a.m. in Brooklyn, so I tried the number he had put on my phone. "You've reached Dean Dean McAfferty, if this is important, please leave a message." I hated to feel so strongly that any colleague of Shep's and benefactor of Redondo Travel was such an unapologetic dick, but there it was.

"Cyd Redondo, Redondo Travel, regarding Shep Helnikov's flat. I'm in it."

I hung up, then assessed the room. Based on my limited experience, England seemed to specialize in smallish rooms and standing wardrobes rather than closets. Who knew closets were American? I was all for them, big ones, but I had to admit, *The Lion, the Witch, and the Closet* didn't have the same ring.

There were two small antique bedside tables stacked with books. The titles were mostly on Victorian and London history, mixed with a couple of contemporary British novels, two no-fiction tomes on American serial killers, and one titled *Cash and Carry: White Collar Crime in the European Union,* which had a folded piece of paper as a placeholder. I tucked it into the side of my purse so I wouldn't lose it. I looked under the bed, as who wouldn't, and found some dust and his L.L.Bean slippers. The slippers broke my heart. I sat down on the lumpy bed and had a proper cry.

When I'd used up half of my travel tissues and could breathe through my nose again, I opened the green wool curtains for more light and walked across the worn Oriental rug to check the wardrobe. It was twice my height and heavy, with small florets carved into the mahogany doors. I took a deep breath and opened them.

The familiar combo of pipe tobacco and Acqua di Parma floated out. Shep said he wore the scent because Cary Grant, Audrey Hepburn, and Ava Gardner couldn't be wrong. He'd given me some on my twenty-fifth birthday.

Inside the armoire hung two suits, one black and one a dark tweed, a stack of shirts in various pastels and stripes, a stack of handkerchiefs, and, of course, a few of his famous waistcoats. Embroidered, corduroy, silk, and wool, they were his signature. As he got larger over the years, he'd loosened the bottom buttons, about one per year. His suitcase lay at the bottom of the cabinet, a carry-on, for which I took credit. There was also a worn shoulder bag, which I thought would fit his papers.

I took the waistcoats down, deciding I wanted to keep the one embroidered with fleur-de-lis. As I set it aside, it jingled. I reached into the tiny front pocket and found a key hanging from a red disc with the number 279 along with a balled-up handkerchief. I checked the other waistcoat pockets, but they were only filled with tiny pieces of pipe tobacco. I put the key with the folded paper in the small pocket of my Balenciaga, checked all the other pockets, then started to fill the carry-on with the contents of the wardrobe.

I opened the bottom drawer and found a picture wrapped in tissue paper of a very young Shep at what looked like . . . his wedding.

He stood in a white puffy shirt and his fleur-de-lis waistcoat, opposite a dark-haired woman with huge eyes and an off-white, crocheted wedding dress, a crown of daisies around her head. A priest stood behind them. What the hell? He'd never mentioned a wife. Was she alive? Should she be here instead of me? I put the watch and photo in my bag.

I left the carry-on in the corner, closed the wardrobe doors, pulled the curtains shut, and put the Yale blue scarf around my neck. His scent was mingled with Tommy-reeking Jemima's, so she had been wearing it. Did she have something of Shep's in her green bag? How long had she been there before I surprised her and how much searching had she done? Was she really there for a photograph? She might have been dating Shep, sure, but something about her being here still felt dodgy.

I took the pens, put all the files and articles into the shoulder bag, and headed for the door. On the chair in the hall, I saw a stack of London's Afoot! signature red pamphlets. I remembered Shep telling me there were so many fake Jack the Ripper guides trying to steal his customers, his bosses had requested their own color stock just so tourists knew they were on the right tour.

I checked the walking tour office address. It was nearby. I decided to stop by in case Shep had left anything there, plus, I wanted to meet the owners, since that would make me feel better about recommending the tours to my clients in the future.

Before I left, I looked around one more time. If Jemima wound up telling anyone the place had been broken into, my fingerprints were everywhere. As far as I knew, my prints weren't in the UK system, but Interpol probably had them, after the whole Tanzania thing. I took one of Shep's handkerchiefs and tried to wipe down everything I'd touched, then used it to relock the door.

As I headed down the stairs, I glimpsed a tall man in a cape in the lift. I hid a floor down and listened. He entered a flat on Shep's floor, but I couldn't tell which one. He had a key, so he was likely a tenant. By the time I got back up the steps to investigate, all the doors were closed. Maybe I was being paranoid. I headed back down the stairs and out into the London afternoon.

Chapter Fourteen

The London's Afoot! offices were up a long, wiggledy staircase off Tottenham Court Road. I lived in an attic room, so I was used to climbing in heels, but the last floor almost conquered even me. And if Shep, given his cholesterol, had to navigate these stairs on a regular basis, I wasn't surprised he had keeled over. I clomped up floor after floor, glimpsing small offices and peeling paint, until I got to the top.

Although it was frigid outside, it still managed to be stuffy on the fifth floor. I spritzed myself with my sample Chanel No. 5 under my nose and on my wrists for a little lift, and knocked on the pockmarked green door.

"Come!" It was astonishing how one word could be bossy, theatrical, and impatient all at once. I guess walkers rarely made it up here, so perhaps there was no need for basic politeness. "Bigby. It's utterly uninspiring, your perennial lateness. I expect you think it's charming?" There was a pause. "Well?"

I poked my head around the door and saw the back of an overblown head of foxlike hair atop a velvet smoking jacket. From the door, it looked like there were a few cigarette burns on the back collar. I didn't want to think about how they got there. The man stood in the middle of a room that was pummeled from ceiling to floor with vintage theatre posters and framed playbills, festooned with overly dramatic, moth-eaten lace drapes, featured at least three antique coat racks—completely full—and smelled like damp wool and vinegar. There were newspapers, brochures, and books on every surface.

"I beg your pardon? Is this the London's Afoot! office?"

The hair swiveled around. From the front, it started well back from the ears, revealed a gleaming bald spot that devolved into a large forehead, and then threw itself off the ski jump of a nose. The man whipped off a pair of reading glasses repaired with masking tape.

I nudged a pile of folders out of the way, walked forward, and held out my hand. "Cyd Redondo, Redondo Travel. I'm here about Shep Helnikov."

He held his hand to his heart before taking mine. "Nigel Hammer-smithson, proprietor. Dear, dear Shep. He was one of our brightest stars, one of our most commanding voices, our Olivier in the guise of Oliver Reed, a vital member of the London's Afoot! family." He shook his half head of hair. "A loss. A tragic loss."

"Yes, it is. He was a lovely man."

"Lovely? Well, that wasn't exactly the way I would describe him, but he was very popular with the ladies. Where are my manners? Please, have a seat." He looked around, lifted an armful of the distinctive red pamphlets, and slopped them onto the floor. Although I would have rather punched him in the face for that comment about Shep, I settled for sitting down.

He gestured around him. "We must keep up with our research, I'm sure you understand. Even though many of our tours are historical, there is constantly new information coming to light, and so we like our guides to keep their walks completely up to date. It's vital in a competitive market." He sat down behind the desk and leaned back in his chair.

"I run a business and you're absolutely right."

"Exactly," Nigel said. He gave a pointed look at Shep's shoulder bag, which I'd put down beside me. "There are always rumors of these types of things, but I had heard Shep might be onto some new evidence himself. Had he mentioned it to you?"

Something told me not to answer this. Perhaps it was the maniacal look in his good eye.

I shrugged. "You know, I was hoping to meet some of Shep's colleagues. You have other guides who do the walk as well?"

"Indeed. Our Ripper Walks are our most popular, they're the only ones we do every day."

"Did Shep have a regular substitute when he was in Brooklyn?"

"We have experts from all walks—no pun intended—of life. We have former MPs, historians, members of the Royal Shakespeare Company and the National Theatre, lawyers, professors, adventurers, students of the world."

Well, that certainly didn't answer my question.

"He had a walk tonight, didn't he? Have you suspended them?"

He hesitated. "We considered going dark, of course, but in the end we felt it would dishonor him and we couldn't let our followers down."

Followers?

"So one of our other experts is taking over tonight. We will have a moment of silence for Shep, of course. And there's a memorial for him tomorrow."

"Yes, Jemima Comstock has already invited me."

"You've seen Jemima?"

At that moment, a woman walked in with the kind of unfortunate perm which had, at least on the east and west coasts of the U.S., gone out of style in the early eighties. She sported—or perhaps I should say endured—an extremely pilled and stretched cardigan in a deliberate chartreuse, which even stretched, wouldn't close in front. It waved above a quilted skirt of many colors, all of them wrong. And at the bottom a pair of sensible—i.e., ugly—shoes.

It was hard to like her right away, or maybe ever. Then she opened her mouth and made it official. "Hello, dear." It was the most sinister use of "dear" since the Wicked Witch of the West. She lowered a huge mug of tea on the desk.

Nigel rose so fast he sent his rolling chair right into my knee. Then grimaced and pushed his spine back into shape. "Ah, Madge. I didn't think you'd be in this morning."

"Yes, that seems clear."

"I'd like to present Miss Cyd Redondo. She appears to know Shep and has come to, well, what is it exactly you've come to do, Miss Redondo?"

I held out my hand to Madge. She took a slurp of her tea.

"Cyd Redondo, Redondo Travel. I'm Shep's designated executor. First, I'm here to wrap up all his affairs." I caught Nigel shooting a quick look to Madge.

It was hard to differentiate between Madge's supercilious, furious, and alarmed looks, as they all involved a pursed mouth and lots of eyebrows, but this one was leaning toward alarmed.

"Miss Redondo was also inquiring about Shep's walk tonight."

"I see. Well, we are fully booked tonight."

"Oh, I didn't know there was a limit?"

"We've had a record number of inquiries," Madge said.

Nigel took her elbow. "What Madge means is that when the walk is so crowded, it isn't always the optimal experience, and of course, Martin, who's doing the tour in Shep's place, won't have as much time to speak with you."

"I understand. That's fine. If you could give me the information and directions, that would be wonderful. I'd like to be able to say firsthand that the alternative guides are wonderful as well."

Madge gave Aunt Helen a run on her harrumph. "Of course they are. We are the premiere tour company in London."

"Yes, on Google, but since most of my clients are elderly, they feel most comfortable with a personal recommendation, rather than random reviews, which, as we know, can be solicited."

This provoked a stare-down between me and Madge that Nigel missed, as he was writing on one of their brochures. He handed it to me with a Tube map.

"Eight o'clock sharp."

"Got it, thank you."

Madge moved closer. "You said first. Is there a second reason you've graced us with your presence?"

"Yes, thank you for reminding me. Jemima Comstock mentioned that Shep occasionally left some things here in the office between visits. Technically, the embassy should collect them, but if there's anything I can retrieve while I'm here, to save you an official interruption, I'd be happy to take care of it."

Madge dropped her cup of tea, sending the tan liquid across a stack of papers. Both of the proprietors tried to recover, after making theatrical "alarm" faces. I figured they must have done what Shep called panto. Or a life-sized Punch and Judy show, which seemed to be the English equivalent of *The Honeymooners.*

I saw Nigel reach for a manila folder and shove it under a pile while Madge mopped up the tea. She stared up at me. "I don't remember his doing that."

Nigel took over the cleanup. "I'd be surprised if he has," Nigel said, in a tone that indicated that was the end of the discussion. "Right, my dear?"

"Correct, there's nothing here." Madge glared at Nigel.

"If you could excuse us for a moment, we'll check in the back just in case?"

"No problem."

The minute they moved into the other room, I dove for Nigel's desk to find the manila folder, but there were dozens of them and none marked with Shep's name or anything about the Ripper Walks. I heard them coming and jumped back to my seat.

"Nothing," Madge said.

"Thank you for looking. I'll have the embassy give you a call, just in case."

Madge put her hands on her hips. "We have a tour, so we must be going."

"Oh, I didn't realize you gave tours as well."

"We all chip in as needed," she said.

"How nice. Nigel, Madge, thank you for your help. I'll see you both at the memorial," I said, just to further freak them out.

I left, closing the door behind me. Why had they been acting so guilty? Or was this just the English eccentricity I'd heard so much about? I hoped to eavesdrop for a minute, as I could hear them arguing, but a tall, sallow man in a floor-length army green trench coat arrived at the top of the stairs and opened the door. He gave me a pointed look, so I commenced my descent.

I found a patisserie—hurrah—just across the street and waited to see if anyone came in or out of the building. A few people went in. One of them looked like Shelagh.

Chapter Fifteen

Maybe Shelagh's office was in the same building. I checked her card, which had a different address. She might be the rental agent for the building. I'd ask her about it when we had a drink.

I left Uncle Leon a message, inviting him to meet me at the walk and thought about what to do about Dean Dean. What could I report? Of course, at the moment I decided I didn't want to talk to him, he called.

The last thing I needed was to have him freak out and question his credit card charges, so I told him the paperwork had been more complicated than I'd anticipated and everyone knocked off early on Fridays, so it would be Monday before I could complete everything. I told him I'd gathered up all the papers I'd found and that I was going to check the British Library in the morning, after I went to the memorial service.

"You have his laptop?"

"No. It wasn't there."

"What do you mean it wasn't there?"

Telling him about the break-in seemed a bad idea. "Well, when I arrived the place was a bit of a mess. I'm hoping it might be among his things at the library or his office at the university. I just checked at the London's Afoot! offices, but no luck."

"Do you think it's been stolen?"

I hesitated. "Who knows? Maybe the embassy got there before I did. I'll see them again on Monday. If it hasn't turned up, I'll report it as stolen to the police, okay?"

"This is all very disappointing."

"Yes, it is. For both of us."

"Keep me posted. I need an ETA for the body in order to organize the department's memorial service. And remember your budget. I'm not a bank."

"I'm aware of that. I'm not happy about the extension either, I need to be back at work."

Dean Dean laughed. "It's just a travel agency. Use the internet."

I considered using the internet to put up fake complaints about McAfferty on rateyourprofessor.com, but remembered the thirty-grand repatriation fee I hadn't collected from him yet and amended my tone. "I'm meeting another Ripper guide tonight to ask about what Shep was doing. I'll let you know."

"Which guide, who is it?"

"I have to run. Use the internet."

The phone pinged again, but it wasn't Dean Dean, it was Shelagh.

"Time for a drink, by any chance?"

"Sure, a quick one. I'm going on Shep's walk tonight."

"Understood." She gave me the address of an underground bar near Charing Cross.

I risked a quick look at my map and saw it was pretty much a straight shot to the Savoy and the bar, since Tottenham Court Road turned into Charing Cross, so I decided to walk. Walking meant I'd see things I'd miss in a cab. In Bay Ridge, that meant seeing who had expired license plates or three empty Scotch bottles in the recycling, but here it could mean all the things I had blindly recommended to my clients—the swinging, glowing lanterns of Chinatown, the National Portrait Gallery, the Catacombs Cafe, and the Spaghetti House. As I didn't want to miss anything, I did two stupid things. I kept my map out, and I paid more attention to all the piggledy alleys, the red mailboxes, and the chimney pots on the top of every building than to my fellow walkers.

At least when someone grabbed for Shep's bag, my self-defense instincts kicked in. Since it seemed the person was behind me, I disengaged them with a throw of my elbow, followed by a backward kick with my spike heel aimed at the ball sack. I heard a yelp as I jammed my purse under my arm, held tight to Shep's bag, and let the momentum of the kick propel me into the nearest doorway, where I proceeded to careen into, knock over, and land on top of a life-sized cutout of chef Jamie Oliver.

I looked up at a laughing security guard, who reached down to help me up.

I took his hand. "Thank you."

"Are you all right, Miss?"

"Yes, I'm fine. Someone tried to grab my purse and I came through the door too fast."

I reached down to try to pick up the cutout Jamie. A couple of the spikes in his hipster haircut were bent. We both looked at it.

"Tosser." He shook his head. "That thing is a menace. It's the fourth time he's gone down this week."

"Really? Same way?"

"Mostly prams," he said. "Are you sure you're all right?"

"Absolutely." I looked around. There were books everywhere and I could see up a staircase to more upstairs. "Where am I?"

"Foyle's. Never been here?"

"First time in London."

"Seven floors of books. Best one in the city, for my money."

"Holy crap." My heart was pounding just to be in a building this big devoted to books. It felt like being in the New York Public Library, but everything was for sale. All I wanted to do was spend the next ten hours here, but I was meeting Shelagh. I asked about their opening hours, thanked the guard, and went out a different exit, just to be safe, then headed back down Charing Cross Road.

I gasped when I saw the Palace Theatre on my right. I had booked over fifty tickets to *Spamalot* there in the last two years. I would have to duck in later.

I passed more bookstores, more theatres and, disappointingly, a Pizza Hut. I continued down the road, jostling against Londoners, past Leicester Square, site of half-price theatre tickets, the National Portrait Gallery, St. Martin-in-the-Fields, and Trafalgar Square without any more assaults on my person, but I still wanted to drop off Shep's bag safely at the hotel before going out for the night. After my stop at the Savoy, I headed down the cobblestone alley Shelagh had directed me to.

I found the address and there was a much-faded sign noting Edward's Wine Bar, but it looked closed. There were bars on the windows and no apparent entrance.

Then, two men being worn by their suits opened a barred door and went in. I followed them, noticing a busy kitchen to my right, and a long narrow staircase going down. At the bottom was another world.

I had landed in what appeared to be a medieval cave. The walls were built from uneven, damp-looking stones with a few tasteful cobwebs blowing in the farthest room. The place was filled with weathered wooden tables, a wine bottle candlestick on each one.

I heard the clunk of court shoes behind me. Shelagh was obviously used to the effect this place had on Americans. She grinned, winked, took my arm, and asked me what kind of plonk I wanted.

"I beg your pardon?"

"Red, white, or bubbly?"

Plonk. Plonk was wine? "Oh, red please."

"If you want the buffet, go ahead."

I was suddenly starving and stacked a plate up with salads, shepherd's pie, bits of cold roast beef, and as much bread and cheese as I could get on top of that. I noticed I was taking about four times as much as anyone else, and headed for a table in the back, so I could snarf it without judgment.

As I waited for Shelagh, I noticed cast-iron gates at the other end of the room, closing off what looked like hundreds of dusty wine bottles. This had it over every dive bar I had ever had the good luck to do shots in. I loved it here so much I felt like crying.

Shelagh arrived with a bottle and two glasses and we settled into uneven chairs and a wobbly table. It was just part of the charm. I raised my glass. "To this place."

"I know. You have to promise me you won't tell anyone about it."

"As a travel agent, that might be the hardest promise I've made this week."

"I've been waiting for that monster, Rick Steves, to ruin it for us regulars."

This was the first time I had heard anyone refer to Rick Steves as a monster, but I could see it. A group of loud Americans in khakis with microfiber backpacks would ruin it.

"It's so romantic." I thought about how my former plus-one, Special Agent Roger Claymore, would have to duck his head all the way through here and got a lump in my throat. His face came back to me at the weirdest times. I wished it would stop.

"Yes, Shep and I used to come here," Shelagh said, taking a swig of wine.

"So you got to know him?"

"In a sense. The second time he stayed in the flat, he asked me out. It was a pretty short-lived thing—I think that was his *forte*—but there were no hard feelings after and we always at least had a drink while he was here."

Wow. Obviously Sister Ellery had been right about Casanova Helnikov. "I had no idea. He said you were lovely to him, but I didn't think it was that kind of lovely."

"Ha." She raised her glass. "To Shep!"

"To Shep!"

Shelagh refilled our glasses. "He was interesting. I think he had quite a following, with the Jack the Ripper thing and all that hair."

"Yes, my mom used to call him Bay Ridge's Alan Bates."

"Exactly. It was so strange his dying right on the Ripper murder site in Mitre Square, don't you think?"

Chapter Sixteen

"Wait, what? I thought he had a heart attack in the flat. He died on one of the Ripper murder sites? Why didn't anyone tell me that?"

"I don't know. They're probably keeping it quiet. Maybe nobody wanted to start a 'copycat' panic, or a rumor that the walk is cursed. Maybe the London's Afoot! people didn't want anyone to appear to have died on one of their tours. I don't know exactly what happened."

This troubled me. As much as Shep might have wanted to die "in harness," this coincidence seemed, well, too coincidental.

Shelagh poured more wine. "When it comes out, it will do wonders for his book."

"But they're sure it was natural causes?"

"I would think so. I'm sure the walking tour people would know more."

"I saw them. They didn't mention anything."

"Was everything all right in the flat?"

"Except for the fact that it had been tossed and there was an actress hiding inside, everything was fine." I told her the story of my encounter with Jemima. She laughed.

"Leave it to Shep to keep a twenty-year-old on the go." Shelagh dumped the rest of the bottle into my glass. I was grateful I had been a complete pig on the buffet or I would have been seriously hammered. "So, did you find what you were looking for?"

I was about to tell her about the key when I noticed the time.

"Oh my God. I'm supposed to be meeting my uncle for a Jack the Ripper walk at eight. I need to get to the Tower Hill station right now."

"Oh. That's too bad. You can catch a District Line train just down the alley, it will take you right there."

"Great, thanks so much. For the fabulous wine and for this place."

"I'll see if my boyfriend can do your Apostille on Sunday and give you a call."

"Thank you so much." I hugged her, sprinted up the stairs to the street, and almost dislocated my ankle jogging down the cobblestones to the Underground station. I checked my watch. The walk was in about five minutes. Dammit.

By the time I got my bearings and figured out the right track, I just missed a train. Five minutes later, I had minded the gap, found a seat near the door, and was headed east. I pulled out my tour schedule to double-check the right stop. I might be a little late, but hoped they might wait for strays who would pay.

I had sent hundreds of older clients to London's Afoot! based on the fact that they called themselves "the first, the best, the premiere walking tours," but were they? After meeting Nigel and Madge, I had to wonder. They did offer the largest selection of tours and they did have several notable British actors and academics like Shep as guides, but when I thought about it, this was possibly the most un-English pamphlet I had ever seen. It was positively seething with self-aggrandizement and exclamation marks. Didn't the English hate bragging? Weren't they supposed to be subtle and understated? And who wrote these bios?

I was glad I didn't have a drink in hand when I read Shep's, or I might have spit-taked it all over the ten-year-old boy kicking his legs beside me. "Dashing Professor Shepard Helnikov, clothed in his signature cape and waistcoat, is the jewel in our crown, our proverbial rock star, the Mick Jagger of Ripperologists, the Elton John of Illusionologists." Illusionologists? Could that even be a word and what the hell were they talking about? "He comes to the bloody cobblestones of Whitechapel via the mean streets of Hoboken and the deepest bowels of the British Library. Let the acclaimed author of the bestseller *Jacked!* and contributor to countless anthologies and academic journals take you into the demented mind of a murderer, where he has spent most of his life. With doctorates in history and psychology and teaching positions on two shores, Shep also enjoys paddle boarding, flavored vodkas, double Gloucester and Renegade Monk cheese, the game Battleship (he was New England champion in 1975, mediocre players beware!) and amateur magician—find him on Thursday nights performing at "Now You See Him" in Clapham.

What the hell? Illusionologist? Paddle boarder? Who were they talking about? If Shep had written this, I didn't know him as well as I thought I did. Just as I was checking the bios for the other Ripper guides, they announced the Tower Hill stop.

Nigel had warned me that there were multiple "fake" tours and to be sure I was with an authentic guide. So, when I emerged from the Tower Hill station, which, I had to admit, looked like a bunker, I expected chaos.

Instead, it was almost completely deserted. No London's Afoot! guide, no fake guides, no tourists, no Uncle Leon.

The area didn't even look particularly Ripperesque. I had imagined crumbling brick buildings, tiny dark alleys, maybe even energy-efficient faux gaslights, like they had at Disney World. Instead, I was surrounded by concrete, neon, and aside from the moldy-looking Royal London Hospital across the street, a decidedly late-twentieth, early-twenty-first century LED-lit vibe. Behind me though, past the round red and blue Underground sign, was the ghoulish, glowing Tower of London—where Anne Boleyn lost her head—hovering amid the modern city like some green-screen special effect across the river.

Where was everybody? I saw brochures on the ground. They must have been here.

Should I try to catch up to the tour? Which way would it go? I stood still and listened. There was melodrama, interrupted by traffic, somewhere, but the streets were so empty, the echoes made it hard to tell where they were coming from. I really didn't want to take out my map at an isolated location, at night.

"Are you lost, love?"

I turned to see a man dressed in black, his face in shadow, lounging by the entrance to the station. My would-be purse snatcher had made me a little paranoid, so I took a semi-kickboxing stance. "No, I'm fine, thanks. Just waiting for someone. We're doing the Jack the Ripper tour."

"They're long gone. They leave at seven thirty, on the dot."

"Oh, well, that explains it. Thank you." I started to back towards the station. Why the hell had Nigel told me eight? I looked down at the second pamphlet, which said the tour was at seven thirty, and at the one he'd given me, where the time was crossed out and replaced. I checked my phone to find a text from Uncle Leon saying he couldn't make it and would meet me at the memorial service in the morning.

I wanted to honor Shep, but I'd never catch up to the tour now. And since I'd arrived seven hours ago, I had stormed the embassy, surprised a burglar, climbed five flights of stairs to be patronized, been almost mugged, had a drink in a cave, and been stood up by a relative. Maybe I could just go back to the hotel. Plus, even with the modern buildings, this place was creepy as hell. And that guy was still hanging around.

I made for the train. He entered behind me, but I managed to get into a different carriage. The cars were significantly more empty going back, now that it was post rush hour and the plays in the West End would have started. I put my roll of quarters in my pocket.

I got out at Temple station, which was on the Embankment. So did my helpful friend. I didn't want to lead him to my hotel, so I headed for the theatre marquees I spotted in the distance. Then wandered towards what I thought was Covent Garden, in search of the shoe sale Delores had mentioned. That killed the next hour. By the time I got back to the Savoy with two patent leather pairs of Louis XIV-heel shoes in wine and navy, I was ready for room service. Unfortunately, it was only four o'clock in Brooklyn.

I arrived in the room to find three messages from Dean Dean dickhead McAfferty, two from Sister Ellery, and one from Aunt Helen. God, what was I going to tell Aunt Helen? I tried Sister Ellery at the office first, in case it was a client emergency.

"Redondo Travel, Ms. Malcomb sitting in for Cyd Redondo."

"Nice phone manner," I said.

She laughed. "It just saves time. How's it going?"

I told her a bit about the embassy issue and Shep's dying on the walk.

"Oh, he was murdered, then?"

"Well, I don't think we can assume that. It could just be a strange coincidence."

"Nope. Not according to my second sight."

"Since when do you have second sight? And shouldn't that have told you he was going to die in advance?"

"That's not the way it works."

"So it's second hindsight?"

"You always were a smart-ass, even at seven. Anyway, it sounds dubious to me, so be careful. How's your uncle?"

I filled her in on that as well. "What should I tell Aunt Helen?"

"He texted you tonight?"

"Yes."

"So he's alive?"

"Well, I don't want to jinx it."

She gave her raucous, non-nunlike laugh. "Then fudge. You don't need to upset her unnecessarily."

"Because she'll come straight to the office, that's why you want me to fudge."

"If you don't fudge, what are you going to tell her?"

"No idea. But you're right, no need to worry her. In fact, do me a favor?"

I made sure Sister Ellery was talking to Aunt Helen when I called her back, so the call went to voicemail. I was a coward, no question. A jet-lagged coward. I left a message saying we'd arrived safely, were going to Shep's memorial in the morning, and would call her after.

Then I practiced the same cowardly behavior by leaving a message for Dean Dean with the History Department secretary.

That's when I noticed that Shep's shoulder bag was not where I'd left it. And it was open.

Chapter Seventeen

I took out my quarters and tiptoed to the bathroom, throwing the door open. Nothing. There wasn't a closet and no one could fit in the armoire, I didn't think. No one under the bed, either. Once I'd double-locked the door, I picked up Shep's bag.

Could I even remember what I'd put inside? I'd just grabbed the papers and shoved them in. It seemed like there were about the same number of them, although they looked neater than they should, given the shoving. At least I'd put the other stuff in my purse, so that was safe.

I hoped. I lifted my bag onto the bed and foraged for everything I'd put there when I'd been in Shep's apartment. I pulled out the key on the red disk, his watch, the handkerchief, the wedding photo, and his waistcoat.

I took out my smallest flat Tupperware and put the vital items inside, then laid the container at the very bottom of my bag, where it was unlikely to be lifted by a random pickpocket. I folded the waistcoat and put it in my carry-on.

Given the Savoy's reputation, I hated to go all hysterical and insist someone had broken into my room, but it did make me nervous. Housekeeping might have moved the bag, but they shouldn't have unlatched it. Maybe I was just experiencing some kind of jet-lagged paranoia. I'd sleep on it and see how I felt in the morning.

• • •

I woke up feeling silly for overreacting and groggy, as it was only two a.m. in Brooklyn. I splurged on a room service breakfast with a whole pot of coffee and tried to figure out what to wear to Shep's memorial service.

Looking through my carry-on, I thought about one of my favorite fictional characters—Kinsey Milhone—and her indestructible little black dress. I had taken a page out of her book, although mine was a bit more delicate. The spandex tended to shed a few sequins every time I wore it. It was essentially backless and perfect for evening, but for funerals, not so much. I decided to "day it down" with my peplum jacket, opaque black tights for the cold, and my new wine-colored pumps from LK Bennett. It was probably a mistake to wear shoes that weren't broken in, but Shep deserved them.

Happily, my dark red Balenciaga went with everything. Well, except orange, but I never wore orange. I double-checked that I had plenty of tissues and donned *Breakfast at Tiffany's*–level waterproof mascara since, let's face it, I was going to cry. I texted Uncle Leon with the address, again. I hoped he was going to show.

On the way out, I had Shep's bag put in the hotel safe.

I splurged on a taxi because it was misting outside and my hair expanded exponentially under those conditions. Plus, apparently the service was on some kind of heath. Although it was a somber occasion, I was strangely looking forward to at least one aspect of it—matching up the guides with their bios.

When the taxi let me off at the top of a hill there were already maybe thirty people milling around. I spotted a blowup of Shep's author photo on a stand, surrounded by black roses.

There was more black around the photo than on the mourners. The outfits almost all included hats that offered a mash-up of every Masterpiece Theatre show from the last ten years. And then I spotted a hat straight out of *The Grinch That Stole Christmas*, complete with pom-pom.

It was atop the head of a woman in a faded pea coat over a long forest green tunic sweater, faded purple leggings, and ankle boots. I figured she was the woman named in the brochure as "Aubrey, our own live elf, ever childlike, with the effervescence of a shaken bottle of champers, ready to explode with her love of panto and knowledge of esoteric alleys on every Dickens walk she leads."

Beside her was a woman with a river of unrealistic black hair and a red velvet cape over a pair of jodhpurs. I pegged her as "Helena, a Blue Plaque guide with vintage velvet capes worthy of *The French Lieutenant's Woman*, a long history of appearances on *Coronation Street*, and a propensity for Jonathan Swift. Let her mellifluous voice guide you through the nooks and overhangs of tony Mayfair."

I walked past a woman in an Empire waist dress with Jane Austen–esque cleavage and figured she was probably Elizabeth Alsbury, "a guide with an impeccable heritage, descendant of Mary Shelley, and leader of the Regency Redux tour who enjoys needlework, country dance, etymology, and cycling down canals."

I also saw how Shep might have developed his waistcoat obsession, as there were lots of them in evidence, under vintage wool suit jackets and over what Jerry Seinfeld would have called pirate shirts.

One deep burgundy waistcoat adorned a tall, athletic figure with fab longish white hair in a Holmby hat. He held his head slightly back and to one side, as if posing for a booking photo or a jaunty mug shot. Could that be Malcom Etheridge, "best known as the original Inspector Hardy in the *Little Village Green* mysteries. A veteran of both the National Theatre and the West End with a weakness for juggling, claret, and basset hounds, his theatre district tours mesmerize. Be ready for randy gossip and perhaps a tap dance or two as he 'detects' the West End's hidden secrets"?

He did resemble a staple on the various **PBS** mysteries I watched with Uncle Leon on Sunday nights. Where was Uncle Leon? I actually hadn't seen him or heard his voice in almost twenty-four hours. Anyone could have been texting me. I searched the crowd, but still no sign.

Finally Nigel Hammersmithson, dressed in a morning coat straight out of *My Fair Lady*, uttered a loud "Ahem," and a "Shall we begin?" This was followed by the flinging of scarves, overly dramatic sighs, and shuffles with hints of ballet. Madge, dressed in an ill-fitting navy blue sack dress and a hat straight out of *Foyle's War* came to stand near him.

He stepped forward in front of the photo, completely blocking it, and held up his hands, then brought them down in a gesture that was half conductor, half NFL referee.

"Thank you all for coming, both those who were invited and those who have stumbled onto this celebration." He gave what seemed like a pointed look in my direction. "We gather here in honor of our fallen comrade, our compatriot, who died, as he lived, diving deep into the Victorian slums of London and the mind of a brutal killer. Shep had much to teach all of us. Happily his books and his research will continue to delight us, even now that he has left us for the Ten Bells in the sky."

There were a few "Hear, hears!" from the crowd, which totally creeped me out.

"Although Shep was only part of our family for a few months every year, he will be in our hearts for all twelve. And now it is up to Martin, Philip, Sean, and Brunhilde to carry on the exemplary Ripper tours that Shep designed and guided so very well."

"And to keep the numbers up," a short man in front of me, in yet another waistcoat, but bald and bareheaded, mumbled. Was he one of the other Ripper guides? Nigel had reeled off their names too quickly for me to identify them all. I'd ask once the service was over.

"I will now yield the stage to our own Ophelia, Jemima Comstock."

Wow. No matter how you cut it, being called Ophelia, even for an actress, was not really a compliment. I caught a couple of smug smiles in the crowd.

Jemima flipped the blonde ringlets that spilled out deliberately from her black beret, and moved toward the podium. Today she was dressed more steampunk, in a tight, long vintage dress, trimmed with black feathers, a tulle jacket, and patent leather lace-up Doc Martens. All she needed was a few sequins and a pop of color and she would have looked fab.

"Dear friends. Dearest guides." She put a piece of dainty lace to her eyes. As her makeup still looked perfect, I imagined it was a bit of a Mock Turtle situation. She lowered the handkerchief, straightened her shoulders, and waited for silence.

"It is our great privilege to be storytellers, to be guides, to be the keepers of the flame. Today, we are here to honor a brief candle which burned brightly, to celebrate the life and legacy of our friend, our inspiration, and my beloved partner, Shep Helnikov. We turn, of course, to the Bard." Jemima paused, then spoke from her corsetted diaphragm, with full projection, and occasional dramatic hand gestures.

"This passion, and the death of a dear friend, would go near to make a man look sad, for in that sleep of death what dreams may come, when we have shuffled off this mortal coil, must give us pause. The valiant never taste of death but once."

Even I, who hadn't studied Shakespeare since high school, could tell Jemima was doing some kind of bizarre mash-up of the Bard's greatest hits. I could identify *Hamlet* and *A Midsummer Night's Dream* so far.

"Out, out, brief candle." Ha. *Macbeth.* Catholic boys hadn't been secure enough to volunteer for Shakespeare, so I had played Macduff in our junior high production. Macduff Redondo. I could tell I wasn't the only one who'd noticed the pattern, as several guides were sharing looks. This didn't deter Jemima.

"Death smiles at all of us. All a man can do is smile back." Wait, wasn't that from *Gladiator*? She leaned forward and threw out her hands, beseechingly. "Every man dies. Not every man truly lives." Okay, that was definitely *Braveheart.* I guess she figured throwing out her hands was enough to transition from classical theatre to period action films.

I could feel a restlessness in the crowd. A few people were looking at papers in their hands, or seemed to be talking to themselves. They were all prepping to go onstage.

"Shep. Shep. Shep." Jemima pulled out her handkerchief again. There was a smattering of applause. At a funeral. Jemima did a half bow as she inched aside to make room for a lanky man in a Victorian morning coat and mohawk.

She gave him a nod. "I yield the stage to our own Stephen Strick."

He bowed to Jemima and stepped up. "Today we honor Shep. An American. America has given much to us. It has not only given us Shep's scholarship and *joie de vivre*, it has given us Arthur Miller." Arthur Miller? Seriously? "So today, I honor the true America, which raised and formed Shep Helnikov."

The man proceeded to launch into a scene between Willy and Biff from *Death of a Salesman*. He performed both parts in the kind of nasally American accent popularized by Anthony Hopkins. Was this a not-at-all-subtle dig that Shep was liked, but not well-liked? I guess we were lucky Strick hadn't chosen a selection from *Who's Afraid of Virginia Woolf?*

Actors. I hadn't had much experience with actors, so this thespian tidal wave was a revelation. They had beautiful, PBS voices, theatrical clothing, and the need to top each other with each speech. An immolation might not be surprising by the time they got to the end. I heard a woman in a watch cap laugh. We were only halfway through the scene.

Finally, Stephen the actor threw back his head. "A man is not a piece of fruit!!!!" I wasn't convinced Mr. Miller had included four exclamation points in that line, but what did I know?

He ended with the most touching bit of all. "For those of you who would like to know more about the dead, pointless American dream that Shep and so many Yanks strive for, the full play is running through Saturday next at the King's Head in Islington. Eight p.m. curtain, one drink minimum." Scattered applause. More scattered than applause.

Another man stepped up. He was wearing a black cape and must have requested an Alan Rickman haircut, which went awry.

"A hit. A palpable hit. Shepard Helnikov was a committed scholar, an effective raconteur, a solid guide. I am gratified that he followed in my footsteps and I was honored to be his mentor."

I heard a snort and turned towards a broad-shouldered, military-looking man holding a flask, whose eyebrows resembled warring fuzzy caterpillars. I raised my own highly curated eyebrows—thanks to Lashes Ahoy! on 4th Avenue—and leaned toward him.

"Who is that?"

"Another Ripper guide. Martin Thompson. They were barely civil.

Shep considered him a hack. His Ripper book is self-published. He's been cited by Nigel twice for trying to sell it on his tours."

"Ouch."

"Precisely."

Jemima had moved back to the podium and looked out at the crowd. As always, she waited for silence, but this time there was the sound of sobbing, then sniffling, then more sobbing. I had just turned to try to find the culprit, when Jemima spoke up.

"Now, I'd like to welcome up one of Shep's dear friends, one who has come all the way from the States to be here today, his travel agent, Cindy Redondo."

My face went white. Really? She was expecting me to follow twelve members of the Royal Shakespeare Company, with an impromptu speech? Wow. She did hate me. Still. I loved Shep and this was for him. Besides, I might not be an actress—Macduff and Tinkerbell notwithstanding—or a London guide, or a professor, but I did have one thing that Jemima Comstock did not have. A miniskirt. I took my time walking up, then turned and looked at the crowd. And saw Uncle Leon. With a date.

Chapter Eighteen

There was my seventy-five-year-old uncle, dressed to the nines in a black gabardine suit, a pale blue shirt, skinny black tie, pale pink pocket square, and pointy shoes shined within an inch of their lives. On his arm was a lovely Asian woman with white hair and horn-rimmed glasses, dressed in an expensive black coat, class all the way except for a hideous brooch spouting peacock feathers—just the kind of thing a taxidermist might give his mistress. Dammit. Seeing this didn't really help my focus. Like the previous speakers, I paused before I began.

Though I often spoke at the Third Avenue Businessperson's Association, I hadn't really performed a eulogy before—certainly not by way of an audition for summer stock. I had learned early not to draw attention to myself in a group of people who make a living trying to draw attention to themselves. My tenth-grade audition for the lead in *Bye Bye Birdie* almost turned fatal when my ex-husband's second, now pregnant, wife, Angela Hepler, president of the Drama Club, noticed our teacher smiling at my rendition of "Old Man River" and loosed a sandbag that missed me by millimeters.

"Miss Redondo?"

I looked out at the crowd. There was no microphone. Actors were trained to project. An entire life trying to be heard above ten teenaged boys would have to do.

"Hello, everyone. As you can tell from my accent, like Shep, I come from the land of Arthur Miller." I smiled at Stephen Strick, who took a deep bow.

"It's been so illuminating to hear about all your experiences with him and to see him through your eyes, as a scholar, as a guide, as a Ripper expert, as a companion." Uncle Leon actually had the nerve to wink at me then. Someone in the back started wailing again.

"These are the things I know about Shep that you may not. He would only sit in a window seat. He was allergic to airline peanuts, he would never reveal the source of his waistcoats, he always had gum in his pocket, and he overtipped at happy hours. He also had the best laugh, ever. I will miss him more than I can say. I could never compete with the lovely readings you've performed today, so I will just add this, from one of Shep's favorite poets."

Thankfully, I knew this one by heart. I channeled my inner Jersey girl and began, "'Baby, this town rips the bones from your back,'" to a carpet of blank faces. I kept going anyway. Springsteen was the bard Shep would have wanted. After thanking them for including me, I put my head down and hurried out of the spotlight to the sound of one Redondo snort and more sobbing. I felt like sobbing myself. Especially since Jemima encouraged all of us to join her in a rendition of the blindingly obvious but still heart-wrenching "We'll Meet Again."

As I joined the crowd, I caught movement out of the corner of my eye, then heard a war cry as a flying object flattened the actress.

"Lying cow!" The assailant, sporting a twin set and pearls, straddled her enemy, jerked Jemima's beret off, and started hitting her with it.

Jemima reached up and grabbed the woman's hair. "He was just using you!"

The twin set slapped her. "We were soul mates!"

"You were not. He was not dowdy!" Jemima grabbed her assailant's necklace. Pearls flew everywhere.

Twin set let out a familiar wail, just louder. "Jezebel! Beelzebub!"

At this point, Nigel and Madge managed to pull the women apart. A woman in a trench coat put her arm around the woman in the twin set and led her away.

In the confusion I'd lost sight of Uncle Leon, possibly because I was still crying a little. I reached for a packet of tissues and pushed my way through the crowd. A man with the black bangs of an early Beatle, a pop art shirt Micky Dolenz might have worn, and peg pants worthy of *Pet Sounds* stepped in front of me. I felt a wave of nausea.

"Here," he said, "let me hold that for you." He took my purse while I freed a tissue from the stubborn packet, dried my eyes, and pulled myself together.

"Thank you," I said, holding out my hand. "Cyd Redondo, Redondo Travel."

"Peter Stacio, tour guide." He had a "Ringo" accent. "Nice speech. I heard from Nigel that you wanted a chat about Shep. I'm doing my Swinging Sixties walk tonight at seven. We stop at some decent pubs."

I admit, I wasn't really paying attention, as Uncle Leon was getting farther and farther away. "Yes, absolutely," I said, taking back my purse and the card he handed me. "I have to run, see you there."

"Don't run. Not in those heels, let me help."

I pointed at Uncle Leon and Stacio took off. He had a pretty bowlegged run. He stopped Uncle Leon just as he was getting into a limo. Once I'd gotten halfway to the car, he nodded at me, then disappeared.

The mystery woman was already inside when I reached Uncle Leon, who hugged me.

"Tough day. You did great, Squid, Shep would be proud."

"Who is that woman?"

"Not important. What's going on with the body?"

I explained. He promised to meet me in the morning at the hotel, when I hoped Shelagh would get us Apostilled. Then he hit the top of the limo and got inside.

As it drove away, my phone buzzed. It was Aunt Helen. I needed a drink.

The speeches were still going, but the crowd was getting restless. I sought out my military-looking friend with the flask.

"Any chance of a sip?"

"My pleasure. It's that kind of day." He offered the antique silver container.

"It certainly is," I said, taking it gratefully, then almost spitting it out. "What is this?"

"Absinthe."

"Oh, right." I didn't think absinthe was something people drank in the morning. I figured it was pretty character-defining if you did. I held out my free hand. "Cyd Redondo, Redondo Travel."

"Roderick Buckminster, OBE. You may call me Sir Rod."

"Don't you usually drink this with water?"

"If you want to dilute its effects."

"Got it. Are you one of the London guides as well?"

"God, no. I teach ancient military tactics at the University of London. Shep and I shared an office."

"And absinthe?"

"On occasion." He grinned. "He spoke about you, you know. He thought of you as a daughter, which was interesting, as he dated a lot of women your age."

"Yes, I'm getting that impression. Jemima, right?"

"She was one of them."

I took another sip of absinthe to be polite, then handed the flask back.

He took a long glug. "You have some relationship to Leon Redondo?"

"He's my uncle."

"I gather he sparked Shep's interest in history. He said you have a singular family."

"Well, that's one way to put it. It's highly male."

"All the best families are."

I didn't really know how to respond to that, except with "Pardon me. It's lovely to meet you. I have to be somewhere."

"Of course. I hope to see you again."

I left him sipping and slogged up the hill, my heels sinking in the wet grass.

I hailed a cab. "The British Library, please."

Chapter Nineteen

I was a library junkie. I loved all of them, from the mobile ice-cream truck versions and flat one-story ranch branches to the lion-guarded New York Public Library. When you're a travel agent who doesn't get to go anywhere, the library is the next best thing, the whole world in one building, your ticket to almost everything you need for your clients. And now I was going to the gold standard. The British Library. The cab seemed to take forever as it wound its way down from Hampstead Heath to the Euston Road.

I exited the cab, feeling a bit off-balance. I figured it was the jet lag or not enough espresso, or maybe it was the British Library itself, which, to be honest, was a shock. I expected an ancient, hallowed building. Instead, I saw a huge new geometric brick edifice, about as unhallowed as you could get.

Then I spotted the statue in the courtyard. It was a monumental brass version of William Blake's drawing of Isaac Newton—a print I'd studied in Art History and You at City College—and it stopped me in my tracks. It was funny how public art could make you go all wobbly. I guess that was the point.

When I finally got to the library entrance, there was a line to get in. And at the end of the line, a security guard checking random bags. I made a quick detour to what looked like the "smoking section" alley and put various metal objects in my bra. I hoped with the peplum jacket, the end of the blowtorch and the penlight might seem nipple-like.

The guard asked me to open the main section of my purse, then said, "Food can only be eaten in the cafes."

"No problem." I wondered what the hell he was talking about—I'd eaten my emergency protein bar in the cab. I could see the line was longer to get out. They were really digging into people's bags there. I guessed they didn't want anyone stealing books.

Once I was inside, I was struck dumb for the second time in ten minutes. Whatever magic the exterior of the building might have lacked, the inside more than made up for it. Gorgeous layers of marble stairs, intercut with escalators, flowed up from the lobby to the floors above. I could see glass cabinets filled with ancient books, floor to ceiling. There were people everywhere, sitting on the floor with their laptops, leaning against standing desks, chatting in the cafe. Signs directed visitors to the

Permanent Exhibitions, the Reading Rooms, Circulation, the Rare Book Collection.

The first thing I did was go down the steps to Circulation, where I got a library card. Technically, if you were from the U.S., you needed to be an academic, but as I had Dean Dean's card, I was able to fudge it and in ten minutes I was official, if washed out. The lighting in the room gave me circles under my eyes the size of coasters, but I knew it was the only way to get into the Reading Rooms, where Shep had spent most of his time.

The clerk reminded me that only computers, notebooks, and pencils were allowed in the Reading Rooms. She directed me down another flight of stairs to place my purse and coat in the locker room. Fat chance, I thought, but as I walked down, I could see everyone walking around with the same see-through plastic British Library bags Shep had in his flat and nothing else. I would actually have to leave my purse in a locker. This filled me with dread. I wrote off my unbalanced feeling to this phobia, as I walked into a new kind of locker room—filled with scholars and absentminded clothing rather than jocks and towels for a change.

I took a plastic bag from a stack by the door, and then noticed the available lockers had red keys hanging from them that were just like the one I'd found in Shep's waistcoat. I was dying to open his locker, but thought it would be smarter on my way out. I popped a pound coin in the slot to remove a key on a locker near the front, took my passport and cash out of the secret side pocket of my bag and, hiding behind the locker door, shoved them in my bra. It was getting crowded in there. I placed my coat over my bag, closed the locker door, and checked that it was locked at least three times. The Balenciaga separation anxiety had begun, so I hurried to the Humanities Reading Room, trying to remember to stay on the "wrong" side of the steps.

I think my sequins got me points with the security guards in the Reading Room, who smiled and waved me through. The room had a busy circulation desk, with lots of people in line to collect stacks of books. The rest of the room had rows and rows of carrels that spread to the walls filled with bookshelves. I spotted the Information Desk and the broad freckled face of the librarian on duty. She had the open, slightly questioning expression of someone about to offer help. She was also wearing a familiar twin set. With grass stains.

She squinted her eyes, then she sent up a familiar wail—which sounded a lot louder in this silent chamber of scholarship than it had on a heath, and threw herself facedown on the counter. Her compatriot gave me a startled look, then patted the woman on the shoulder, while the entire room of readers looked on.

"There, there, Evelyn." The other librarian looked up at me. "She's had a loss."

I approached the kiosk. "Yes, I know," I said. "I'm so sorry. I think we've both just come from Shep's service. That's why I'm here." Evelyn turned her flattened head to look at me.

"Cyd Redondo, Redondo Travel. If you could spare a minute, I would love to buy you a cup of tea or something?"

"Yes," the other librarian said, "that's a marvelous idea. Thanks." She peeled her compatriot off the polished oak surface and got her vertical. "I did suggest she take the day off."

Ms. Twin Set settled her shoulders. "I'm perfectly capable of working, thank you very much. Hello, Evelyn Woodhouse. Collections Specialist."

Much of her lipstick had migrated to her cheek. I held out my hand. After we shook, she kept hold of it as we moved toward the exit. The security guards had the kindness not to check my plastic bag and I managed to get my trauma victim to a wooden chair in the adjacent cafe.

I reached toward my purse for tissues and got nothing but air. It was like a phantom limb. I grabbed some napkins for her and said I'd be right back. By the time I returned, she had stopped crying, but still had a bit of orange-red on her cheek. I didn't have the heart to tell her and hoped she would inadvertently wipe it away after eating the chocolate croissant I'd brought back for her. She kept touching her breastbone in search of the missing pearls.

"Thank you." She took the tea, poured in tons of milk and sugar, and sucked it down.

"You're welcome." I took a sip of my cappuccino.

"He talked about you," Evelyn said. "You were the one who found him his flat, right?"

"Yes, well, I was the person who found the person who found his flat."

I didn't want to provoke more tears. I had to tread carefully. But the longer I was here, the longer my purse was in a locker. "I assume you two were close?"

She raised a napkin to her eyes and nodded. "Ever since I found him the Whitechapel tax rolls from 1888," she said. "They were a cornerstone of his first book."

"Yes, that sounds very romantic. Were you helping him with the new book, too?"

"Of course. He called me his Muse from Hell." She sniffled. "We shared a lot of Ripper humor."

"I'm sure you did. It must have been wonderful for him to have someone who shared his passion that way."

"Yes. That's why I don't believe he would have had anything to do with that ridiculous actress. She knows nothing."

I wasn't going down this road. "One of the reasons I'm here in London is because the dean of his department at Brooklyn College has asked me to bring back his research."

"Why?"

"I'm not completely sure. Maybe he's designated someone there to finish his work?"

"How dare they? No one could possibly do that."

"That's probably not it. I honestly don't know. But I'm his designated executor and everything of his that's here in London is supposed to go back with me." She got a little frown between her eyebrows. "Since you're clearly the person who is most involved with and up to date on his research, I was just hoping you could tell me a bit about the new book and maybe point me to any notes or anything else he might have left here? Or to show me what he was reading lately?"

She gave me a long look. "You didn't date him, did you?"

"No. God no. He was more like an uncle. A completely platonic uncle."

"I did keep a few things for him behind the desk. If you had a library card, I could let you take a look at the books he had on hold. But none of those can leave the Reading Room."

I held up my unflattering photo card. "I think I should look at them, at least."

I pointed out Evelyn's straying lipstick before sending her to the restroom. Then she set me up in a carrel with the items Shep had on hold.

I couldn't believe I was actually sitting in a Reading Room, with my own stack of books, surrounded by people brimming with knowledge, degrees, and dandruff. The truth was, though I had officially graduated from City College of New York with dual degrees in hospitality and accounting, I'd worked full-time through my whole college career, so it had taken me six years to finish. And I'd never gotten to take enough humanities classes to feel really educated.

I looked at the books in front of me. I didn't actually know what I was looking for. I could at least give Dean Dean a list of the sources Shep had been using, so I proceeded to write down the titles on a British Library notebook Evelyn had been kind enough to give me. She'd also handed me the folder Shep had asked her to keep.

As I opened the fourth book, I found two pieces of paper, one in Shep's distinctive writing and the other much older, faded, and official. They were folded together. I figured Shep wouldn't do anything dodgy when it came to scholarship, so they must belong to him, and so, now to me. I waited until no one was looking and slipped both into Shep's folder. I didn't find anything else in the books, so returned them to the circulation desk. Evelyn was busy with a patron as I left, but I waved and held up Shep's folder in my plastic bag, mouthing *thank you*. The security guards gave the bag a cursory look, thank God.

So I had something, at least, that I could look at back at the hotel, although it might take a Ripper expert to decipher it. Now, I was ready to see what Shep had locked in the bowels of the library.

First, I had to liberate my purse. The locker room was quieter now, except for a large teenager with a buzz cut and pants five times too big, talking on his phone right where I needed to be.

"Excuse me," I said, trying to ease in. He didn't budge. I restrained myself from giving him a roundhouse kick to the head and stood, tapping my heel, until he finally moved down toward the "staging table" that I was going to need next. Was it politically incorrect to hate adolescents? Too bad.

I opened the locker, my heart doing flip-flops until I found my Balenciaga safe beneath my coat and scarf. Keeping an eye out for the discourteous teen, I took it out, turning the key to lock and leaving my coat and scarf where they were for now.

I carried my purse and the plastic bag to a long table on the other side of the room. I could hear a strange snuffling noise. Maybe it was the library filtration system.

I reached for the other locker key and wandered around until I found its match on the bottom row at the back of the room. My tight, sequined skirt might be great for distracting security guards, but for squatting by the lowest locker, not so much. Without my kickboxing background it would have been impossible.

Shep's locker, like his living room, was a mess. Had someone already been in here, or was this just the way he kept it? The first thing I found was a sandwich. Thankfully, it was double ziplocked. There was a battered notebook with a British Library cloakroom claim ticket as a bookmark. I noticed the teen was coming my way again. Could he be the purse snatcher?

I eased Shep's things into the plastic bag, returned the key, retrieving the pound coin deposit, threw my purse over my shoulder, and hurried out, deciding on the ladies' room on another floor as the place to reorganize all Shep's stuff.

As I walked up the stairs, I still felt something was off with my bag. It might look random to anyone who opened it, but it was a highly calibrated, technical environment, ruled by various Tupperware containers. I had a few extra things when I traveled, but the basic checklist included moisturized tissues, a penlight, a glow stick, a mini-lint roller, a mini-bottle of neutral nail color, plastic tweezers and nail clippers, a roll of quarters, which doubled as a sap, a small bottle of Jack Daniel's, which doubled as hand sanitizer, plastic zip tie handcuffs—courtesy of the 68th Precinct—my regular wallet, my emergency emergency wallet, Band-Aids, travel deodorant, a black silk scarf, nesting Atlantic City shot glasses, a small blowtorch, Neosporin, Advil, Tylenol, dental floss, mini-toothpaste, mini-Listerine, push-up pads for my bra, Responsible Raisin lipstick, a pocket translator, various stationery supplies, a set of lock picks, my passport and my dad's compass as well as two new additions in honor of my trip: a paperback Dickens novel and fold-up ballet flats, for stealth.

Since my last two trips, I had spent time in my attic room, practicing walking in flats. It was torture. No woman who was five-foot-two should have to do it.

So, when I felt a bit of extra weight, approximately five ounces, that hadn't been there when I went to Shep's service, I was concerned. I hurried through the bathroom door, checked under doors for occupants, and entered a stall. I sat down on the lowered seat, put the British Library bag and my purse on my lap. When I did, I felt a vibration against my thigh. I tried to feel through the bottom of the purse as, given that I had been known to be a reptile magnet, I wasn't keen to open it to an asp or something. Whatever it was felt roundish—could be a curled-up snake—but also warm, which made it potentially less snaky. God, what was warm and that small? Nothing good.

Happily, my penlight and quarters were in an outside pocket, for easy access. I tried to balance them on top of the toilet paper dispenser, really wishing it were flat instead of those stupid round ones. I popped the snap on my purse and eased the top zipper open.

The first thing I saw was a torn, empty quart ziplock knockoff that had holes in it. What the hell? I grabbed the penlight and shone it in. In the very bottom, wedged between a powder blue flat Tupperware and my abridged copy of *David Copperfield*, I spotted something that looked like a breathing hunk of bread pudding. With whiskers.

Chapter Twenty

It's amazing how loud a scream can be when it's bouncing off tile. The door opened. Clunky shoes ran toward my stall.

"I beg your pardon, are you all right?" The very posh English voice sounded like it didn't really want to know. "I don't suppose you need any help?"

"No. Sorry. It's nothing."

"But you screamed."

"Yes." I was wracking my brains. "It was just a small miscarriage."

"Good God. Should I call someone?"

"No. No! I meant a miscarriage of justice. A case I was working on. I'm a police officer."

"With the Met? I'm DCI Sarah Hamilton."

"No. NYPD. Francis Redondo. Seriously, I'm fine. No worries."

"You're sure?"

"You know what it's like when the bad guys win. Really, I just need some time alone."

"Right." Finally, she walked out.

I opened the top of the purse a bit wider. The creature inside was brownish gold, mouselike, and about three inches long. It was lying on its back with squinched eyes, holding on for dear life—with all four teensy paws—to a sparse and fuzzy tail pressed over its face.

It was possibly the cutest thing I had ever seen.

This helped with the whole rodent aspect, but cute or not, what was it doing there? Had it crawled in somehow? And if so, when? Had it been hiding in the empty locker?

My purse had passed through many high rodent areas, not only in Bay Ridge but in Tanzania, and the not so delicious bowels of a cruise ship. Never had any of that species been able to penetrate the sanctity of my bag. So, how the hell did it get there and what should I do with it? My first impulse was just to let it loose, but I could hardly do it here. It might get stepped on. Or eat books.

I checked the generic plastic bag which appeared to have deliberate holes punched into it, and then one large, chewed hole. Had the creature been inside and chewed its way out? As I moved a few items around it, it snuffled and squeaked, but its eyes stayed closed. Was it snoring? Was that the sound I'd been hearing? I went to throw the plastic bag away, when I saw writing on the white label.

It read "Keep him safe. GH."

GH? GH. The bowlegs. The wig. Of course. Grey Hazelnut, extreme animal activist, aka the Unavet. Swinging Sixties guide "Pete Stacio" was my part-time nemesis. No wonder I'd felt nauseous when I saw him.

We'd tangled in Tanzania and briefly joined forces in Tasmania. Why was he in London and why on earth had he planted this tiny thing on me? And how was I going to get a snoring rodent, and the rest of Shep's contraband, through the bag check at the exit? I sat on the toilet, as a few more women came and went, until I formulated a plan.

I might be versed in smuggling snakes in my bra, but mammals were a whole different dilemma. I could squeeze Shep's notes and ziplocks into my dress, but not anything I needed to keep alive. Then I remembered the guard's comment about food in my purse.

Minutes later, I was in line again at the cafe. I considered a Danish or muffin, but in the end erred on the side of safety and went with a doughnut for the built-in breathing hole. I carried it in a small brown paper bag back to the restroom. Once inside the stall, I took the doughnut out, made sure the creature was still asleep, and tried to suppress the memory of Bobby Pinkowsi putting a white mouse from the biology lab down my shirt in second grade. I could still feel it scrabbling in there. I took a breath and lifted my stowaway, cupping it in both hands to make sure it didn't commit inadvertent hari-kari by rolling into the toilet bowl. I was able to lower it into the paper bag and place the doughnut over it, then tucked it near the top on my purse, so it wouldn't be crushed.

I fit the rest of Shep's stuff into his folder and slid that into the outside pocket of my bag, exited the bathroom, retrieved my coat and scarf, and got in line.

I arrived at what appeared to be, literally, the changing of the guard.

As the new guard took over, I watched in horror as he began to take everything out of everyone's bag and put it on the table. Everything. There were a lot of things about this that were bad. For starters, a mouse was heavier than a doughnut. Plus, even if the guard didn't notice that, the little thing could escape. Or get trampled by scholars. When I was one person away from the Balenciaga cavity search, I did the only thing I could think of—took off my peplum jacket, to reveal my backless, Spanx-like cocktail dress. I took the mouse/doughnut out of the purse, as if I were about to take a bite, and tried to act naturally.

The guard reached for my bag without looking at me, foiling my plan to stupefy him with sequins. I always tell my clients, if they're stopped in Customs or anywhere else in a foreign country, just be quiet, and don't volunteer any information, as it makes you look suspicious at best and guilty at worst. This is sound advice, which I promptly ignored, partly to drown out the academic slut shaming happening behind my naked back and partly out of panic.

"Hi," I said, as loudly as I could. "Just visiting this gorgeous library for the first time. First time in jolly old England, in fact. Could you tell me a few good restaurants to visit? Or any good places to stay? Any theatre recommendations?"

He finally gave me an annoyed look, then shoved the purse at me. I nearly dropped the rodent bag taking it.

As I hit the door, I heard him say, "Bloody Yanks."

I returned to my old pal, the Newton statue, and eased the paper bag back into my purse, then hailed a cab back to the Savoy, waving gaily to concierge Kent on my way in, since I might well need some discreet vermin assistance in the foreseeable future.

It was only three o'clock, but it felt like midnight. And I had to stay awake at least through the Swinging Sixties London walk. I wasn't interested in Twiggy, but I was very interested in returning my traveling companion to Hazelnut or Stacio, or whoever he'd decided he was today. In the meantime, I didn't know what the tiny creature might do when it woke up. It had already demolished a ziplock, what might be next?

I opened my bag. It was still curled up in a protective position. Was it alive, or had it died of fright? I looked closer. It gave a small snort. Alive.

I wondered what it ate, if it were thirsty, and if it needed a diaper treatment, such as I had managed with the Tasmanian tiger cub who had resided in my purse for a few days. Thank goodness, after that experience, I made sure most of the things in the purse were either in Tupperware or plastic.

And what was it? It was mouselike, but its tale was too bushy for a mouse and not bushy enough for a mini-squirrel. Plus, I had never seen anything sleep that way. No matter what the creature ate, it needed water.

I took one of the teacup saucers and filled it with water, then made sure the bathtub bottom was dry, laid down a hand towel, set my Balenciaga down on top of it, and opened the top to its full, extended position.

I spotted the bushy tail and found the creature lying on top of one of my tissue packs, like a mouse mattress. I lifted it from on top of the tissue pack and laid it on the towel.

I squealed for a second time as it popped awake and ran, trying to scurry up the tub walls. It was frantic and I felt incredibly guilty. I tried to steer it towards the saucer, and finally it found it and began drinking. At least there was that, but I was sure it was hungry and scared. I knew wild animals shouldn't eat people food, but it had to be better than nothing. I called down and ordered some room service, making sure I ordered something with lettuce.

Now for containment. If it had chewed through the baggie, I needed something tougher, but with airholes. I hated to ruin another Tupperware, but I didn't have much of a choice unless there was something in the room I could use. Could I keep it in a drawer for safety, so it could run around a bit? Poor little thing, it looked so fragile. And, if Grey Hazelnut had anything to do with it, it was likely endangered.

After it had been watered and fed, I put a layer of napkins and toilet paper in the second drawer of the dresser. The creature was asleep again. I lifted it gently, laid it down on the bed of paper products, then eased the drawer shut. There would be plenty of oxygen there for now. By then I had an hour before I had to leave for the tour. There was just time to look at Shep's things.

I figured either there wasn't anything important in his shoulder bag, or if there had been, it was gone. So what was left? I opened the folder Evelyn had given me. It was full of handwritten notes that were barely decipherable, but seemed to be listed under the years 1887 and 1890 and included a lot of question marks. There were also two xeroxed pages from an 1887 *Illustrated Police News* with the headlines "Female Fiends Beat Man to Death with Fenders" and "Man Sleeps with Mad Dog." What these had to do with Jack the Ripper was anyone's guess, but I took pictures of all of it, just in case someone tried to nab it again.

Tucked in the middle, I found an ancient, almost see-through pamphlet stamped "Do Not Remove from Reading Room." Shit. Shep must have had a reason for hiding it, but it was actually me who had stolen it. I had desecrated the British Library. I was scum. And would Dean Dean even know what it was? I didn't have time to read it now, but I could always return it to Evelyn later. She might even have gotten it for him. I was afraid to open it, in case it might get damaged. When I lifted it, something fell out.

Inside a plastic bag was a letter covered in cramped Victorian script.

The ink was a bit smudged at the bottom, so I couldn't make out the signature. Was it Jack the Ripper's? I laughed at myself, then stopped. Had Shep found something that could be tested for DNA? Was this what Dean Dean wanted? Was this what all the break-ins and bag grabs were about? I was just about to compare it to the two notes I'd found in Shep's stack of books when I noticed the time. I had a date with Ringo.

Chapter Twenty-one

I put all of Shep's items into my rolling backpack to take down to the hotel safe and checked on my rodent roommate, who was still pressing his tail through his legs and over his face and snuffling. Should I bring him? Or leave him? I didn't really think he was safe in my purse, and besides, he'd had a rough day. I would let him sleep until I knew what the hell was going on.

I put on my Bendel coat and red scarf and swapped my heels for my boots. I put the *Do Not Disturb* sign on the door and left the TV on low, just to make sure housekeeping didn't come in to turn down the bed. I observed a moment of silence for the chocolate that would not be left on my pillow and jerked on the door to make sure it was locked.

I had just enough time to walk. I had to grab every inch of London I could. I turned left on the Strand and fought my way through focused, efficient Londoners and inefficient, interminable Americans to Piccadilly Circus and then right up Regent's Street, which was, in travel agent speak, a "prestigious lifestyle destination." It was famous for its upscale shopping, from Liberty London—a bit too chintzy for my style, but the perfect kind of dowdy for my ex-husband's wife, Angela Hepler—to Tiffany—completely my style, but not my budget—to the newest and biggest Apple Store in the world. That was a bit depressing, but helped with the Graduates Ahoy! package tours my clients bought for their grandkids. I kept my eye out in vain for *Winter Sale* signs as I curved around with the street, until I spotted the legendary, curlicued cast-iron sign for Carnaby Street that Uncle Leon had told me about. He said he'd actually seen the Beatles singing in a club, back in the day. I wondered whether the mystery woman on his arm was a former Twiggy wannabe from his past or the current threat to his marriage Aunt Helen was worried about. Or both?

The street itself was just as narrow and charming as Uncle Leon had promised. Most of the buildings had brightly painted doors and were Regency or Victorian or something. These were words English travel agents threw around all the time, but honestly, I was not always sure which was which. They were old. The street was purely pedestrian, paved in brick with trees planted in the middle. It was magical until you spotted the hideous square buildings at the end that appeared to be Early Administrative, an architectural era I was familiar with. By then, it was time for me to find my rodent-hiding tour guide.

I could hear Hazelnut's exaggerated Liverpool accent before I saw his wig and sunglasses. In many ways, he was a master of disguise—he had tricked me as a FedEx driver, a cruise ship gigolo, and today as a London's Afoot! employee. I had to give it to him, he was skillful with wigs and makeup and attitude. But there was one thing he couldn't hide unless he wore a maxi-skirt: bowlegs that formed parentheses wide enough for Tweedledum to roll through. They looked particularly parenthetical tonight, in the kind of tight sixties trousers that Uncle Leon favored. How had I not recognized him at the memorial service?

He was in the middle of a modest crowd, holding up the scarlet rectangle and taking money from the walkers. It was clear the walks only took cash and I wondered where the guides kept it, as it seemed like they would be sitting ducks walking home. When did they turn it in?

I stood there while he rambled on about Julie Christie and *Alfie*, until he noticed me. His scowl looked relieved. This was quite a change from the time I had completely ruined one of his undercover operations and he had declared me the female Anti-Christ—i.e., AntiChristine.

He led the walkers down an alley past what he said was Terence Stamp's favorite bar and allowed them to ogle it as he found me in the back. "Meet me at the end for the handoff."

"For the what?"

"Don't be an ass," he said to me. To the group, he declared, "And here we are at Regent's Street, originally designed by John Nash and named after George, Prince Regent, later George the Fourth."

While I soaked up sixties history, I figured I could drum up some new business. I chatted with Ted and Gwynn from Derry, Angelique and Pierre from Marseilles, and Betty and Bert from Perth. I gave away five business cards and got an open invitation to both Mt. Buggery and the town of Useless Loop in Western Australia.

We passed a club where the Who used to play as well as Mick Jagger's house and Mary Quant's first store. I could completely see Uncle Leon, snappy retro dresser that he was, here.

I noticed someone who was definitely not a snappy dresser—Madge—hovering at the back of the walk, watching Hazelnut with the concentration of a cobra. When she noticed me, she practically coiled.

Kill them with kindness, I thought. "Madge! How lovely to see you. I didn't realize you went on the tours yourself."

"We have certain standards, so we like to check in with some of the newer guides, watch them interact with the public, get a sense of their research."

"That makes sense. So, Mr. Stacio is a new guide?"

"Yes. We took him on at the last minute when our most popular sixties guide broke his leg on a holiday cruise."

"Oh, that's too bad. Where was he?"

"Australia."

Oh God. "How lucky that you found Mr. Stacio."

"He was recommended by our injured guide. Apparently he toured with the Dave Clark Five."

"Did he? How interesting." Bastard.

"You will excuse me?"

"Of course."

She worked her way towards "Stacio." I watched the exchange, a monetary one. Finally Madge headed off and Hazelnut continued his banter as we moved toward what he promised would be our final stop, a pub where Richard Harris threw a chair through a window.

As I entered, Hazelnut, beer in hand, waved to me, and pointed to the stairs. As the pub didn't have Jack Daniel's, I took possibly the worst glass of wine I'd ever had, including during communion, to the stuffy second floor. It had a smoke-stained, timbered ceiling right out of *Shakespeare in Love*.

He threw his hands up. "Well?"

"Well what, Mr. Stacio. Pete Stacio, really?"

"It was that or Mac Adamia. There aren't that many nuts."

"I beg to differ," I said, reaching for my glass, then thinking better of it. "Did you break someone's leg to get this job?"

He shrugged. "It's a war. There are injuries."

"Oh, come off it. What did you do, throw him down some stairs?"

"Tripped him in the conga line. Oldest trick in the book."

"What is wrong with you?"

"Look, I'm not interested in arguing tactics with you, or even talking to you, to be honest. Just give Bruce back to me and we can go our separate ways."

"Who's Bruce?"

"*Muscardinus avellanrius*, the only living species in the genus *Muscardinus*."

"My Latin's a little rusty, from lack of use."

"My hazel dormouse."

"Oh, that's what it is. Like an *Alice in Wonderland* mouse?"

"If you want to cheapen it."

"Bruce? His name is Bruce?"

He shrugged. "He's a stud. He's the Boss."

"Oh, did you tell Madge you toured with Springsteen too? And why are you even doing this job? What does this have to do with your work?"

Just then, a thin woman in a tie-dyed dress oozed up to the table and asked if she could join us. I took one for the team and finished my wine as the woman told Hazelnut how much she liked his sunglasses.

After he had finally dispensed with his groupies and gotten what seemed like a lot of five-pound notes in tips, he asked me to hand him my purse.

"Absolutely not. You've violated the sanctity of my Balenciaga once already today. Why would you do that anyway, put him in my purse without telling me?"

"It was an emergency. Someone was tailing me at Shep's service and I couldn't have him on me. You just happened to be there."

"Yeah, and you hate me. Why would you trust me with it. I mean him?"

"I don't trust you. I trust your purse. It has more brains. Plus, I know you never let it out of your sight. It's like a growth. Hand it over."

"But why didn't you tell me it was there? I could have crushed it."

"I couldn't risk your screaming."

"I beg your pardon. Why do you assume I would have screamed?"

"Did you or did you not scream when you found him?"

I could still hear my terrified cry echoing off the British Library bathroom tiles. "No. Not really."

Hazelnut snorted. "Right. So just give him back."

"He's not in there."

Hazelnut slammed his pint glass down on the bumpy wooden table. "What!"

"He's in my chest of drawers. At the hotel."

"Tell me you didn't put him in a drawer!" Hazelnut shook his head so hard both his wig and sunglasses shifted to the left.

"What's the matter? He's perfectly safe, I gave him a blanket and closed the drawer."

"Oh God, let's go. Which hotel?"

"The Savoy."

"That's pricey."

"I'm not paying."

"Ah, concubine."

"Executor. Shep's."

Hazelnut grabbed my hand and pulled me down the pub stairs. "Poor Shep. Which one of them killed him, do you think?"

Chapter Twenty-two

"You think Shep was murdered?" I tried to keep up with his bowlegs as he took me down a series of small alleys. "And where are we going?"

"Shortcut. Yes, of course he was murdered. He knew what was going on."

"He knew what was going on? What are you talking about?"

"I can't discuss it, I have more important things on my mind."

"Oh come on. I've kept your dormouse alive all day."

"That remains to be seen."

He went down another small street, past the stage doors of two theatres, and then down another alley. He either knew the city or was trying to lose me.

"Fine. Will you at least tell me if Howard is okay?"

Hazelnut and I, initially mortal enemies, had joined forces over Christmas to save a "functionally extinct" Tasmanian tiger cub named Howard. The last time I'd seen the cub, he was on a boat with Hazelnut, headed to a tiny island.

"The package is alive." He swung his head around, checking behind him. "Not safe to talk about it. Come on, get the lead out!"

We made two more turns and suddenly we were at the Savoy. I caught a shocked look on Kent the concierge's face as we sped by and Hazelnut practically threw me into the elevator.

Once we reached my floor, and my room, he tapped his foot as I searched for my key. It wasn't in the regular place. As I dug around in alternate pockets, he jerked his Ringo wig off and started hitting it against the wall.

"Calm down. You're making it worse," I said, finally finding the key. "And put that back on, for God's sake," I said, glimpsing the collapsed pompadour underneath.

Just to torture him, I took off my coat and scarf, hung them up, and put my purse on the bed. Then I went to the designated dormouse drawer and eased it open.

There was plenty of shredded paper, but no Bruce. "Shit."

"You bloody breadhead! Why couldn't you leave him in your purse?"

There was a crash behind me. A tiny piece of china bounced near my foot. I turned to see one of the Savoy floral teacups in bits on the carpet.

Hazelnut was reaching for the pot. I slapped him as hard as I could. He stumbled back, like a dancing wishbone.

"I'll get charged for those. One more peep out of you and I am calling the concierge to have you removed and you will never get your rodent back. Do you understand me?"

He stabilized and rubbed his cheek. I kept one eye on him while opening the next drawer, also empty, and the next.

I finally found Bruce in the bottom drawer, in his standard ass-up position.

"See? He's here. He's snoring. He's fine." I moved some of his bedding to the new drawer, hoping he would roll onto it.

Hazelnut let out a long breath and collapsed onto the bed. I shoved him over and sat down. "Now, are you going to tell me what the hell is going on?"

He shook his head. "Don't any Americans watch David Attenborough? Don't you know that the hazel dormouse is the only dormouse native to Great Britain, that they're vital to the ecosystem, that they're being obliterated?"

"Look, I watch PBS as much as anyone. I just missed the dormouse episode, okay?"

"They're amazing creatures. Disney, of course, trivialized them. When he's awake, and motivated in mating season, that little guy can jump ten meters."

I assessed all the spots that were ten meters from the drawer. There were a lot of them.

"They sing to the females at night with this trilling kind of sound. And their pheromones are so strong that humans can smell them."

Perhaps I needed more bedding for Bruce. I had grown up in a house full of male pheromones. It wasn't pretty.

"When a creature has that kind of sexual enthusiasm, it doesn't make sense that the population is down fifty percent in two years."

"He's been pretty dozy most of the time."

"That's because he's supposed to be hibernating. He's not supposed to wake up until June."

"Then how did he get into the other drawer? Teleportation?"

"No, like I said, obliteration. Someone is messing with them. I mean the loss of the hedgerow network alone is doing irreparable damage."

There was no way I was going to admit I didn't actually know what a hedgerow was. "Right, but that still doesn't explain why you're doing a Paris Hilton with Bruce."

"Catch up! One of my contacts at the London Zoo's been assigned to a new secret breeding program for dormice. Wait for it," he said, rolling his eyes. "Operation Alice. Idiots! It turns out they gathered up almost all of the existing population from one of their last habitats in the Yorkshire Dales. It all looks aboveboard, right? Remove, save, breed, repopulate. Wrong! It's supposed to be run by the People's Trust for Endangered Species, and they're pretty aboveboard. But then I found out the initiative was sponsored by a shell company called Nature Free. And the company behind that is a foreign real estate firm called WOCAM International— looking to build a huge development right next to that habitat. Fishy, right?"

I didn't completely get this, but for the sake of the Savoy china, I nodded.

"That was bad enough, but they're not just breeding. Those bastards didn't want to wait until spring, so they're keeping their subjects awake, messing with their hibernation patterns, pumping them with hormones, farming sperm, possibly doing some kind of genetic modification. Who knows what else. I mean Bruce is supposed to be completely asleep right now and for the next four months, not crawling from drawer to drawer. He has no bloody clue if it's spring, winter or fall."

"So that's why he acts like a part-time narcoleptic?" I had a couple of clients with this problem. "But surely the zoo wouldn't do anything to hurt animals. I mean, it's a zoo."

He started pacing again. I eased the tea tray away from the edge of the bedside table.

"Do you live on this planet? Who do you think runs the zoos? Governments! Who do you think sponsors the exhibits? Corporations! Welcome to the Military Industrial Reptile Complex! Anna the elephant, courtesy of Fastfood McChicken! This zebra is provided to you by the newest 'keep your dick in the air' drug. Get the picture?"

I thought about how the chameleon exhibit where my old pal Barry and her children lived had a plaque that read "Sponsored by Redondo Travel." Shit. At least it was us, not Hepler Heating, Air Conditioning, and Roto-Rooting, but Hazelnut was right.

"Bruce was my first rescue because, believe it or not, that snuffling little ball is the best hope for the species."

Bruce was resettling. He rolled onto his paper bed, gave one long, completely splayed stretch, and recurled.

"He has the highest sperm count of all the dormice in the study and top-rate genetics. He's a super stud. You can't screw with that. So I had to get him out first, before they did too much damage. Then we figure out the rest."

"Okay, but what does this have to do with Swinging Sixties London?"

"Guess who's one of the major investors in the mysterious real estate firm? Bloody London's Afoot!"

"What? How can you possibly know that?"

"You probably noticed that Madge has a crush on me."

"Ewww!"

"Seriously. Didn't you see her drop by tonight? She wanted to have a drink after."

"Well, you are a cruise ship gigolo, I suppose you have your charms."

"Ask Sister Ellery. So, Madge lets me hang around the office and I've managed to get a look at their books."

"What do you know about books?"

"I did a two-year course in forensic accounting. The smuggling, the destruction of habitat, the poaching, it's always about money. That's the way I'm going to get real evidence to take them down."

"Like Al Capone."

"Exactly." He sat back down and sighed. "Why do people have to screw with everything good?" This is a question I had often asked myself. I looked at Hazelnut, his wig barely hanging on. His heart was mostly in the right place, except for the leg-breaking part.

"Well, I'm glad you are going to save him. He is quite cute."

"I hate that word. Cute. It's so American. Can't you just call him handsome or virile?"

"Not really, no. Where will you take him now?"

Hazelnut didn't answer. Instead, he took a pillow from my bed and put it in front of the door. Then he opened the armoire and took a blanket from the top shelf.

"What exactly do you think you're doing?"

"You going to begrudge me a pillow, AntiChristine?"

"Why do you need a pillow?"

"I'm sleeping here."

"You absolutely are not."

"I'm just going to lie down in front of the door. That way, Bruce stays in and everyone else stays out."

"This is my hotel room." I pointed to Bruce's drawer. "This is your dormouse. Take him with you and go away."

"They know where I'm staying."

"Who knows?"

"Forces."

"Forces rallying against dormice?"

"Something like that."

"Putting the ridiculousness of that aside, isn't there somewhere else you can go?"

"Not unless I can trust you to keep him here."

"I thought this whole evening was for your getting him back."

"Well, since you didn't actually kill him, he's probably safer with you."

"Look. I have my own issues to deal with. You just told me Shep might have been murdered. It looks like his research has been stolen. And if I can't sort this out, it's the end of Redondo Travel."

"It's always about money with you Americans."

"It's not just money. It's my whole family, they all depend on me. So if you want me to help you with Bruce, then you've got to help me find out what happened to Shep."

"I barely knew the guy."

"I think it's all tied up with the walking tours too, and you have access. Deal?" I held out my hand.

"I don't make deals."

"Learn. Or I swear, I will let Bruce out in the Embankment Gardens."

There was a long moment. Then he held out his hand, too.

I shook it and got up "Alright, fine, I will keep him tonight until you can find someone else. Now, just get the hell out. Please." I dug a tiny vodka bottle out of my Balenciaga and screwed off the top.

"I'll be in touch." He moved to the door.

"Wait, if he wakes up, what does he like to eat? What's his favorite thing?"

Hazelnut looked away.

"Well? What is it? What does he eat, worms?"

"Hazelnuts."

I spit out my vodka all over the white bedspread. Thank God it wasn't bourbon.

Hazelnut made his exit, leaving me alone with the Casanova of rodents. It was clear that, at least today, he hadn't been getting any action. Neither had I. Neither of us slept much.

Chapter Twenty-three

I secured Bruce in the armoire, where he'd have room to leap and trill if he woke up feeling romantic and called down to housekeeping to request no service today. Then I descended to the lobby, where I drank a triple espresso waiting for Uncle Leon, pretending it was 1967 and that Peter O'Toole would walk in any minute. I had a fresh set of the consular paperwork and a bottle of Dom Perignon to give Shelagh's boyfriend in my bag, both thanks to the fabulous front desk staff. God knows how much they would charge me for it, but I had bigger things to worry about—like that Uncle Leon wouldn't show.

Granted, he had rarely let me down when it mattered, none of my uncles had, until lately. The last few months had shaken my faith in everything I trusted growing up and I had to face that my role models were only human, had secrets, and made mistakes. I tried not to think about the woman from the memorial service or what I was going to tell Aunt Helen.

Then I saw him push through one of the gilded revolving doors, dapper as ever. He looked around at the gorgeous room and grinned. "I had a few drinks here back in the day."

"With Hemingway, I suppose?" I kissed him on the cheek.

He winked. "I never drink and tell. McAfferty is paying for this?"

"He's paying for part of it. I cashed in a lot of coupons, points, and miles. It added up to just enough for the nights we're here."

"Ray always said you had the gift. Now, what is it we're doing?"

I explained as we walked out to the taxi. I was racking up cab charges, but I felt like I was missing too much traveling underground. I explained about the Apostille, but also caught him up on most of the strange things that had happened over the last two days. I didn't mention Bruce, as I didn't want Hazelnut breaking one of my legs, or worse.

"What do you think? Did Shep ever mention these threats? Do you think someone was actually out to get him?"

Uncle Leon smoothed his skinny brown and turquoise tie. "He definitely said it was competitive, the Jack the Ripper business. Lots of nasty internet comments, lots of backstabbing, but I never thought he meant actual stabbing."

I told him I'd met some Ripperologists and other guides at the memorial service. "You might have met them too, if you and whoever that woman was had stuck around."

"Enh. Any suspects, you think?"

"Well, they were pretty creepy. And there was that catfight you missed, between a couple of his girlfriends."

Leon laughed. "Was one of them the bird you found in the apartment?"

"Bird? Yeah."

"That seems dodgy to me. Her being there."

"I know. Look, speaking of dodgy, I'm trying to give you your privacy, I'm covering for you with Aunt Helen, and I'm not trying to boss you around, but how could you bring a date to Shep's funeral? Seriously?"

"It wasn't a date. It's work. I told you, I'm working."

"Well, do you think you could take a night off and come with me tonight on the Ripper Walk? There's a guide who was there the night Shep died leading it. Please? For Shep's sake. I just want to know everything's on the up-and-up before we bring him home."

He patted my hand. Just then, we pulled up in front of a house in Knightsbridge—the home of Harrod's, which supposedly had the best selection of Chantelle bras, ever.

We got out and headed up to the narrow, freshly painted three-story stucco house, with a shiny black door with paint so thick it must have been reapplied yearly since the Magna Carta.

I banged the oversized lion head knocker. Shelagh opened the door, smiled, and gestured us into the narrow entryway. This one had black and white check marble floors, an overbright chandelier, and smelled more like gin than bacon. She shook Uncle Leon's hand, I handed her the champagne, and she took us into another bright room, reeking of money and lit by a fire in a molded cast-iron fireplace.

"Derek, look, champagne. How lovely."

Standing by the fire was a man with sandy, thinning hair, deeply etched worry lines on his forehead, and a dusky blue fisherman's sweater tied around his shoulders that had probably set him back five hundred pounds. He turned.

"Cyd Redondo, Redondo Travel."

"Derek Lancaster." He had a mildly effective shake, which was probably a good thing for Shelagh.

Uncle Leon stepped up. "Leon Redondo, pleased to meet you."

"Drink?"

Once we were seated with Scotches in hand, I turned to Derek and smiled. "It's very kind of you to do this, especially on a Sunday."

"Anything for a friend of Shelagh's," he said, raising his eyebrows at her. "Do you have all the documents?"

"I certainly hope so. They did look them over at the embassy."

"That Texan halfwit?"

"His executive assistant."

"Delores? Well, they'll be all right, then."

I pulled out the stack and handed them to him. He looked them over, humming slightly, while we all sipped our Scotch. Shelagh turned to Uncle Leon.

"And what is it that you do, Mr. Redondo?"

"I'm a taxidermist." As usual, that was a conversation stopper. I used to add "for the Museum of Natural History," but it never really helped.

Derek looked up. "So this is a transfer of executorship?"

"Temporary, just so the embassy will allow me to make the arrangements."

"And you need to do this, why?"

"I've been asked to handle the arrangements by Shep's department head."

"Plus, she's the family whiz with these kinds of things," Uncle Leon said. Bless him.

"Is she? Then it will revert to you upon return to the U.S.?" He looked at Uncle Leon. They seemed to be sizing each other up. What was going on? "Do you want to stipulate a date for the return of executorship?"

Uncle Leon shrugged. "Anytime is fine. Two weeks, just to be safe?" He gave me a look.

Derek made a small note on the document.

Shelagh brought another round of Scotch. "How's the Savoy?"

"It does not disappoint."

Derek opened his drawer. "I had my assistant prepare the Apostille in advance, I just need to fill a few things in."

He asked for both of our passports very formally—this was not stamping something over lasagna, which often happened in Bay Bridge. It was interesting to me that it was so much more complex here, but in the end it was probably less subject to fraud.

He leaned over a table and gestured for us to come by and sign.

I asked to see it. He had added the word *indefinite* to the transfer. I guessed that was all right. We signed. He stamped it and then attached the Apostille, which was a separate document.

"You shouldn't have any problem with the embassy now. Shelagh says you're going back there in the morning?"

"Yes, first thing."

He handed me a very expensive embossed business card and told me to call him if any problems arose.

"That's very kind. We won't take up any more of your time. Thank you again."

"Yes, thank you." Uncle Leon rose.

Shelagh saw us out. "Good luck. Let me know if you need Shep's flat?"

"Thanks." I had learned enough online to know how to give a two-cheek European kiss, so I tried it out on Shelagh. Then Uncle Leon and I walked out and I used him as a shield while I checked my Streetwise London.

"I don't like him," Uncle Leon said.

"Noted. Of course, if you hadn't run off, we wouldn't have had to do this."

He concentrated on hailing a cab, which, as someone who worked for forty years in central Manhattan, was one of his skills.

I stood, amazed, as one pulled over right away. "I'm the whiz, huh? Are you coming with me on this walk or not?"

"I need to make a call."

I gave him the appearance of privacy for the call, actually eavesdropping as much as I possibly could. I only caught a few phrases, "What time?" and "Unlikely." Was he talking to the woman with the taxidermy brooch?

We went back to the Savoy, where we had high tea. The pastries and sandwiches were amazing, but the tea itself only reinforced my feeling that, no matter how expensive Earl Grey was, it still tasted like soap.

We had a bit of time before the Ripper Walk, so I asked Uncle Leon if he would take me to the British Museum. He made another call while Kent got us a cab.

We drove through Covent Garden and then onto Holborn and Great Russell Street, where the cab dropped us off just in front of the cast-iron gates of the museum. Uncle Leon took my hand like he used to when I was a little girl and we just stood there for a minute, taking it in. There were people and pigeons everywhere. We zigzagged around students sitting on the steps and moved toward the entrance. I threw a five-pound note into the donation bucket.

"That's my girl," Uncle Leon said, guiding me into the dark classical entrance, with veined marble stairs the shade of tobacco. In front of us was a startling, white, wide-open atrium, with a domed skylight. On one side of the space were the kind of lion statues I associated with everything British. On the other side were the Easter Island statues I'd seen on *Nova*. I took a deep breath and checked my watch. "We only have an hour and a half."

"Well, we better get to it. And, here's our guide."

Uncle Leon waved to a short man with a fuzz of white hair surrounding his bald spot like a halo. He pulled my uncle into a tight embrace and they both laughed.

"Jeremy, this is my niece, Cyd. Cyd, Jeremy is one of the curators here and he's promised us a whirlwind tour of the highlights, as well as a special surprise for you." Jeremy offered his arm and propelled us both into the Egyptian Hall, where I saw the honest-to-God Rosetta Stone, a far cry from the software I'd used to learn Swahili. It was only feet away from the massive head of Ramesses II. The weight of these ancient things, the idea of how they had even traveled here blew my mind. We passed the Assyrians and went straight to the Parthenon Gallery, where the famed Elgin Marbles lined the walls. Pictures couldn't do them justice. How could someone make stone look like it was flying? I was pretty much beside myself and could have stayed in that one room for days.

Jeremy looked at his watch and at Uncle Leon. "Shall we?"

I followed them. "Where are we going?"

Uncle Leon winked as Jeremy led us up the marble stairs and down a few hallways, then stopped outside a room that I had heard about my whole childhood—the place where Uncle Leon had taken his youngest brother, the merchant seaman, my dad. The clock room.

My father was the one who'd made me want to travel. When he'd put me to bed in my attic room, we'd spin my light-up globe, talking about all the places he'd take me someday. Even though I was only four, he made sure I knew the difference between latitude and longitude, about how hard they were to figure out, and about the amazing inventors and their magical machines that helped save sailors' lives. He said one day he'd bring me to this room.

And here it was. A world of wonders. Filigree, shining brass, gleaming wood, a sparkling silver celestial globe, with the constellations etched in black, a solid gold clock in the shape of a ship, complete with tiny men marching in and out of a tower. There were pocket watches and sextants and the things my dad had loved the most: compasses and chronometers.

After I'd soaked it in, Jeremy led us to a door in the wall. He unlocked it and gestured us in. "We can't display everything," he said, "but we keep them going just the same." This room was filled to bursting with every manner of instrument, all ticking or swinging, but none behind glass. I could get right next to them and really watch them work.

After I'd been mesmerized by a few, he took me to a corner, where he opened a case and took out a compass. I gasped, then reached into my Balenciaga and took out the suede bag with my father's 1929 Wilcox Crittenham compass, the one I always carried with me. I held it next to the one in Jeremy's hand. They were identical.

"I saw his face when he saw it," Uncle Leon said. "The only other time I saw it light up like that was the first time he saw you. So Jeremy helped me find one for him."

I didn't get a lot of opportunities to feel close to my father. I had been so small when he died and, out of an abundance of love, or caution, my other male relatives had worked hard to replace him, even in my memory. Here, I got him back.

"I don't know what to say. Thank you, Jeremy. I can't tell you what this means."

He blushed, then gave me his card. "Miss Cyd, I am at your service. If you need anything at all while you're here, museum-related or otherwise, just give me a call." He looked at Uncle Leon. "I owe your uncle many debts, and now another one, for the privilege of meeting you."

I squeezed my uncle's hand as we went down the stairs and began to make our way to Tower Hill.

Chapter Twenty-four

We decided to walk down King's Way to the Temple Underground station. Uncle Leon pointed out a few things as we got nearer to the Thames. He sounded wistful.

I squeezed his arm. "How long were you here?"

"Just about long enough to fall in love. With the city, I mean."

"What did you love most?"

"You know me, I like old. There's part of the Roman wall by the Museum of London, Viking ships came up this river, there's real history here. Every kind. Like look over there." He pointed to a series of brick and stone buildings that rose up at the top of a long lawn. "That's part of the Inns of Court. They were started by the Knights Templar."

"Like the Crusades Knights Templars?"

"Yep. Wowser, right?"

"Yes, wowser." I loved him very much at this moment and it made me want to know more than anything what the hell he'd been doing here.

"How about you, Squid? Like it so far?"

"I feel like crying all the time, if that makes sense."

"Yeah. It does. So what's our assignment tonight?"

I told him. This time, I was determined to get there early, and instead of a deserted station, I found at least four groups gathered, with various levels of volume. I knew now to look for the brochure.

I caught sight of one in the raised hand of a tall man I recognized from the memorial service. He was backlit by the Tower Bridge, in true horror movie style, and surrounded by well-wrapped-up tourists of all shapes, sizes, and accents. I moved through them to the front. The guide had about a foot and a half on me, even in my heels, so I had to tug on his coat to get his attention.

"Cyd Redondo, Redondo Travel. You're Philip Babcock? We met briefly at Shep's service? I'm his executor, just hoped we might speak a bit about him on the way, or after?"

"The fee is five pounds."

I held out twenty. "This is for me and my uncle."

"Thank you. Much appreciated. It's still hard to talk about Shep."

"I understand. It's okay. For us as well. I thought just going on the walk would help me understand it all a bit better, his life here. I hear you did the tour with him that night?" I had often heard the term *recoil*, but this was about the first time I had seen it in action. Babcock moved back and curled inward at the same moment, bringing him momentarily closer to my height.

"How did you know that?"

I took a chance. "Nigel told me."

Just then a solid woman in a Greater Cleveland baseball hat shoved past me. "I thought this was supposed to start at seven. Where's Professor Helnikov?"

"He won't be with us tonight. We are just leaving, madam." By this time, Uncle Leon had found me. I took his arm as Babcock moved to the front of the group.

"Everyone! Welcome to London's Afoot! And the city's premiere Jack the Ripper walk. I'll be your guide for this evening, Philip Babcock."

I heard a distinct "Boo!"

Babcock sighed. "I know many of you were expecting Professor Shepard Helnikov, but unfortunately he cannot be here this evening. Professor Helnikov trained me, so I promise you, I will give you the walk as he would have done and do my utmost to honor him."

A few people started walking away. I had a moment of pity for Babcock.

Uncle Leon leaned down to whisper, "Why aren't they just saying he's dead?"

"I'm not sure. Maybe he doesn't want hysterical groupies on the walk? Or maybe it's orders from on high?"

Babcock raised his voice. "My special area of research concerns one of the most vital figures in the Ripper Murders—Superintendent Thomas Arnold."

"You mean the idiot that had the graffiti erased?" There were murmurs of assent.

"I mean the policeman who may have saved countless additional lives by heading off a racist riot. Imagine being crushed in these tiny lanes, pushed to the cobblestones, wet with sewage, imagine the numbers trampled, the innocents slaughtered, the blood, had Arnold not made a command decision."

The ghoulish look on people's faces as soon as they heard the word *blood* was somewhat disturbing, I can't lie.

"So, let's begin. I'm sure those of you familiar with the history of the murders know that if we did the walk in the order they were committed, it would take about four hours, so we will do a more logical route and I'll be reminding you of the order of each victim as we go. Of course, we start here, not only for the scenery—the Tower of London, site of countless beheadings—but here where we can still find dark corners that existed in the fateful year of 1888. Shall we?" He gestured towards a dark alley. Several walkers shot through, and I was happy to let them.

Babcock led on, pontificating about the squalor and desperation of the Victorian city, how it was filled with eighty thousand prostitutes, many living on the streets, who had no other way to afford a bed or to feed their children. It was clear that *From Hell* had whitewashed this a bit, since Heather Graham's hair always looked like she'd stepped out of a L'Oréal ad.

"And here is a piece of the original London Wall. Likely the killer himself made his way through this hole in his travels." As Babcock gestured us through the opening, I could see Uncle Leon grinning like a six-year-old. I, on the other hand, was a bit creeped out, as this looked like rodent country to me. Rodents. I hoped Bruce was all right.

We squished into a single-file line down a few alleys, then finally crossed Aldersgate, a street I recognized from my map, and headed into Mitre Square. Babcock made sure to point out that we had crossed into the "Square Mile," the official City of London. He insisted that the tale of "two Londons" might have determined the fate of the Ripper case, as the square-mile City of London had one police force, and the broader city another. They weren't known for their cooperation.

"So when Jack the Ripper spread his bloody entrails over both jurisdictions, he increased the chances he wouldn't be caught. And, as you know, he wasn't. Was this intentional?" Babcock shrugged. "We will never know. Or will we?"

I had tuned Babcock out by that point, as I was staring at the place where he said Catherine Eddowes, the fourth victim, had fallen. I grabbed Uncle Leon's hand.

"This is it."

"What is it?"

"This is where Shep died. On the spot. Over there. Shelagh told me." I pointed to the space where everyone was looking. "It's too weird, right? He saw this place multiple times a week, it's not like it should have freaked him out. Why would he have a heart attack here?"

Uncle Leon frowned. "You're saying one of the world's foremost Jack the Ripper experts collapsed on one of the murder sites and that wasn't on the news? How could that be? Did someone cover it up?"

"We'll have to ask Babcock, I guess."

We both crossed ourselves as we neared the fateful spot, and made sure to step around it, then followed Babcock to what my map said was Middlesex Street. On the way, Madge, in yet another sad, stretched cardigan and a scarf that trailed on the ground, emerged from the fog, spoke to Babcock, took his money, then disappeared.

Although he claimed to be following Shep's tour, some of the things Babcock was saying about the suspects contradicted what I'd read in *Jacked!* and this kind of pissed me off. He clearly had an agenda and seemed to be using the tour as an opportunity, not an homage. He walked us into Goulston Street, where the police had found a victim's bloody apron and chalk writing, possibly by the Ripper himself. Babcock's featured superintendent, Thomas Arnold, was the one who'd insisted it be erased. I heard several walkers gasp when they heard this, that the police had tampered with evidence. Had they never watched *The Shield?* Or any cop film ever made?

Babcock ended at the site of the last, horrific murder, the one with the maximum violence. I moved us to the very back, as a blow by blow of the mutilations was not my kind of tourist porn. I wondered how Shep, who had been so charming and kind, had managed to spend all his time steeped in this kind of gore? What had started his fascination with these murders?

Finally, we stopped at the legendary Spitalfields market, which was sadly closed. Most of the walkers crossed the road and entered the Ten Bells Pub, where Babcock said victim Annie Chapman drank the night she died. That seemed to rev everyone up. I figured this walk was the closest to "dark tourism" I ever wanted to get.

Uncle Leon and I stopped opposite the pub to gaze at Christ Church, with its spikey spire and grounds that, at least at night, were as creepy as anything we'd seen.

Someone touched me on the shoulder. I have to admit, I was halfway into a jab and uppercut when I saw it was Babcock. He jumped back. "Buy you two a drink?"

"We should buy you one, you're the one who's been doing the heavy lifting." His face went white. I wondered why. "I'm sorry, did I say something wrong?"

"No, no, of course not. The Ten Bells will be crowded, but I'm supposed to linger to direct people to the Tube. Is that all right?"

"Absolutely." We walked across the street toward the four-story white building that housed the pub on the ground floor. The packed place vibrated with sound. The whole place, including the ceiling, was covered in Victorian tile. It was great-looking, but it amplified everything.

Babcock had a pint waiting for him on the bar, and he ordered two for us. For the eight hundredth time, I wished I didn't hate beer. He led us to a table near the entrance, where his attitude became strangely friendly. He raised his glass.

"Cheers. So you are in charge of Shep's estate?"

Well, that wasn't a subtle opener. I looked at Uncle Leon. "We are, the two of us."

"Oh. What will happen to his research? His books?"

"They'll go back to Brooklyn College. They have proprietary interest."

"Who told you that? They're going to America? To that Dean McAfferty clown? That's completely unfair. Shep would have wanted scholars to have his work, to continue his work. He often told me he wanted me to continue his work. In fact, we had made a discovery in the last week or so, a big one which might change everything, all the scholarship."

"The two of you made the discovery? Together?" I would definitely have a word with Evelyn about this.

"Yes. Of course, I let Shep hang on to it but I would like it back. I should look through his things. You wouldn't know what to look for, as a travel agent."

"As a travel agent, perhaps I know more than you think. I know, for example, that Shep actually died in Mitre Square."

This time his face color hit morgue level. He took a long drink, then threw up his hands.

"Look, you knew Shep. He was a walking time bomb—his diet, the drinking, the women. We were walking back to Tower Hill and he just collapsed. I tried CPR, then called 999, then called Nigel. He's the one who made me."

"Made you what?"

He leaned in so the walkers couldn't hear. "Move the body."

Chapter Twenty-five

Uncle Leon and I stared at him in disbelief.

"Just around the corner. Not far. It wasn't my idea. Nigel thought it would be bad for our image. We're the respected walks, the scholarly walks, not the sensational walks. It would have been in such poor taste. So I got him out to Aldersgate and the ambulance picked him up there. I rode to the hospital with him. I didn't abandon him, I promise you. How did you know? Did Nigel tell you?"

I really wanted to cream this guy with a poker. He jumped up a little too eagerly to give directions to some walkers, which gave me time to remember the break-in with no forced entry at Shep's flat. Babcock came back with another pint. I let him sit down and take a few sips before my interrogation.

"What happened to his things? His clothes, keys?"

He hesitated. "Um, I'm not sure. They must still be at the hospital, you know, unless there was some kind of mistake."

The mistake had been not punching this guy the minute he changed Shep's script. I would bide my time. Probably. Then, I didn't have to.

Uncle Leon put his glass down harder than was necessary, then took out his handkerchief. He was the most mellow guy in the world, until he wasn't.

I had only heard him take this tone a few times with his sons, but I was always glad I'd never been on the receiving end of it. It was a tone that carried. I saw a few of our fellow walkers look over.

"Look, Buzzcock, or whatever your name is. Be straight with my niece or she'll have Shep's apartment fingerprinted. I assume we have yours on this pamphlet," he said, picking it up with the pocket square. "My son is a lieutenant with the NYPD."

Uncle Leon looked at me. I reached into my Balenciaga for one of my brousin Frank's evidence bags. I kept two, along with plastic zip ties. Uncle Leon put the brochure inside.

Babcock might be a scholar, but he had no common sense, since he fell for this ridiculous piece of theatre, hung his head, and admitted he had kept the keys to look for their "discovery."

Uncle Leon leaned in. "Did you find it? You didn't, did you?"

"No. It didn't appear to be there."

Uncle Leon gave him the look. "Because you don't actually know what it is."

"Okay. He wouldn't tell me. He knew better. No pun intended, but this is a cutthroat world, Ripperology. Everyone is just looking for a leg up, one tiny piece of evidence no one else has. It wasn't fair Shep already having a best seller and then finding something else. I mean, I was his protégé, it should be mine now, and it certainly shouldn't leave the country."

Uncle Leon shook his head and rose. "We'll see how the police feel about all this."

"I didn't want to move him. Really. I thought it would help his legacy, dying there."

We just looked at him and walked out. He ran out after us and stopped us in the middle of the street.

"I'm sorry. You aren't going to tell anyone, are you? You can't."

"Shep would be ashamed of you," I said, as Uncle Leon and I walked away, having absolutely no idea where we were going.

After we got about a block, Uncle Leon looked around at the creepy, empty market and foggy streets. "Do you know where we are?"

"Cover me," I said, using the light on my phone to check for the nearest Tube station. It took awhile, due to jet lag and alcohol. Luckily the Aldgate East station, on the District Line, was only blocks away, so we headed there, surrounded by mostly empty and unlit streets. I kept all my self-defense skills on alert, but we got there in one piece and a train came within ten minutes.

The late-night Tube wasn't that different than it was in New York: a motley combination of drunken twenty-year-olds and cleaners going to work.

"What do you think?"

Uncle Leon didn't say anything for a minute.

"Fishy."

"Just Babcock, or the whole thing?"

"The whole thing."

"That's what I think, too. Murder fishy?"

He shrugged.

"Shep left us in charge. What should I do?"

"Let me sleep on it. Call me before you go to the embassy?"

"Okay."

He got off with me at the Covent Garden station and we fought our way through overdressed theatregoers to the marquis lights of the Savoy. He caught a cab there, but still wouldn't tell me where he was going.

I walked into the lobby, which couldn't help but cheer you up. Until I saw something that made me suicidal. Hazelnut.

His wig, as ever, was slightly askew as he veered in front of me. "Is Bruce okay?"

"I hope so."

"You were supposed to look after him."

"You said he was hibernating. He's supposed to be asleep, right?"

It was his turn to sigh. I saw the night concierge give me a look as we got into the elevator. Great.

When we arrived at my room, I unlocked the door and turned on the light. Bruce was fast asleep. On my pillow. The Savoy chocolate had tiny chew marks on the wrapping.

"Oh God, that's not going to kill him, is it? And how the hell did he get out, again? Those experiments might make him wake up, but they don't make him a three-inch Houdini." I shoved a finger in Hazelnut's chest. "Ha! You knew he was an escape artist. That's why you wanted someone else to watch him, isn't it?"

"He doesn't really like being confined."

"How aware can he be that he's confined if he's in a state of torpor?"

"Torpor, really?"

"Yes. I looked it up, all right? I assume you're taking him now, so he will be your problem."

"Actually, no. I have to fly to Paris in the morning."

"How am I supposed to keep him safe? What if whoever put this chocolate on my pillow had seen him? Or the housekeeper had opened the door and let him out?"

"Just say you don't want service."

"I did that this morning, and they still turned down the bed. Look. I am staying for just a few nights, at the Savoy Hotel. The whole point of a hotel is that you come back to the room and everything is perfect again, with no effort from you, unlike in life. I am not giving that up because you sprung some super sperm-king mouse."

Bruce was snoring. It was so adorable, it was very hard to insult him.

"Seriously. This is twice he's escaped. I have to be out all day tomorrow and I'm leaving the day after, so I don't think he'll be safe."

"Take him with you tomorrow. If that purse held Howard, it should have no problem with this. As much as I hate to admit it, I took a page out of the AntiChristine handbook."

I gasped as Hazelnut pulled out a battered lime green Tupperware mini-bowl with lid, circa 1995. I saw, to my horror, that it was mutilated with air slashes on the top. The pain I had felt doing this to one of my beloved containers to keep Barry the chameleon alive was still fresh. At least this wasn't my bowl.

Hazelnut had put a bit of shredded newspaper on top of what looked like a washcloth in the bottom. "See if this fits."

I took it, rearranged one compartment, and managed to fit it in the bottom of my bag.

"Won't he hate being bounced around? It's very hard to keep it still when I'm walking everywhere."

"Perhaps you might comport yourself with dignity, for once."

"Perhaps you might wear something flattering, for once."

"This, I will have you know, is the epitome of Mod. Here are a few nuts and berries, if he wakes up." He handed me a small paper bag.

"What about water?"

"Ah, look at you, the accidental activist, saving a species at a time. By default."

On that, he exited. I fell back on the bed, almost bouncing Bruce off. He wobbled, then fell back into the "holding his tail between his legs and over his eyes" position.

I eased him into the Tupperware, then put it into the deep bathtub, figuring it would be too slippery for him to crawl out. Just to be safe, after I brushed my teeth and put on night cream, I pulled the door closed, hoping he couldn't flatten himself enough to get out.

• • •

The next morning, I found him snoring in the bathroom sink. At least he wasn't missing. Was he doing all this moving while he was asleep? Like a sleepwalker? Or sleep-scurrier? You weren't supposed to wake up sleepwalkers, so I lifted him carefully and laid him back into the Tupperware. I left a couple of nuts in the bottom, then put on the lid. I almost burped it out of habit, but stopped myself just in time. I took my plastic nail scissors and made the air slits a bit bigger. I didn't want Bruce's torpor to be permanent.

Then I tried on all the outfits I'd brought with me, which took some time. I settled on a leopard-print silk shirt with a bow at the neck, over my pencil skirt, and black stilettos.

I checked that all my paperwork was good and with me, put the Bruce container in my purse, and added the biscuits from the tea tray in case my blood sugar dropped. With any luck this morning I could actually get a start on getting Shep home and Dean Dean off my back.

I called Uncle Leon from the cab. This time, he picked up. "Any thoughts?" I asked.

"Still fishy."

"I know. But just because someone moved the body, it doesn't mean there was actually any foul play, right? Surely the paramedics would have noticed something. Do I say anything to the embassy? You know I have to get him home or we're going to lose Redondo Travel. Uncle Ray will never forgive me."

"You've forgiven him."

"I haven't actually. Not altogether."

"Oh. Well, why don't you just go and see what they say. Ask a few nonpressing questions, just to see?"

"Got it. I'll call you when I'm done."

I didn't tell him that I was going somewhere else first.

After last night, I wanted another look at Shep's apartment. I was worried that Babcock still had Shep's key and might have tried again. If I could find proof he'd been there, great. If not, at least I could head him off and have another look for whatever the Ripperologists wanted. This was probably what Dean Dean wanted too, so two birds with one stone.

I got to Red Lion Square, checked to make sure no one was watching, and slipped inside and up the narrow stairs, the smell of bacon still prevalent. This time, I used my mini WD-40 spray on the lock. Then I eased the door open, but heard no scrabbling this time.

I entered to see the place was trashed. Again. Was it Babcock? Jemima? Or had it been someone else? Surely not the embassy, but if Harley had been hungover, all bets might be off. The kitchen was trashed this time, cookie tins opened with the cookies poured out, a cereal box turned upside down. I still didn't know whether the intruder had found what they were looking for. Or did I already have it? But if I had the treasure, what was it? I did one more turn around the apartment, checking, then locked up and headed to Grosvenor Square.

Chapter Twenty-six

I stopped on the way into the embassy because I couldn't remember whether they opened and checked bags or just put them through the metal detector. Could the X-rays injure Bruce's mighty manhood? Or worse? What to do? I called Delores.

"Deputy Deputy Consular Office."

"Delores? This is Cyd Redondo. I'm downstairs and afraid my new Agent Provocateur bra is going to set off the alarm. Can you help me out?"

She laughed. "Be right down."

She arrived, gestured to the guard, and took me to the elevator. "Do you have a gun or something?"

"You wouldn't believe me if I told you." I looked down at yet another pair of fabulous shoes, navy blue suede with a red leather tie on top. "Oh my God, Delores. Same store?"

"No. Hobbs. It's like the J.Crew of England. Everyone here has them, but no one at home will. There's one in Covent Garden, too. How long are you here?"

"Due to go back tomorrow, but there might be more delays, so who knows?"

"Yes, there might be a few of those." She opened the office door and announced that I was there. Harley emerged, looking even more hungover than he had on Friday.

I went in. I already had my paperwork half out of my purse. "Hi, Harley. I was able to get the notarization and the Apostille—it's all right here. I'm all set, right?"

"About that," Harley said. He handed me a copy of the *Daily Mail* with the headline "Copycat or Curse? Second Jack the Ripper Guide Dies on Famous East End Murder Site."

I slumped into the chair behind me. There was a picture of Philip Babcock beside a photo of the last murder site we had visited on last night's tour, complete with crime scene tape and something that looked like a long body bag. I didn't want to read the text, but I knew I had to.

Sources reveal that the suspected homicide last night of London's Afoot! tour guide Philip Babcock, on the site of the second "canonical" Jack the Ripper murder on Hanbury Street, is the second death of a guide on a Jack the Ripper walk this week.

Last Tuesday, notable Ripperologist Shepard Helnikov, also with the tour company, died on the exact site of the Catherine Eddowes murder in Mitre Square. Scotland Yard is now investigating both these deaths as suspicious. Babcock was last seen in the company of the couple caught here on CCTV. Anyone who recognizes these people or who has any information should call the Metropolitan Police.

At the bottom of the page was a grainy, underexposed photo of me and Uncle Leon talking to Babcock outside the Ten Bells. Fricking surveillance.

Harley was talking. I tried to focus. "So, we don't have jurisdiction over the body at the moment. At least until the Met's done with the autopsy. We can't release it to you until they're done with whatever they're doing. If they can find these witnesses, it may speed things up."

Delores raised her eyebrows at me. My mind was racing.

"I can get the death certificates at least, right?"

Harley handed me the document. Under Cause of Death it read: Pending.

"Where are the other copies?"

"You need more than one?"

"You really haven't done this before, have you? You need about ten or fifteen, and because I'm going to have to file in two countries, I want twenty to be safe. Can you arrange for that, at least?"

"Delores? Can you get Ms. Redondo nineteen more death certificates?"

"Of course. She can pick them up tomorrow."

"What about his belongings?" I said.

"The police will want to search the flat, so for now, we should leave everything there."

Had that mess been a police search? I guessed I could write off Babcock as the most recent burglar. Had I wiped off all my fingerprints? Harley saw my face and handed me a packet of Alka-Seltzer. "You were right, it helps." He now had a whole drawer full. I ate three, dry, in solidarity and thanked him, then walked to the outer office.

I sat in front of Delores's desk. She looked over my documents, then took out a form, filled it in. We could hear Harley snoring. She shook her head and forged his signature.

"I don't mean to be rude, but could that be problematic down the road, that he didn't actually sign it?"

"Are you kidding? This is the signature on file. He was at Ascot the day he was supposed to fill in his employment paperwork. You'd have a bigger problem if he actually did sign it. This should be everything you'll need for Scotland Yard, and to register the death, if they'll let you."

She made copies of everything and handed them to me in an envelope the perfect size to slide into the side of my Balenciaga. She was nothing if not efficient.

"Thanks, Delores."

She picked up the phone, then held it for a second. "That's you in the photo, isn't it, doll?"

I sighed. The shoes. They were a dead giveaway. "We had a drink with him after the tour to talk about Shep. He was alive when we left him. Best advice?"

"Where did you go after?"

"We walked about a block down Commercial Road, then figured out how to get to the Aldgate Tube. Took it to Covent Garden, then walked to the Savoy."

"Good. With any luck there'll be enough CCTV to verify your movements. Anyone who can prove you stayed there all night?"

Bruce, I thought. I didn't know how they'd feel about the whole torpor thing. "I know the concierge saw me come in, and I think the key cards show all entrances and exits."

"Okay. It's not that they don't think Americans are dumb, they do, but they don't consider it an excuse. Better to go there, fess up, and, in British parlance, assist the police with their inquiries."

"Right. I owe you about forty drinks. Where are you from, anyway?"

"Teaneck."

"Of course. That's why I like you."

She made the call to Scotland Yard and said I might have information on last night's death. They could call the Deputy Deputy's office with any questions. I was glad Harley was snoring, as it covered up the increasing squeaking and snuffling coming from my purse.

She hung up. "Ask for Inspector Blethly. Good luck."

"Thanks. Restroom?"

"Down the hall to your left. The code is 456."

I went into the bathroom, which was empty, and headed into the farthest stall to check on Bruce. By some miracle, he was still in the Tupperware and snoring peacefully. I counted my blessings, until I remembered Dean Dean. I could only imagine his rage over a further delay. And the impending emptiness of my bank account that could result. I thought about calling him, but it was still three in the morning in Brooklyn. It could wait. In the meantime, I needed to avoid being arrested for murder.

Chapter Twenty-seven

Because it was nearby and because it would postpone my walking into Scotland Yard as a suspect, I took the death certificate and my executor paperwork to the Registry Office. As promised, in half an hour I emerged with a Certificate of Registration of a Death and a Certificate for Burial or Cremation—both worthless without a body.

I checked my Streetwise London and Underground Map and saw that Scotland Yard would be a forty-minute walk or two station changes. I hailed a cab.

Once inside, I asked if he could take me to Scotland Yard via Buckingham Palace. At least I would get a royal drive-by before I was hauled off to the clink. God, I hadn't even called Uncle Leon. Had he seen the papers? I checked both my phones, but no one had called. I tried practicing my speech as we passed St. James Park and Big Ben, and then we were there.

The building was more *2001* than Sherlock Holmes, chrome and glass and inset lighting. It did have low brown benches that looked out the huge windows onto the London Eye, so there was that. I looked up at the large space-age set of stairs leading from the lobby and stopped.

I had dated plenty of men and married one, briefly, but I'd only really been in love once. Unfortunately, it was with the perpetual liar with the Raisinet eyes who stood, also stock-still, at the top of the stairs—Roger "Mr. Bad Sandals" Claymore.

I felt like someone had jabbed a tweezer between my ribs.

I was frozen on a level surface. Roger froze halfway between two steps and tumbled, elbows first, down the chrome stairs. As I ran towards him, so did a blonde woman in a tailored suit and a chignon. Operating on instinct, I managed to trip her so I could get to him first. I fell to my knees. He looked unconscious. I slapped him.

His eyes flew open. Oh thank God, I thought.

"Cyd? It is you. Cyd? It's me, Roger."

"Yes, I know that." I knew that mainly because the moment I touched him my heart stopped, I went pale, and my ovaries went into overdrive, just like always.

"Roger? Roger, are you all right?" The woman with the perfect blonde hair, impeccably tailored suit, tasteful jewelry, and definitely nothing that had ever been on sale, was gorgeous. She bent down on the other side of Roger. I almost slapped her too.

She seemed about to ask me a question when Roger started to struggle up. We fought to help him, almost dislocating his arms.

"Hey," he said. "I'm okay." Of course, as soon as he stood up, he almost fell over. We helped him over to a chair in the lobby and I reached into my purse for my emergency dry ice pack, which I slapped onto the knot that was forming on his forehead.

"I've missed that purse," he said. "You don't have a beer in there, do you?"

"Just a mini-tequila." He held my eye for a minute.

"So, I assume you two know each other," the woman said.

"Slightly," I said.

The last time I'd seen him, we'd been kissing desperately at the curb at JFK, after having spent a night of wild sex in a tent, complete with vervet monkeys. He'd asked me to come to Indonesia with him. I'd said no and stayed to save the family business. Given today's news, that might have been the wrong decision.

Just then, an officer in an actual uniform and pigeon gray hair came towards us, laughing. "Claymore! What the devil happened?"

"Nothing. Just lost my footing. Mike, I'd like you to meet Cyd Redondo, Redondo Travel. Cyd, this is Sergeant Mike Kendall and Detective Felicity Hubbard from the Wildlife Crime Prevention Unit."

Sergeant Mike grabbed my hand and shook it up and down rhythmically. "Cyd Redondo? The woman who took down the Fisher/Wu smuggling ring? You're quite a legend in our circles. Are you here to help us with the dormouse situation?"

My face went slack. "The dormouse situation?"

"Some lunatic broke into a breeding facility at the London Zoo. You two were just heading over there, weren't you, Detective?"

"Yes, we were. We must get on." She moved toward the exit.

"Wait. Roger you're here working on dormice?"

"I've been seconded to the unit on something else. This just came up, so I'm helping out."

"Yes, Roger has been an enormous help." The female detective took his elbow. "Are you here to apply for our staff as well, Ms. Redondo?"

"No. I'm here on a nonanimal matter," I said, hoping they couldn't hear Bruce letting out a particularly fluttery snort. Roger looked puzzled. Could he recognize dormouse snoring?

He pointed behind me. "Isn't that your uncle?"
I turned to see Uncle Leon walk through the door. In handcuffs.

Chapter Twenty-eight

I waved. Uncle Leon waved with his cuffs, then followed a policeman through a door. I turned to Roger's colleagues. "Nice to meet you both. I'm sorry, I have an appointment. Good luck at the zoo."

Sergeant Kendall gave me another enthusiastic shake, then went back up the stairs. Roger turned to the detective. "You go on and get the car, I'll be right there." She frowned, but went.

Roger got a card out of his wallet. "Here's my UK number, in case you have time to catch up while you're here. Or if your uncle needs anything."

All I wanted to do was throw my arms around Roger, but I was never going to do that from Holloway Women's Prison. "Thanks. Gotta go." I hurried to the reception desk.

If there were ever an embodiment of jaded, it was the man in the cheap short-sleeve shirt behind the counter. I stood there for at least two interminable minutes before he raised his beady eyes at me. "Yes?"

It didn't look like a hand-shaking situation. "Cyd Redondo, Redondo Travel. I'm here to see an Inspector Blethly? They called from the embassy. I believe he's expecting me."

"Ah, from the embassy. I see." Any response to that seemed to be a mistake, so I kept my mouth shut. That became harder when I saw Uncle Leon pass by in the offices behind. Aunt Helen was going to kill me.

"I'll let Inspector Blethly know that someone from the 'embassy' is here," the officer said. "You did say the embassy?"

"That's very kind of you, thanks." I refrained from finishing my sentence, which otherwise would have included "you supercilious shithead."

At least I had dressed formally, which meant my knees were covered until I sat down.

I was expecting someone somewhere between John Thaw's Inspector Morse and Robson Green's Dave Creegan. What I got was closer to Benny Hill.

Inspector Blethly was small, round, and looked like he could explode at any moment. I gave what was left of his gray hair about two years.

"Ms. Redondo?"

"Yes, Cyd Redondo, Redondo Travel."

"What can I do for you?"

"Well, two things. I'm here in London, as an executor, to arrange for the return of one of my clients to the States—Shepard Helnikov. The embassy said you've initiated an investigation into events surrounding his death?"

"Yes, we have. What's the other thing? You said two things."

"Right. Yes. I'm here to confess."

He actually laughed. "To what, may I ask?"

"That's me in the CCTV shot in the *Daily Mail*. My uncle and I were on the tour and spoke to Mr. Babcock afterwards."

"Yes, we already know that. Leon Redondo is your uncle?"

"Yes."

"We've spoken to him."

"How could you arrest him? He's seventy-five years old!"

"Arrest him? Hmmm." Blethly picked up his phone. "Could you bring the witness in?"

He must have seen the panic on my face. "Ms. Redondo, while we're waiting, why don't you run me through last evening. Your interaction with Mr. Babcock, any conversations you might have had?"

I have law enforcement officers in my family, including Uncle Leon's son, Detective Frank Redondo. Luckily, I've had to lie to them about my dating situation, the amount of milk left in the fridge, and how many times I've been shot, so I was able to withhold information from the Met, no problem.

I thought it was safe to say that Babcock was Shep's protégé and had been on the walk the night Shep died, which is why we'd wanted to talk to him. I said we had left him alive and taken the Underground back to Covent Garden. I held back a few things—the stuff in the British Museum locker, the burglary of Shep's flat, and the fact that he was rumored to have something a Ripperologist might kill for. I don't know why. I just wasn't ready for them to start poking into Shep's life, or mine. I felt protective, not only of my client's possessions, but of Bruce, currently Number One on the Yard's Rodent Most Wanted List.

They must have known Shep's body was moved, since the paper has said he was killed in Mitre Square. But I didn't know if they knew Babcock had moved the body. Telling them that would implicate Nigel, and I might need him. I wasn't sure what to do.

Uncle Leon entered. "Hi, Squid. You tell them about Babcock moving the body?"

I shot up. "Are you okay?" I turned to Blethly. "Why is he still in hand-cuffs? For that matter, why was he in them to begin with?"

"Sit down, Ms. Redondo. You too, sir."

Uncle Leon sat down, cool as ever, his handcuffed hands in his lap.

"So, you have information about the body you haven't told me?"

"I was just about to." I explained what Babcock had told us.

The inspector leaned forward. "Anything else you were just about to tell us?"

I thought fast. It was going to be better for me if the police knew Babcock had been in Shep's apartment. "Babcock said he took Shep's keys when he collapsed, if that helps."

He gave me a long look. "And that's everything?"

I nodded. "I think so. Do you think Shep was murdered?"

"I can't really discuss the investigation with you, I'm sure you understand. Particularly because you seem to be connected to both of these deaths."

"Not intentionally! Look, Inspector, the idea that something happened to Shep on a trip I booked makes me physically ill. If someone killed him, I want to know."

"I'll know more after the autopsy scheduled for later today." He must have seen my face. "It's necessary." He stood up. "Well, thank you for coming forward. We'll be checking the CCTV cameras on your route, of course. I'd suggest you stay in London until then."

"Right. As I said, I'm the one arranging for Shep's body to be returned to the U.S. Can you please keep me posted on when that might be possible?" I gave him my card and wrote my English cell phone number on the back.

"I'm sure we'll be speaking again," he said.

Uncle Leon stood up. I turned to him. "Do you need bail?"

Uncle Leon wiggled his hands and the handcuffs came off. I just stared at him. He and Blethly looked at each other and laughed.

"Shep's trick handcuffs. I did it to Frank once, too, walked right through the precinct. You should have seen his face."

I turned to Blethly. "And you let him do this? What kind of public servant are you?"

"We take the laughs where we can in Homicide."

I just shook my head and walked out. Uncle Leon caught up with me. His neck was so scrawny, it was unsafe to even fake strangle him, as much as I wanted to. It didn't keep me from screaming, though. "Alright, that's it! You almost gave me a coronary."

"Aw, come on, kiddo. Don't lose your sense of humor."

"My sense of humor? Seriously, you are stressing me out. Making me avoid, or outright lie to, Aunt Helen. I have no idea where you're staying or what you're doing, you have the nerve to show up at Shep's service with a date, and now this. What is going on?"

"It's work, Squid. Honest. I'm not supposed to discuss it. They hired me because I'm discreet."

"Discreet? You just walked, handcuffed, through Scotland Yard. You are a material witness in a murder investigation. You're like an animated foghorn!" He laughed. I didn't. "Okay, who is she? That woman with the taxidermy brooch."

"An old friend and colleague. Like Jeremy. We all studied together. She's the head of the Taxidermy Department at the Natural History Museum. Right now, she's my boss."

"Well, why did she come to Shep's service? Did she know him?"

"I'd put them in touch one time he was over. I guess they had a few drinks."

"Stop, just stop. I guess we're lucky she didn't join in the memorial catfight."

"Why do you think I got her out of there?"

I snorted. So did Bruce. Oh God, Bruce.

"What was that?"

"Nothing. Indigestion."

He patted my arm. "I have to go back to work. What are you doing?"

"Trying to speed up this investigation. I'm going to talk to some of the guides."

"Be careful."

He kissed me on the top of the head just as his perpetual black town car pulled up. Whoever did the fundraising for the Natural History Museum, I wanted as a client.

I looked at my watch and figured I had four hours before Dean Dean would be in the office. Maybe I could solve the crime by then and he'd never know about this blip.

I checked the walking tour schedule. Jemima was giving a theatre walk in ten minutes.

Chapter Twenty-nine

I figured if Jemima had killed Shep, she'd have admitted it already for the publicity. Still, there was Babcock. Maybe she wanted three or four murders under her belt so she'd qualify as the female Ripper. I wouldn't put it past her.

I joined the clutch of tourists who were waiting by the Leicester Square Underground station. Jemima was in yet another unripped bodice, one I recognized. It was Shep's tartan waistcoat. That trollop. It only reinforced my distrust of Ms. Curlilocks.

She was busy taking cash and putting it into a small purse. Eventually she stuffed the purse into said bodice, moved to the front of the crowd, and began to project from her encased diaphragm.

"In case some of you might not recognize me, I am Jemima Comstock. C-o-m-s-t-o-c-k. Actor. I am delighted to be your guide through the magical streets of London's Theatre District, where we are surrounded by the ghosts, and heroes, and heroines, of the tragedy and comedy that is life. Welcome to the land of Shakespeare, of Marlowe, of Gilbert and Sullivan, the city of Andrew Lloyd Webber."

I knew Andrew Lloyd Webber had his fans, but I'd hardly put him up there with Shakespeare.

"In the words of Oscar Wilde, 'I regard the theatre as the greatest of all art forms, the most immediate way in which a human being can share with another the sense of what it is to be a human being.'" She paused and rearranged herself, throwing out one arm. "'All the world's a stage and all the men and women merely players. They have their exits and their entrances. And one man in his time plays many parts.' Women, as well, of course. As a performer, I am uniquely qualified to lead this tour, as I've had the privilege to strut upon many of these hallowed stages."

"Have you been on the telly?" A small man with a big voice waved his hand near the back.

"Of course," she said. "*Casualty* and *The Bill*. Moving on, we will first visit the historic Theatre Royal, Drury Lane, the oldest in London, originally built in 1663, and end our tour at the fabulous Savoy Theatre."

After her speech there, she made a few extravagant gestures leading the motley group onward. "On our left, you can see another historic building, the Royal Opera House, built in 1732. I visited the Opera House for the first time as a precocious child of five."

Sigh. Cobblestone streets and heels were not the best match, but I managed to make my way to the front and receive a surprised nod of recognition from Jemima as she turned for her next speech. In between a detailed version of her résumé, the walk was filled with tedious, obvious questions, or with people who felt they knew more than she did. Which was certainly possible. Still, it made me feel for these guides.

She continued as we walked toward the Strand. "Many of our beloved spaces were built in the 1880s, including the Comedy Theatre, the Prince of Wales, and the gorgeous Savoy Theatre, inside the hotel you see before you."

After the tour, many of the tourists tipped Jemima. She took that significant roll of cash and put it in a separate compartment of her bag. Then she distributed cards—i.e., mini headshots—to the participants. I took one. "Jemima? I was wondering whether you'd let me buy you a drink in the American Bar. If you are not too tired from the tour, of course."

"He who is tired of London, is tired of life," she said, with a toss of her blonde curls.

Honestly, with the quotes? Samuel Johnson would be appalled. I rolled my eyes so hard it's astounding they didn't wind up in France.

We entered the lobby. As we passed Kent, he tipped his hat. "Ms. Redondo."

Jemima stared at me. "You're staying here?"

"Yes, of course. Would you mind if I dropped off my things?" I got into the elevator and pressed five. "You can order me a White Lady, put it on room 567." It was only lunchtime, but given my morning, a drink was in order.

I ran to my room. Happily, it had already been serviced. It was safe to leave Bruce. I made sure he was still breathing, then took the top off the Tupperware and put the bowl in an empty drawer at the top of the armoire. I headed to the elevator, considering how best to handle Jemima. She reminded me a bit of Angela Hepler, my ex-husband's second wife. So I would use my Hepler-coping skill: insincere flattery.

I arrived at the door of the famous bar and sighed. If they were about to remodel, I'd be one of the last thousands of people to have an overpriced cocktail on chairs that might have contained the bottoms of Hemingway or Streisand. I tried to memorize the room.

The carpet was a bit busy, but I wasn't complaining. It had a deep brown border, with blue grids full of cream-colored circles. All the leather club chairs and bar stools were a soothing, brownish gold. It felt like being inside a glass of bourbon. I wanted a bourbon, after the morning I'd had, but legend had it one of the bartenders had buried the bar's signature White Lady cocktail, in its shaker, inside the foundation of the building, so a White Lady it would be.

In normal circumstances, I'm a person who likes to sit at the bar. If you befriend the bartender, you not only get free drinks, but the leftovers from their cocktails. Of course, Jemima had chosen a chair in the center of the bar, where everyone would see her as they walked in.

She was flirting with the waiter. What a shock.

"Ah, Cyd, how kind of you to join me. This is Luke."

"Lovely to meet you," Luke said, giving a small bow. "Your drinks will be coming shortly."

I could see that Jemima didn't like another woman getting attention, so I was going to have to unruffle her feathers before I got anything out of her. "They are so lovely here, aren't they? Even to Americans like me. That must be tough, given the kind of behavior some of my fellow citizens engage in. Is it hard for you on the tours?"

"Yes, sometimes." She narrowed her very green eyes. "How is it you are staying here? Is Shep's estate handling it?"

"Oh no. His college, plus some travel agent skills." Our drinks arrived. She had ordered a martini. I hoped she didn't want to clink, as the small glasses were filled to the brim and we'd both lose half our cocktails that way. She was no fool, and didn't.

"Cheers," I said, taking a sip. "How are you holding up?" I was expecting actor's tears and I got them. How people could just spout like that on demand was beyond me.

"Of course I'm devastated." Sniff. Blow. "It's hard to imagine continuing on without him."

"At least until March," I said.

"How could you say that? Our relationship wasn't just physical. Our spiritual connection transversed the Atlantic." I took a very deep sip of my White Lady and gestured to Luke for another one. I could have done without the egg white. I kept thinking about it curdling in concrete for a decade. That was one time capsule reveal I might skip.

I was losing my focus. I tried again. "So, you arranged such a lovely service on Saturday. I know Shep would have appreciated it. It seems he was pretty beloved by the guides?"

She smiled. "By most of them. Some, of course, were jealous of our relationship."

"Yes, I saw that words were exchanged."

"Just another lonely, deluded spinster. He was so charming that anyone who met him might create an imaginary situation in which they were special. We often laughed about it." At this point I was hoping she would choke on her olive, but not before I got more information.

"How about Philip Babcock? He said Shep had taken him on as a kind of protégé?"

She finished off her martini with a slurp heard round the bar. "Philip? He wanted to be Shep. He was working on his own Ripper book, and of course pursued me. In the end, he was just too immature."

I guessed Jemima hadn't read the news this morning, so at least I was spared more CliffsNotes Shakespeare. "And who were Shep's other friends and colleagues? I just wanted to thank them for coming, on behalf of the estate."

"I can thank them for you."

"That's very kind, but Shep would want me to do it, I think. So, who else?"

Two more drinks arrived. I was going to have to be careful. Having two cocktails at lunch was unheard of for me, except during tax and hurricane seasons.

"There's Martin Thompson. He led the most popular Ripper tours before Shep took over."

"The one in the cape. Did Shep take his job?"

"Not on purpose. Martin had just gotten a part in the touring company for *The Buddy Holly Story* and asked for a break. Shep was teaching in London, so Nigel got in touch. By the time Martin returned, Shep was the darling of the walking tour world. Of course, Martin was furious, but he needed the money, so he came back. The Ripper tours are the cash cows of London's Afoot! Some guides, like Shep, get bigger crowds than others, but it's the tour everyone wants. Well, maybe except for Lady Di's London. Nigel and Madge insist that we're all trained for both, just in case a regular is ill. God forbid they miss out on the cash."

"So all the guides know the murder spots, the names of the Canonical Five, etc." Well, that didn't exactly narrow it down. And it made Madge or Nigel less likely to bump Shep and Babcock off. It was going to cost them money. I saw Madge taking Babcock's cash.

"So London's Afoot! only operates on cash?"

"Yes. Tickets and tips."

"How good are the tips?"

"Good, since we have a lot of Americans. That's why there's so much competition for the most popular tours, especially for the full-timers. For them it can be very uneven—weather, Tube delays, strikes, you know. It can make some of the older guides quite desperate."

Like Martin Thompson, I thought. "So how many people, max, can come on the walk?"

"It's hard to manage more than thirty and keep track of who's paid and who hasn't. Shep had a 'From Hell' stamp for their hands."

I wondered what had happened to Shep's cash on the night he died. "You said Shep was getting threats. And you don't think Philip Babcock could have sent them?"

"No. I can't see that."

"It's just that I went on his tour last night and he said he wound up with Shep's keys. So he could have been the one who was in Shep's flat." I watched for her reaction. She sucked down the rest of her drink.

Her phone buzzed. "Would you pardon me? It might be my agent."

She took out her phone, appeared to read a text, then clutched her heart, screamed, and slid gradually off the leather chair until she was an attractively arranged lump on the floor.

Chapter Thirty

I looked at Luke the waiter. He took his time coming over.

I was about to drop to the floor and help her, when he held up his hand. "Just give it a minute. We were at RADA together. I think fainting is actually listed with fencing and conversational Mandarin as one of the skills on her CV. Though, it's usually when there's a bigger audience. Anything provoke it?"

"She got a text." He picked up the phone and read it to me.

"Phil is dead. Come immediately."

Jemima started to come around. Luke and I got her back in her chair and I gave her a sip of my White Lady. At least it had protein. "Here. Are you all right?"

"Philip Babcock is dead. He's dead!" She grabbed my hands. "I must go to the others."

"Of course," I said. "Luke, can you put our drinks and a generous gratuity on my room?"

"You don't have to rush off," Jemima said, gathering her coat and scarf.

"Don't be silly. You just fainted. I just want to make sure you get there safely. It's the least I can do."

Downstairs, I enlisted Kent's help in bustling her into a cab, climbed in and asked her for the address. It was the London's Afoot! office.

We stopped on Tottenham Court Road, where Jemima tried to leave me in the cab. I insisted on helping her up the stairs, due to her delicate condition. She did get her revenge, however, deciding to do "method" fainting about twice on each of the five flights and insisting that I pull all her weight so she would know how it felt. On the third floor, I gave her one method slap to revive her, followed by a splash of mouthwash from my Balenciaga on her face, so she could experience the full effect of being revived from the vapors.

We were on the verge of fisticuffs by the time we got to the office, which was filled with several guides, including the Jane Austen Empire waist woman, and Ripper guide Martin Thompson, wearing a cape I recognized. Was he the man following me at Tower Hill?

"Jemima, there you are. You should have been here an hour ago. And why are you wet?"

Jemima blushed, handed Madge the cash, and pointed to me. "I think you all know Cyd Redondo, Shep's executor?"

The room went silent.

"Hi. Cyd Redondo, Redondo Travel. I saw some of you at the lovely service for Shep."

"Yes, Miss Redondo," Nigel said. "Tragedy has struck us yet again. I hope you'll pardon us in our grief."

"Of course. I'm so sorry for your loss. I was on Mr. Babcock's very informative walk last night. He told us all about what happened to Shep, his final moments," I said, watching for Nigel's reaction. It was swift.

"Oh, I'm so sorry, where are my manners? Please, have a seat." He elbowed Madge, who moved papers from a chair.

"Oh, I wouldn't dream of interrupting. If you do find anything of Shep's that I should take home for his family, you will call me?" I gave him my card again and noticed Madge putting Jemima's cash in a safe. It was full of stacks of bills. She slammed it shut and twirled the combination lock.

I walked out, pulled the door almost shut, then listened. Happily, actors project. "It's not my fault," Jemima said.

Nigel's voice went into an upper register. "We're not canceling the walks. Absolutely not. We have a fiduciary responsibility. It's not fiscally sound."

Fiscally sound? Two dead guides in a week. I heard a thump as someone else headed up the stairs. I sprang away from the wall. Hazelnut practically knocked me over. We both stopped.

He just threw up his hands. "What are you doing here? Trying to blow my cover?"

"Cover? Your wig does that all on its own."

"Is Bruce okay?"

"Yes, except that the Wildlife Crime Prevention Unit is looking for him."

"What? How do you know?"

"I spent the morning at Scotland Yard. Now, get into that meeting. They're talking about Shep and I need you to take notes. You owe me."

"I'll find you later," he snarled as he went in and slammed the door.

I looked at my watch. One more hour before I had to call my employer. Hazelnut was covering the suspect guides and girlfriend. Jemima had me thinking about Martin Thompson and the other Ripperologists. There was one person I figured who knew the most about that group of morbid delinquents. Evelyn, the librarian.

Chapter Thirty-one

This time, I got into the line at the entrance of the British Library with confidence. I was so relieved not to have a living creature to conceal that I missed the new sign outside saying liquids were prohibited. I plopped down the minibar that was my Balenciaga on the security table and it clinked. The guard pointed to the sign. Before he could open the bag, I said I'd be right back and ran out to sit at the feet of giant Isaac Newton, who was stuck in a position that made him a cert for sciatica.

I opened my bag to see all the airline bottles I'd managed to get not only off the plane but through Customs. I couldn't bear the idea of throwing away perfectly good, free liquor. At least I was on vacation. I chugged the Cuervo Silver and Jack Daniel's. I couldn't quite face the gin, too. I knew it was a British favorite, so I left it at the base of the statue. I spritzed myself, especially my neck, with Chanel No. 5, popped three Altoids, and got back in line.

No clinks this time. The guard let me through.

I smiled at him and took the marble steps down to the locker room, where I left most of my possessions. For the first time in my life, I saw the attraction of cargo pants.

The security guards in the Humanities Reading Room checked my library card while I looked for Evelyn. She was wearing a dark navy twin set with white trim, minus pearls, in what could only be called a moping pose. When she saw me, she pulled out her handkerchief.

The other librarian shoved her out from behind the counter, said, "She's all yours," and went back to her post. Evelyn fell into my arms. I helped her out of the Reading Room and sat her down at a table in the cafe outside. "Don't move. Tea or coffee?" She shook her head.

"Nothing?"

"Wine. Have a glass of wine with me."

At this point, I'd had four drinks and it was barely two in the afternoon. I got her wine and asked if they had any nonalcoholic beer.

The guy behind the counter laughed. I took a white wine and plopped in an ice cube to water it down. I handed Evelyn hers. As she reached for it, I saw the bruises on her knuckles, where she'd punched Jemima and hit one of the gravestones.

I raised my watery wine. "To Shep. How are you feeling?"

"Heartbroken, of course. How are you?"

"Same."

"When will you be taking him back?"

"Well, that's complicated." As I didn't really consider her a suspect, I took the risk of telling her what was going on.

"You mean they think he was murdered? And Philip, too?"

"That's the way it looks. Two guides die on the murder sites, it seems too much of a coincidence. It could be a rival, another tour guide, I guess."

"Oh no." She went pale.

"What's wrong? Do you know who it is?"

"No, but if it's a Ripperologist, I've probably helped him. Before I met Shep, I helped all of them. I might have helped his killer." She looked down at her bruised knuckles. "I have blood on my hands!"

People in the cafe looked around. I patted her arm. How did this woman keep her job? She was, hands down, the loudest librarian in the known world.

"Don't be silly. There's no way you could have known what would happen. But you might be able to help me, I mean the police, figure out who some of the suspects are. Any names would be great."

She took a big gulp of wine. My phone pinged. It was Uncle Leon. Now he wanted me? I'd have to call him back. "Sorry, please go ahead."

She wiped her eyes. "Well, there's Brunhilde, she's a guide too, but she couldn't possibly hurt Shep, he was the only one of the scholars who was kind to her. It's a very, very sexist bunch, as you might imagine. There are seven other walking tour guides who have books or are working on them. One is the head of the Beyond Ripperology site. He's a Leachan. It's the given name of one of the suspects. Each of the rival authors favor a different killer. It's the only way to make a name for themselves. They all hated Shep. Because of the book, because he was American, of course. And he had a full head of hair, rare among the Ripper guides. As is personal hygiene. Under the right circumstances, it could be any of them."

"What about Jemima? Or any other women he might have seen in the past?"

"Any of us might have killed one another, but not him."

She wrote down the scholars' names, then got up. "Thank you for the wine."

"You're very welcome. Just one more thing. You didn't mention Martin Thompson. A few people have said he might harbor a grudge?"

She went pale again. "That snake? Of course he's a suspect! He was caught trying to smuggle out something from the Rare Book room. He's banned for life from the British Library. Can you imagine anything more despicable?" I guess that meant that Evelyn hadn't helped Shep smuggle the things he'd taken. I definitely couldn't ask her about those now.

"He's a very sneaky person altogether, Martin Thompson. And I should know."

"From helping him at the library?"

"From being his ex-wife."

Well, that pretty much confirmed Evelyn as a Ripper groupie, so maybe she had protested too much and was back on the suspect list. Who knew? As soon as I'd thanked her and retrieved my Balenciaga, I remembered Shep's claim check. I'd left it in the safe. Damn. I'd have to come back later.

I checked my phone to find a text from Uncle Leon saying he had something he needed to show me. Another girlfriend? I tried calling him back, but he didn't answer. I stopped for a bacon sandwich, to soak up my two liquid lunches, sat down on the steps of St. Martin-in-the-Fields, and called Dean Dean. The History Department secretary put me through, sadly.

"So, when is the flight arriving?"

"I'm not sure. There's been another hiccup."

There was a long silence. "That's not acceptable."

"I agree. But honestly, Dean McAfferty, I was at the embassy when they opened this morning with every piece of paperwork they needed to have him on a plane tomorrow."

"So, what's the problem?"

"Scotland Yard has taken charge of the body. They think it might have been a homicide."

I heard something break at the other end of the phone.

"And why do they think that?"

I explained about Babcock. "The embassy is doing everything they can, I've got a call into the coroner. I met with the inspector in charge this morning. I promise you I am pushing as hard as I can for a resolution. But these are governments I'm dealing with, not airlines."

"Have you spoken to the Heeps yet?"

"No, I was waiting for the go-ahead for them to pick up the body."

"Please call them and let them know what's happening. As soon as possible."

"I will."

"You'd better."

Dial tone. Great. I doubted I could count on Dean Dean to extend my stay at a five-star hotel, and I had already used up all my favors, coupons, and miles. I walked back down the Strand, soaking in every storefront, every chimney pot, until I made it back to the Savoy.

I stopped in front of the revolving doors and took a deep breath. This would be my last night as Cinderella, complete with mice. I didn't think my particular mouse was up to making me a ball gown, but there was only so much fairy tale one girl could take. I went in.

Standing in the middle of the lobby was Uncle Leon, in shirtsleeves. He always wore a jacket. This was bad. I hurried over to him.

He looked worried. "I need your help."

"Of course. With what?"

"This." He held up a plastic bag filled with what looked like cocaine.

Chapter Thirty-two

I jerked his arm down and hustled him into the nearest elevator, which smelled as though someone had been sick inside. Too many White Ladies, I thought. Thankfully I was only on the fifth floor. When the elevator door opened, I waited until the housekeeper was looking the other way to push him into my room. I gestured to an armchair. He sat down and crossed his stick-insect legs, revealing silk socks and garters above his pointy shoes.

"Nice," he said, looking around. I sniffed the air. The stench had followed us in. I thought I heard a chirp from Bruce and hoped it wasn't pheromones. A leaping rodent was the last thing I needed right now. I was grateful, for once, that Uncle Leon was a little deaf in one ear.

"What the hell is that?"

"I don't know for sure. I thought you might."

He held out the baggie. Even from an arm's length away, it smelled like wet dog and vomit. I got up and grabbed a few tissues and used them to take it from him.

"Ewww. Where did you get this?"

"It was inside something else."

"What, an intestine?"

"No. Colon."

I dropped it to the floor. "What the hell?"

"Are you going to sit down?"

"I'd prefer to pace right now, thank you."

He shrugged. "It's involved with the job I'm doing. It's kind of a specialty item."

"A specialty item with a colon? And this is why you can't stay in the hotel, because of the smell?"

"No. Accommodations were included."

"Where?"

"I'd rather not say."

"I forgot. You're Mr. Discretion. That's why you stood in the lobby of a hotel with a huge bag of cocaine in your hand. Good job."

"As I said, I'm not supposed to talk about the job itself. This was an unexpected wrinkle in my mission."

"Your mission? What? Are you MI-6 now?"

He raised one Redondo eyebrow. All my uncles had the Redondo eyebrow raise.

I looked down at the baggie, hoping the Savoy team had something to remove odors from their carpets. "So, to review, this was inside the colon of an animal you are preparing?"

He nodded.

"Is it for the museum?"

"It's for a museum. Of sorts."

"Stop it."

"It's a private museum. It's a family pet."

"With drugs inside. Have you asked them about it?"

"Not yet. Knowing the family, I don't really think they're involved. The pet died while they were on holiday and it was frozen and sent to Heathrow. Look, Squid, this looks like cocaine, right? I didn't want to tell anyone in case it was something else. I'm old, what do I know? Will you help me?"

"What makes you think I'd know whether or not this is drugs?"

"Because I was the one who dropped you and Barry Manzoni off at CBGB on your eighteenth birthday. Something I never told your mother or your Uncle Ray, by the way."

I sighed, got two disposable gloves out of the side of my purse, and took the baggie to the bathroom sink. Uncle Leon stayed in his chair.

As I unzipped the bag, a tiny bit of the powder flew up and into my nose. I hate drugs, but Uncle Leon was right. I'd seen *Scarface*, I was once in the bathroom at CBGB, and I do live in Brooklyn. It was pretty clear from the instant freeze I felt that this was indeed cocaine. Or something worse. I instantly rinsed my nose inside and out. I'd already had five drinks. I didn't want this day turning into an English version of *Less Than Zero*.

I came back out. He was still in the chair, eating my Savoy cookies.

"It's drugs. So explain. Seriously. And not vaguely. Because we are already in trouble with the police and for all I know, might be under surveillance."

"Okay. This project required a quick turnaround. It was frozen on the other end, but as you know, once it thaws, I only have seventy-two hours to stretch the skin, and it hadn't even been skinned yet. There was no one on that end qualified to do it. And since it was an animal, it had to be inside a pet coffin and air tray, enveloped in dry ice. Instead of waiting for the driver to take his time getting it to the museum, I went to Heathrow to pick it up myself. Well, with my driver."

"Of course, your driver."

"He's very nice."

"I bet. So you signed for the package at Heathrow, for this drug-smuggling package?"

He shrugged. Christ on a bike. "Looking back, it would have been smarter to wait for the delivery. I've probably messed up the chain of criminality."

"The chain of criminality?"

"I watch PBS."

"So do I."

"Not enough." He was probably right.

"And do you know who packed it at the other end?"

"I just have the shipment number. I don't know anything. I'm just a taxidermist."

"Apparently now the El Chapo of taxidermists."

He kissed the top of my head. "I need to get back and finish. Can I leave this with you?"

"Do I look like a fricking evidence locker? No. I have no intention of being part of the chain of criminality. Here." I put the baggie in one of my own ziplocks, then put both inside one of the hotel's plastic laundry bags.

"I'm going back with you. I need to make a phone call. Give me a minute."

I dug around in my special cards pocket, found what I was looking for, and dialed. I did a surreptitious check on Bruce. For once, he was still in the Tupperware, but this time in a splayed position, like a leaping cheerleader. It was my last night in the Savoy. I wanted Housekeeping. I eased the Tupperware into my purse as Roger's voicemail beeped.

"Hi. Can you meet me in the basement of the Natural History Museum? I have some pet guts you need to see."

Chapter Thirty-three

I thought it would be faster to take the Tube, plus commuters could blame the smell on someone else. At this time of day, the District Line would take us right to Kensington station, a block from the Natural History Museum.

I looked over at Uncle Leon. He looked tired.

"Have you talked to Aunt Helen?"

"Yep."

Well, that was a lie. But I understood. I'd ignored two of her calls today already and it was only ten in the morning in Bay Ridge.

"So, the museum here, is it as good as ours?"

"What are you, nuts?" He grinned.

He had always promised me that "our" museum, on 77th Street in Manhattan, was the best in the world. "It has its charms," he said. "We have more square footage, but their central building is really something."

Suddenly, I was six again. The Natural History Museum was my first love, because it was about the only place I ever got to go outside the neighborhood, but mostly because it was the most wonderful place on earth.

When my mother needed to go into Manhattan, she would drop off me and my stroller at the museum with Uncle Leon. He would give me dead animals to play with, which is probably why I have such a strong immune system. As soon as I could walk, I had free run of the whole building—even at night. It was like living in *From the Mixed-Up Files of Mrs. Basil E. Frankweiler*, with bison. *Night at the Museum* had nothing on me. To be honest, that film pissed me off. It didn't keep me from being Uncle Leon's date at the premiere, though. It was one of the last times we'd gone to the museum together, now that he was retired. So, even though this visit probably involved an international criminal conspiracy, the six-year-old in me was excited.

We walked through an endless tunnel, filled with buskers, shoppers, and flurries of schoolkids, until we finally found the right exit.

And there it was. Their building was grander than ours. And, of course, like all museums to museum lovers, it had a churchlike quality. Uncle Leon understood and let me stand for a minute, until I caused a sidewalk jam and he moved me aside.

I grinned. "Is there any way we could walk through the main hall first?"

He'd always said the entrance of any public institution meant everything——if it didn't provoke delight and awe, it was worthless. Its purpose was to jump-start the wonder, and certainly seeing the complete skeleton of the famous Dippy the dinosaur did that, even though Uncle Leon said it was only a plaster cast of Andrew Carnegie's real one. In spite of one dead client, one furious client, and whatever Uncle Leon was up to, I was happy. My uncle nodded to a guard, and we headed for some back elevators.

Every city has its own smell. So does every museum. Uncle Leon's stuffing rooms in New York smelled like pipe smoke, wet clay, damp fur, and garlic. This one smelled like wet fur too, but with formaldehyde forward, and an undernote of stale ale.

We moved through the workroom, where several assistants smiled at him. He stopped to say something to one of them, who took out some kind of walkie-talkie.

At the end of the room was a large tented table and several work trays beside it. There was also a curtain on a long rail, which Uncle Leon gestured me through and pulled closed behind us, separating us from the rest of the space.

"They'll let your boyfriend in."

"He's not my boyfriend."

"When all you have to say is 'Hi,' and he's showed up for an unannounced dinner with your family, he's your boyfriend."

There was some logic to that, but I didn't really want to hear it. I looked around.

The top of a pressed-wood air tray with the silhouette of a dog was propped against the wall. The rest of it was still around a smallish, red-silk-lined coffin right out of *Sunset Boulevard*—a movie Uncle Leon had made me watch. There wasn't a limp monkey hand hanging out of it, at least.

"That looks like a new air tray model. Did it hold up?" The one Ginger had sent for the pet alligator the Woodleys had backed over while in Florida had been much flimsier-looking.

"Very sturdy, actually." Very gently, my uncle lifted the sheet on the worktable, revealing the orange, white, and in this case gray fur of an obese corgi.

"Wow. That's the kind of dog the Queen has, isn't it? Aren't there always like three of them following her around, yapping?" He didn't say anything. "Uncle Leon?"

He gave me the Redondo gesture for "lower your voice."

"Currently two," he whispered.

"Holy crap!" I grabbed the back of a chair, sending a half-done hedgehog flying. My uncle was stuffing the Royal dog. Well, that explained a lot. Except for the drugs. It didn't explain the drugs at all.

"Wait. Are you telling me that someone smuggled drugs inside a monarch's corgi. This is a Royal air tray?" No wonder it was sturdy. "Holy crap!"

"You already said that."

"Well, it bears repeating. Roger. God, what are we going to tell Roger?"

"To ask you out?" Uncle Leon said.

"It's the twenty-first century, I think women can take the lead," Roger said, pulling back the curtain.

Chapter Thirty-four

I had no idea how long he'd been standing there. I tried to control my heart rate. In vain. When I ran my hand over my hair, Uncle Leon snorted, then wiped his hands and held one out.

"Leon Redondo. We met in Brooklyn."

"Of course. Nice to see you." Roger shook, then turned to me.

"Cyd Redondo, Redondo Travel. We met in Atlantic City."

To his credit, he blushed. "I remember." It would have been a romantic moment if we hadn't had a canine carcass between us.

Uncle Leon gestured to the bag as he put on gloves and turned the poor corgi on its back, revealing the incision and releasing a few more unlovely smells. Roger looked a little green.

"Sorry, he's starting to thaw, I'll have to work while we talk." He put on his apron and lifted a scalpel. As always, he started the skinning process at the scalp.

Roger stared in horror. "Perhaps you two can tell me why I need to be here for this?"

I took out a tissue from my Balenciaga and pulled out the plastic bag. "This was inside the dog." Roger tried to take the baggie and, for a second, our fingers touched. He shook his head, then lay the baggie back on the table.

"What's that wooden thing? Or is it cardboard? The thing around the coffin?"

We explained about the air tray, how coffins had to be shipped in them and why they had them for pets. The look of disbelief on Roger's face never wavered.

"Sorry to have bothered you, Roger, but I know you've looked into people using animals to smuggle other things, so I thought you were the right person to call. Also, you come to mind when I see animal intestines." Roger and I had once attended a tribal ceremony involving the guts of a goat.

Roger laughed. "Back at you," he said, wrinkling his nose. "Is there someplace not in the corpse vicinity we could talk?"

"If it's quick. As I said, I have a time limit on this skin." Uncle Leon directed us past a half-restored platypus towards a tiny office crammed with stuffed crows and cobras, lots of wooden filing cabinets, and an actual typewriter.

"Old school," Roger said, looking around. "I love it. So, just take me through the pickup, step by step." Uncle Leon did. Roger took notes. "Do you have the waybill?"

"It'll be up in Accounting. I'll ask them for it."

"I know this is a weird question, but there wasn't any cash, currency of any kind in the shipment, was there?"

"No. But I did find this stuck to the underside of the fur." Uncle Leon lifted another baggie with what looked like a piece of a hundred-dollar euro.

Roger looked at the euro and the baggie for a long time. "Is it okay for me to take these? I probably need the air tray too, but I'll come back for that. And I need to know the dog's owner, of course."

Uncle Leon and I looked at each other, not quick enough for Roger to miss it.

"It was addressed to the museum. I'm just the errand boy. Got to get back to work. Leave your card and I'll call when I find the waybill. Thank you for coming. Cyd will walk you out." He winked. Unbelievable.

Roger turned back to him. "Mr. Redondo? We're going to need to preserve the dog as evidence. Can you do that?"

"Preserve it, yes. Absolutely. Preserve it as evidence? No. I answer to a higher power."

"Higher than Scotland Yard?"

Uncle Leon nodded.

Roger looked at me. I nodded too. "Seriously, he does."

"Can I get photos, then?"

I took some on my phone, with a close-up on the location of the cocaine, and Uncle Leon promised to have his assistant take better ones.

"I'll be working all night. Call you later, Squid."

Roger stared at me. "Squid?"

We got coffees on our way out, as Roger had already asked me if I were drunk. I was. We exited, sucking down the caffeine. Roger stopped me at the bottom of the stairs.

"What the hell is going on?"

"I'm not sure I can tell you. I mean, I know he can't tell you. And from me, it would just be a supposition and not based on anything he's told me, understand?"

"For the love of God, Cyd, cough it up."

"I think that's one of the Queen's corgis."

Roger spit out his coffee. "So it was sent by someone working for the Crown?"

"I guess. Who knows? Maybe they delegate. Whatever it is, you cannot get Uncle Leon in trouble. I'm the one who called you, he didn't want to say anything, but I was afraid if he didn't, it might look like he was involved."

"I don't know how I can keep him out of it."

"By not making a report, that's how."

"I don't know if that's possible, now that I've seen it. And especially because there's a chance it's tied into what I'm over here to investigate."

"Dormice?"

"I'm just helping with that, I'm mainly here for something else. Smugglers have always put drugs into animal shipments, but now there's something else going on."

"What? What else?"

"They might be using animals to move cash. There are two ways to move illegal cash around. Either launder it or smuggle it, right? There are lots of ways to launder money, filter it through shell companies or real estate investments. Cash businesses, if you can find legitimate ones. Smuggling is riskier, but faster. You know about putting drugs inside snakes and other animal shipments, but we've never had cash move that way, until lately. That's why I'm here."

"But this was drugs, not money, so you don't have to report it, right?"

"If you didn't want it reported, then what am I doing here?"

"I don't know. I don't know why I called you. I saw him holding that bag in the Savoy lobby and panicked."

"Why was he in the Savoy lobby?"

"I'm staying there."

"You're staying at the Savoy? Wow."

"I know, it's incredible. Tonight's my last night." We looked at each other for too long. "Can you just forget you saw it? Just don't follow up. Or not yet. At least until we're off the suspect list for that other thing?"

"The double murder thing?"

"Yeah. I have enough to worry about."

We stood on the sidewalk. There was a wicked wind that blew Roger's dark hair into his face. I hated to say it, but I really wanted him to kiss me.

Instead, he put his hand on my elbow. I practically heard it sizzle.

"Let's take a walk. There's a spot near here I think you'd like. Come on."

He pointed me toward a park in the distance. We walked past the Victoria and Albert Museum, which had an actual fashion section, into Kensington Gardens. I remembered, suddenly, that Bruce was in my purse and was thankful there were enough joyful and/or miserable kids in the park to cover his snoring.

I figured talking would help cover the noise, too, so I told Roger about Shep and what I was trying to find out. I had forgotten what a good listener he was. When I was done, I asked for his opinion, as a law enforcement professional.

"I don't think the Yard would have stepped in if they didn't suspect something. And it does sound suspicious, two guides dying on the tour in a week. On the murder sites. I mean, if I were them, especially given the kind of negative publicity something like this would generate, I would do a quiet investigation. Who are your suspects?"

I tried to focus on his question, rather than his arm, which had snuck around mine. Having had five drinks didn't help with my self-control, caffeine notwithstanding.

"Jealous scholars? But scholars are fairly sedentary, right?"

Roger grinned. "Probably, but I would imagine they're sitting on a lot of rage."

"True. Shep was always talking about how much schools took advantage of adjunct professors. That's why he wrote the book and did the tours—to be able to afford to live in Brooklyn."

"Anybody else?"

"When it was just Shep, I thought it might be a jealous girlfriend, he had several, but why would they kill Babcock?"

"Maybe he knew more than he told you."

"Or was sleeping with more than one of Shep's girlfriends I know about."

"Wow. What kind of woman fixates on Jack the Ripper guides?"

I thought about the catfight at the memorial service. "You'd be surprised. So far, librarians, unemployed actresses, museum curators, and former nuns."

Roger laughed.

"It's actually not that funny."

"Sorry."

"It could also be one of the London's Afoot! guides wanting to pick up extra walks. Or guides from less famous companies wanting to move up."

"That seems unlikely, doesn't it?"

"I met some of them. It is a cutthroat business."

"That joke is beneath you."

"Apparently not anymore."

Roger slowed us down. Was he going to kiss me? "Who else?"

"It could always be some random Jack the Ripper–obsessed psychopath."

"Well, you've certainly narrowed it down."

"Shut up. Seriously. What am I going to do?"

"You're going to close your eyes. Just close them for a minute. Trust me." He actually said this without irony. I let him lead me for several steps and began to hear what sounded like running water. "Okay, open."

We were standing in front of the kind of magical spot I'd only seen in high-end brochures—an elevated pond with fountains and sculptures and what looked like dormant water lilies. Roger walked me to the structure at the end, a charming little house with benches, which looked over the fountains and beyond over what Roger told me was the Serpentine. I was thrilled to see it, as several of my hardiest clients had participated in the Polar Bear swims there in winter, and not died.

Although it was January, the trees were still gorgeous, like something out of a Redondo, travel-deprived fairy tale. We sat on a bench, our arms and thighs just touching, not talking for a minute. I could feel the slight vibration of Bruce's snoring, but the fountain was loud enough to drown it out, so I relaxed and leaned a tiny bit into Roger's arm on my non-Bruce side.

"It's not quite Tanzania," he said.

He was right. In Tanzania I'd almost been arrested at the airport, had been stuck in a leopard trap, and had to be hypnotized so I could smuggle snakes in my bra. Although none of those things sounded particularly enjoyable, somehow they had been, because of him.

I was about to tell him this, when his phone buzzed. He ignored it, which was one point in his favor. It buzzed again. He sighed and looked at the number. "We have a lead on our rodent theft. I've gotta go."

"Anything you can tell me?"

"Not really. It's not my case. You haven't run into Hazelnut while you've been here, have you? Or anyone who reminds you of him?"

"God, no. What would he be doing here?" I clutched Bruce to my side.

"He moves around a lot," Roger said, standing up. "What are doing the rest of the day?"

"I'm going to do another Ripper walk to see if I can get more info."

"Is that smart? To go on another tour? What if another guide dies? You're already a suspect. And with this situation with your uncle and everything else, someone might be setting you up. As you know, it's not great to be under scrutiny in a foreign country. And I don't have the jurisdiction to help as much as I would at home." He took my arm and turned me toward him. "Seriously, Cyd, be careful."

"Okay. I will. Go ahead. I'm going to sit here for a minute."

"You sure?"

We stood up and came about as close to a kiss as I had at any seventh-grade bowling party, which is really, really close. In the end, he pecked me on the head and walked away. He turned once, and waved. Bastard.

I had to find Hazelnut.

Chapter Thirty-five

This time, I knew the way to Carnaby Street and was able to head off my favorite ecoterrorist before the starting point.

He gave a violent head shake when he saw me, strong enough to slightly dislodge his Ringo wig. "We should not be seen together!" He looked around and pulled me into yet another historical doorway. "Where's Bruce? Is he all right?"

"He's right here."

"I thought you were going to leave him in the room."

"I didn't know how long I'd be gone."

"Well, get him back there, you're going to screw up his circadian rhythms with all this jogging around."

"I'm not the one who screwed up his rhythms!"

"Well, you're keeping them from normalizing."

Was I? Damn. "Look, your name came up with the Wildlife Crime Prevention Unit and I just thought you should know."

"My name came up how? Because you gave it to them?"

"Of course not. It's, it's Roger. Cleghorn. I mean Claymore. You said he was working with them. Whoa." I felt a little dizzy and leaned against the doorway. Hazelnut backed away.

"You smell like tequila. And bourbon. And something else."

"Gin and egg white."

"You're drunk? During the day?"

"Kind of. So?"

"How could you be so irresponsible? Isn't Mothers Against Drunk Drivers an American thing? How can you careen around, pissed to the gills, with Bruce in your purse?"

"I don't have gills. And you have never seen me really pissed. Not even close! Do you want him, right now?"

He looked around. Walkers were gathering. "No."

"Then cool it. Every drink I had today was for work. And I just had two double espressos. Which is probably why I'm dizzy. Believe me, no matter what happens, my purse does not hit the ground."

"So what's all this about Claymore?"

"He's working with the Wildlife Crime team. He asked me if I'd seen you. Of course I said no, but just be careful."

"I'm being careful. Now, get Bruce home. Do it, go now."

"I'm not going until you tell me what got said at the tour office. Is there any gossip about Shep and Babcock? Any likely suspects?"

"I don't give a flying squirrel's fuck about Ripper guides. I have more important things on my mind. But if it has anything to do with the walking tours, like I told you before, it's all about the money."

"What about the money?"

"Follow it!"

"Oh God, did you actually just say follow the money?"

"Yes! Now get out of here, I have widows waiting for me."

I reached up and straightened his wig. "There. I have to leave the Savoy after tonight, so you need to figure out something else to do with Bruce."

I wanted to trounce off, but I had taken the circadian rhythm comment seriously. The last thing I wanted was to mess up any species, anywhere. Hazelnut might be unhinged, but he had taught me that much.

I had forgotten to get nuts from him, so I went back to the room via the American Bar, where Luke put a White Lady down in front of me before I could slip some cashews and almonds into my pocket.

"Hello, Ms. Redondo. How are you?"

"Very well, thanks. Look, you said you went to drama school with Jemima, right?"

"Before she dropped out."

"She dropped out? She told me she was a graduate."

"Slight exaggeration. She received two bad reviews in a student production and abandoned ship to work for her father's accounting firm. I think she still works there part-time. It happens. We had a few fellow students who gave up and went civilian. One of them became a chef, one married a lord, and one's working at the British Library." A ding went off in my brain.

"She wasn't named Evelyn, by any chance?"

"Yes. How did you know?"

"Lucky guess. Thanks so very much. I'm checking out tomorrow, so thank you for all your kindness. And best of luck with your career."

"Cheers. You're a travel agent, Jemima said? You book tours to England?"

I perked up at that one. "Yes. Can I help you with travel plans?"

"No," he said, reaching behind the bar and handing me a flyer. "I thought maybe you could recommend our theatre company—we work out of a mental institution in Camden Town."

Actors. Sigh. I took it and shook his hand, then headed to the room, which I was delighted to see was fully serviced, including the replenishment of cookies, which went straight into my purse.

I got my snoring charge back into the armoire and left him the nuts and a bit of water in case he took a hibernation break. At least I wouldn't be endangering any rodents on board for this disturbing and frigid outing, which I hoped would only feature historical murders.

Chapter Thirty-six

I took the now-familiar walk to the Temple Underground station and caught a Circle Line train. I wondered which of the guides would be leading the tour tonight, with both Shep and Babcock DOA. The trains were more crowded than before, and so was the station. I exited into a hoard of tourists and press milling about. Also a few police. I guess the news stories had whipped all the Ripper fans into a frenzy.

At least every possible Ripper guide and con person would be out tonight. Since the killer could be from an alternate company, or even a rogue walker—which would make my suspect list untenable—I needed to keep my eyes open.

A guide dressed like a hiker, with a walking stick and a handlebar mustache, was in front of a group of about fifteen people, off to the left of the station. I was just taking a photo of him when he locked eyes with another man dressed in an English bobby outfit from the late nineteenth century. The faux policeman made a rude gesture, turned back toward the Underground entrance, and yelled out in what sounded like a *Mary Poppins* version of a Cockney accent, "Get it right 'ere. From the 'orse's mouth! Secrets from the files of Scotland Yard!" This cry only garnered about three people. I took a chance and joined them.

"Excuse me, sir? I can't take your tour today, but will you be doing it again this week?"

He was with Murderers' Row Tours and led tours on alternate Mondays and Wednesdays. He also did a *A Fish Called Wanda*: The Locations tour on Thursdays. He offered his card and I shoved it in my bag.

"Who's that other guy, the one with the walking stick?"

"A bloody poser," he said, and turned back to his faithful few.

I squeezed into the enormous group gathered around a red-brochure-waving, gray-haired woman in a fedora, a red wool poncho, and what could only be called sturdy boots. She had worn them to Shep's memorial service. She put a few more bills inside a fanny pack under her poncho, then stepped up on a bench to get everyone's attention. Her clipped, commanding voice echoed over the Thames.

"Welcome to London's Afoot!, the original and still the best Jack the Ripper walk, created by a member of the Metropolitan Police and tonight led by one of Detective Frederick Abbeline's own descendants." There were gasps in the crowd. She took a deep bow.

"I'm Brunhilde Hyde, his great-great-grandniece." More gasps. If this were true, it was a big deal, as Abbeline was the one portrayed by Johnny Depp in *From Hell* and the most well-known policeman from the case. She would be mobbed on the tour. She gave a bit more of the Ripper spiel, then said, "If you'll just follow me up Seething Lane, we'll begin."

Seething Lane. You couldn't make this stuff up. As our group passed the other two guides, handlebar mustache yelled, "Stupid cow!"

"Wanker," Brunhilde responded, as the group started up the street.

I worked my way to the front and tried to match the woman's significant strides. She gave me a questioning look.

"Cyd Redondo, Redondo Travel. Ms. Hyde, I wanted to pay, but also perhaps talk to you. I'm over handling Shep Helnikov's affairs."

She stared at me, then shook her head. "I saw you at the service. Call me Hildy. You don't need to pay. I wouldn't dream of it. Shep was the only one of these bastards who was ever kind to me. Bless his soul."

"Yes, he was pretty wonderful. I can't believe he's gone."

"I know. I was hoping it was one of his magic tricks."

"Did you ever see him perform? At Now You See Him?"

She grinned. "It was the standard doves and top hat stuff, but he loved it. He'd always do a tiny piece of magic or two on his tours, flowers for one of the women, a Victorian coin behind the ear of a pensioner. The walkers ate it up." We came to a crossing. "If you'll excuse me, I need to stop here, but perhaps we can speak at the end? I wind up at the Ten Bells at about nine thirty."

"Perfect, see you there."

She reminded everyone to be careful at the crossing and described what the neighborhood had been like when "my great-grand-uncle walked these dark and dangerous streets."

I followed the tour for a bit, hearing other guides in the distance. I could see how important it was that every guide had a hook, a costume, a theory, a piece of information no one else had. And how they all gave each other the stink eye at every traffic crossing.

Hildy leaned towards Dr. James Maybrick as the primary suspect. As expected, she humanized the women more than the male guides did. When she got to the "hours of disemboweling" part, I figured I would just go ahead to the Ten Bells and wait. Maybe one of the bartenders might remember the last time Shep had been there.

I remembered the way and headed down the creepy half-modern, half-

Victorian streets. A couple of times I thought I heard footsteps behind me and wondered whether I'd ever done a reverse kick after six drinks? Yes, I had. Angela Hepler had showed up at Chadwick's on Tiki Night after I'd had three two-for-one mai tais and called me just another "slutty-ass recipient of nepotism." I hadn't connected with her head, but I did receive a resounding round of applause from the regulars before I got thrown out.

Still, Angela hadn't killed anyone that I knew of. Well, maybe with despair.

I moved from the cobblestones to the sidewalk, for a more stable kicking surface. The footsteps stopped. They started back, but I spotted Christ Church and the pub and made it inside without hand-to-hand, or heel, combat.

It was busy. I elbowed my way onto a bar stool between one end of what I guessed was a bachelorette party—five overdressed women in tiaras—and a sullen man in a work jacket, who just kept shaking his head and looking into his pint.

I caught the eye of the bartender, the same one who'd been here the night we drank with Babcock. Oh God, was that just last night? This had been the longest day in history.

The barman headed my way. "I'm sorry, love, I'm going to have to cut you off."

What was he, psychic? I hadn't even ordered yet. "I beg your pardon?"

"Not you, her," he said, nodding towards the woman beside me, who was now waving a light-up sex toy in the air and singing an out-of-tune version of Kylie Minogue's "Can't Get You Out of My Head."

"Out of your mouth, more like," muttered my sullen bar mate. I was glad I didn't have a drink yet to spit out. The woman tried to spin around on the stool. It wasn't a spinning one.

The bartender shook his head and asked what I was going to have. If I asked for a Coke or a club soda, I'd never get any information out of him. I needed to go relatively high-end. I scanned the shelves behind the bar. "A shot of Jameson, please," I said. He poured me a double shot. Great. I should have smiled less. "Thank you. I'm Cyd Redondo, Redondo Travel."

"Gus."

"I'm actually Shep Helnikov's travel agent. He might have come in here at the end of his Ripper walks?"

"Of course." He poured himself a shot and raised it. I had to raise mine. "To Shep," he said and shot his drink. I shot mine too, not to be rude. He poured me another one, dammit. "Yes, he came in all the time. And never once paid for a drink. Tourists were always buying him a round. He'd leave a tip for me, though. He was in here the night he died, may he rest in peace."

"Do you remember anything special about that night, anyone in particular who bought him a drink?"

"There were a few. It was mostly women, and to be honest, in my line of work, they all start to blur together. But there was one man who stood a round that night. I can't quite remember his face. He was wearing a cape, though."

Martin Thompson. "That helps. Thank you so much."

"My pleasure." He headed off to the other end of the bar. I placed the rest of my drink in the pathway of the twirling sex toy and, as planned, the pink battery-operated missile knocked it over. By the time Gus was back, my glass was empty, and before he could pour me another, Hildy arrived and dragged me to a booth in the back.

"We need to hide or they won't leave me alone. It's bad enough on a regular night, but after the news about Philip's death, it's just mad. These people are animals."

"Are you nervous now? About doing the walks?"

She shrugged. "You have to be a bit morbid to do this to begin with. I can't shy away from homicide at this point, can I?"

"I guess not."

"Besides, it sounds like they were both killed on their way home, so the walk itself and a drink or two are safe, at least."

I wasn't entirely sure about the drink part, so I would get hers myself. "What are you having? It's on me."

"Gus will have it waiting. Ta."

Taking the chance that Gus wouldn't have poisoned someone who overtipped him, I brought back her pint and a water for myself, which I hoped she would think was vodka. I had read in tourist guides that the English didn't trust people who didn't drink.

"I really want to find out what happened to Shep. Do you think it could be a rival guide?"

"Of course. We'd all heard he'd found something big. I figure he was going to unveil it next week. One of these bastards was likely trying to prevent that, or get whatever it was and reveal it themselves."

"Unveil it where?"

"Annual Rips event. It's in Paris this year, so likely to be bigger than the one in Latvia."

That was why Shep had added the Paris leg to the trip. "Are you going? To the conference?"

"Can't afford it, but all the big Rips will. They'll have a full list of attendees on the website." She wrote the web address down for me. I gave her my card in case she remembered anything else. Or needed travel arrangements.

"By the way, are you really Abbeline's great-great-grandniece?"

She winked and lowered her voice. "Of course not. That was Shep's idea. He figured I needed a leg up. I will miss him." She raised her glass, then drained it.

"Me, too. Thanks. Do you want me to walk you to wherever you're going?"

"And get us both killed?" She laughed. "No, tonight I have cab fare."

We shook hands and I walked to the Tube with throat and purse intact.

The weaving motion of the train wasn't doing great things for my balance, but I finally made it to the hotel, up the elevator, and into my room, where I promptly collapsed on the bed. Possibly a mistake.

I couldn't remember the last time I'd had to lie on a bed with one foot on the floor to stop my head spinning. 1994? I couldn't even remember how many drinks I'd had. Once the room stopped moving and I'd chugged what was probably a fifteen-dollar bottle of water, I checked on Bruce. He appeared to be asleep, but I knew I could look back in ten minutes and he'd be leaping from chair to chair. Poor little guy. I hoped he wasn't screwed up for life.

I was too tired to take my makeup off, but had just managed to wriggle out of my clothes when I heard a knock. Oh God, Hazelnut. Maybe he was finally going to take Bruce off my hands. I had to admit, part of me didn't want him to. Maybe I could apply for joint custody. I threw on my Savoy robe and opened the door.

It was Roger.

Chapter Thirty-seven

"Hi," he said. "Can I come in?"

My head started swimming again. This just seemed like a bad idea. But it was my last night at the Savoy. And it was Roger. I could blame it on the eight drinks, couldn't I? Or was it nine? I gestured him in.

He closed the door and leaned against it.

I looked at him. "Do you want anything?"

He looked at me for a long time.

"Are you still tipsy?"

Yes. "No, of course not."

He picked me up and pushed me against the wall, kissing me senseless. Well, not quite senseless, as my senses were pretty much on high alert. I wrapped my legs around him and we hobbled forward to the bed. We fell onto it, laughing.

Roger's weight on me was so familiar. And incendiary. He propped himself up on his elbows and looked me in the eye. "How was your day?"

I snorted.

"Seriously," he said, "are you all right?"

"It's a long story."

He rolled off me and we lay side by side looking up at the ceiling and holding hands. He ran his thumb over mine.

"How about your uncle?"

"Who knows?"

He pulled my hand to him and kissed it, making me breathe a little harder. "Cyd? I was so glad you called today. It scared the shit out of me, too. I know why you didn't come to Indonesia with me. I understand." He squeezed my hand. "You did let me hypnotize you, though."

"I would have let Hannibal Lecter hypnotize me if Interpol was putting snakes in my bra."

"Fair enough."

I turned on my side. Our chemistry had sparked from forty feet the first time we saw each other. At this proximity, it was nuclear fission level. I restrained myself, mostly because he didn't seem to be finished talking and it seemed impolite.

"I swear, I couldn't tell you the whole truth when we were in Tanzania. I don't know anyone who takes their job more seriously than you, so I hoped you'd understand. You know, after giving it some thought. I mean, it's not an excuse, but if there were one, that would be it. And I'm so sorry about your Uncle Ray, I would have done anything to spare you that."

"Yeah, well, if you can spare Uncle Leon, I might call it even."

He kissed me for just long enough to discombobulate me completely, then stopped. "I just, I think about you all the time, I keep remembering our first night in Atlantic City. You remember, right?"

"I remember." I was remembering so much that I was practically hysterical. "And the leopard trap. And JFK." The last, and second time we'd really spent the night together the sex had been mind- and heart-blowing, but sad too. I was still confused. I knew he cared about me. He had probably saved my life and definitely kept me out of jail. Still, while his deception didn't put as much of a blight on the sex as it should've, it had put a blight on the love.

He waited for more, but I kept quiet.

"Could we start over? You know my job now. I can't imagine a situation where I'd need to lie to you again. We can be honest with each other from now on. Deal?"

At that moment, there was a squeak and snuffle. He didn't seem to hear it. I wished I hadn't.

He took my face in his hands and looked right at me. It's kind of strange how rarely we look into another person's eyes. Really look. Dammit, I was still in love with him. That was just a fact, no matter what he'd done.

"I forgive you," I said.

He kissed the top of my head, my forehead, my eyelids, my nose, and then pulled me to him until the lengths of our bodies were touching in all the places that rendered me helpless.

Then he kissed me properly, for a long time, before he untied my robe and ran his finger over my nipple, at which point I squeaked. "Are you planning on taking off your coat?"

He laughed, pulled it off, and tossed it on a chair.

"And your shoes?"

He undid his work boots and put them by the armoire, then shrugged off his sweater and lay back on top of me, his chest against mine, his belt pressing into my hips. I rolled on top of him and proceeded to undo it. He eased down his pants.

The whole time, I could hear a faint beeping noise. Maybe it was the whiskey. It kept getting louder. I sat up. "Do you have a beeper?"

"Not really."

"What does 'not really' mean?"

"I have a tracker with me, but I turned it off."

The beeping got louder. "It sounds like it's in the hall. Do you think it's a fire alarm?"

"It's not loud enough. No flashing lights."

"Speak for yourself," I said, kissing his knee. The beeping got louder. He sat up, too, his pants halfway to his ankles, and looked around the room.

There was a violent knock on the door. "Metropolitan Police!"

I stared at Roger. "What the hell?"

Before either of us could move, someone kicked it in.

Chapter Thirty-eight

There stood Detective Felicity Hubbard, blonde ice queen, baton over her head, with a beeper on her belt that was going berserk.

We all froze. Unfortunately, I froze topless.

Hubbard lowered her baton, slightly. "Roger?"

He didn't answer. He was too busy pulling up his pants. He gave me a desperate look. I threw him his sweater with one hand, while I pulled the sheet up around my neck with the other.

Roger rose. "Detective Hubbard."

"I didn't realize you were still working. Sir. Have you secured it?"

Well, that was a piece of English slang I was unfamiliar with, but no, he hadn't.

Roger's sweater was inside out. "I'm not sure what you're referring to, Detective?"

She held up her beeper. "The dormouse. I assume you secured it before you, well, took a break?"

Crap. Was that actually a dormouse beeper? When the hell were those invented? The closer she got to the armoire, the louder the beeper got.

"There must be a glitch in the device," Roger said, throwing me my robe.

I did a Jennifer Beals *Flashdance* in reverse, putting the robe on under the sheet. I pulled it tight around my neck and got up.

"Hi, Detective." I thought I would start out with courtesy, and find a way to ingest some sobering caffeine at the same time. "Would you like a cup of tea?"

"No," she said. "Thank you. Could you please open that?" She pointed to the armoire.

I laughed unconvincingly. "You think I'm harboring a fugitive in there? What did you say it was? A titmouse?"

"Dormouse. The chip in the creature emits a tracking signal and that signal has brought me to your hotel room, so yes, I do believe you are harboring something." How could Hazelnut not tell me Bruce was chipped?

"Flick, seriously, there must be a mistake."

"If there's a mistake, what are you doing here?" She threw up her hands and almost lost control of the baton.

I stared at Roger. "Flick? What does that mean?"

Roger shrugged. "It's a nickname for Felicity."

"You gave her a nickname? Are you sleeping with her?"

"No!" they both said at the same time, but Flick had turned a sickly red and Roger wouldn't look at me.

"Well, perhaps she's just stalking you, then." I turned to our intruder, or the two of them I was seeing in my still-sloshed state. "Detective Constable Flick. This is my private hotel room. In America you would need a warrant to barge in here." I heard a snort that sounded almost human. Was Bruce getting louder, or was it my completely justified paranoia? I hoped they couldn't hear it over the incessant beeping, which was not improving my headache or my mood.

My rival was all business. "As apparently Special Agent Claymore was invited in, that's not necessary. I'm asking you one more time, please open the wardrobe."

I walked over, trying to pull off drunken casual. What did the English really know about Tupperware anyway? I opened the doors of the armoire, but I was still dizzy when I moved. I wound up swinging back and forth on one of them.

She gave an initial look. "Where is all your luggage?"

"I only do carry-on. Like any sensible person."

"I can verify that," Roger said.

"Really? How convenient." She moved to the armoire. "Special Agent Claymore? Assistance, please?"

Was Roger going to go through my underwear? I hadn't even brought my best stuff. He noticed the green Tupperware on the top shelf and looked at me. The detective was not aware of its nonfood uses. Roger was.

She opened the bottom drawer. Bruce's favorite. If he wasn't in the Tupperware, he was in there. I turned away and crossed myself.

I heard the armoire doors slam.

God bless you and your sleep-scurrying, I thought. I love you, Bruce. The policewoman moved into the bathroom. Unless you're in the sink.

Roger had the top off of the Tupperware.

The detective emerged from the bathroom, tapping her baton on her thigh. She went back to the armoire, rifling through my unmentionables and shoes again, and then moved around the room, jerking anything that would open, including the curtains. The machine was still beeping.

Roger still had the Tupperware in his hand. He cleared his throat. "Detective, I believe you can turn the beeper off. There are other guests in the hotel."

She stared at him, then hit the button. I instantly heard snuffling. Maybe they would think it was the central heating.

The detective moved closer to me. "Where is it?"

Two could play this game. I picked up my phone and closed the gap between us even more. I took a photo, then hit voice memo. "I don't know what your relationship is with Special Agent Claymore, but it's clear you've stalked him here under false pretenses and kicked in a door in a five-star hotel without giving the resident, myself, the time to answer your knock. I assume the Metropolitan Police will be paying for the damage and for my pain, suffering, and inconvenience." I neglected to add sexual frustration, as I was pretty sure that wasn't covered. "I will be making a formal complaint to Scotland Yard for conduct unbecoming and possibly sexual harassment of Special Agent Claymore as well, with the special agent as my witness."

I realized that my being naked under the hotel robe and the fact that I might be slurring my words probably hurt my case, but she moved back.

Roger was looking at the holes in the top of the Tupperware. He shook the bowl. It rattled. Damn. Bruce hadn't eaten all the nuts. And where was he? Had he escaped into the hallway?

"Clearly there have been mistakes on several levels." She gave Roger a look I was glad was not directed at me. "I deeply apologize, Ms. Redondo. I will leave you both to whatever you were doing."

Roger put down the Tupperware and turned to her. "Ms. Redondo is upset. Understandably. I'm sure she'll reconsider her complaint. There has clearly been a technical glitch in the equipment, which is no fault of yours."

"Ha!"

"Seriously, Cyd. Some decorum?"

"I didn't say anything."

"I will see you at the Yard in the morning, Detective?"

She was just heading for the door when a man in a tweed cape and deerstalker hat flew into the room, pulled out a taser, and sent her twitching to the floor.

Chapter Thirty-nine

Deerstalker Hat turned to me. I put my hands up, only because he could zap me faster than I could get into position to kick him.

"Where is he? Is he okay?"

"Who are you?" I tried to gesture with my head toward Roger, who still held the air-holed Tupperware top.

"Don't be an idiot. Where is he?"

"Where is who?" I tried to signal Hazelnut with my mind, as well as a swift "cut it out" gesture to my throat. Neither worked.

"Bruce. Bruce! Is he alright?"

"I don't know who you're referring to. Who are you?"

"Stop screwing around!"

Roger moved towards us. Hazelnut held out his taser.

Roger sighed. "Put it down."

He didn't.

"Look, your charge light is flashing. Enough. Hazelnut, you're under arrest."

"I beg your pardon. My name is Peter Stacio, walking tour guide."

Roger shook his head. "Cut it out, I saw your legs. As I said, you're coming with me."

"You can't arrest me, you're out of your jurisdiction. And where are your shoes?"

"None of your business." Roger pointed to the prone Detective Hubbard. "She's not out of her jurisdiction."

"She's unconscious."

"Exactly. And that means we can add assaulting a police officer to all the charges Interpol already has against you."

"Try it. Cyd, where is he?"

"How do you know where Cyd's room is, anyway?"

"Wouldn't you like to know?"

Roger turned to me. "Cyd?" Although my gestures didn't seem to be working, I tried a rotating finger to indicate Hazelnut was out of his mind.

"Where is he, where's Bruce?"

I threw up my hands and told the absolute truth. "No idea."

"No idea? What do you mean? He was your responsibility."

"He was not. And what the hell are you wearing?"

"I had to cover the 221b Baker Street tour tonight, one of the halfwit guides called in sick."

I heard what sounded like the word *Pissant!* None of us had said it.

It was followed by a loud sneeze. And another. None of us had sneezed.

We looked at each other. I reached behind my back and hit the concierge number and speaker button on the room phone.

When Kent answered, I screamed, then hung up.

Something moved under the bed. It was too big to be Bruce.

"Hazelnut?" I pointed to the bed.

Hazelnut bent down, grabbed something, and started pulling.

"Unhand me, you troll!"

Hazelnut pulled harder. A hand and part of a forearm emerged.

The voice under the bed screamed, "I am not a halfwit!" There was a strangled war cry.

"Hey! The bastard bit me. Claymore? Some assistance?"

Roger shook his head and bent down. Together, they pulled out a man in a cape and an unflattering Alan Rickman rip-off haircut—Martin Thompson. As soon as he stood up, I slapped him as hard as I could.

"I beg your pardon." He rubbed his cheek. "That was completely unnecessary."

"No, it was not. Have you been under the bed since I got back?"

He shrugged.

"Tase him. In the balls."

"Cyd!" Roger moved forward.

"Are you the one who broke in before?"

"Don't be ridiculous. I'm only here now because Shep promised it to me."

"Yes, well, he promised it to Philip Babcock too and look what happened to him."

Thompson paled for a moment. "It needs to be handled by someone who truly understands its value. And at the very least not an alcoholic travel agent with the IQ of a vole."

At that moment, Kent arrived. "Ms. Redondo, how can I be of assistance?"

"Kent! Thank you so much for coming." I pointed to Thompson. "We've just found this man hiding under the bed. He's also a suspect in a double murder. And on top of all that, he's wanted for stealing a rare item from the British Library."

"It was an accident, it just fell into my book."

We all just stared at him. Kent looked particularly stern.

"Perhaps you might call Inspector Blethly at Scotland Yard and hold Mr. Thompson until one of his constables arrives?"

"You do have Sherlock Holmes here, madam, are you sure you need me?"

"Marry me, Kent," I said.

He took Thompson by the arm and dragged him towards the door. On the way out, Kent turned. "I'll have this lock sorted right away, madam, as soon as I've dealt with this, if you will excuse the redundancy, this ungentlemanly fopdoodle." He managed to close the broken door with a minimum of noise. If he'd noticed the detective unconscious beside the bed, he'd been too polite, or too discreet, to mention it.

That left Hazelnut, me, and Roger. And I hoped, Bruce.

"Great job, Claymore," Hazelnut said. He pointed to Detective Hubbard. "And she must be a real brain trust. You two searched the room and never looked under the bed? It just confirms your Wildlife Crime Prevention Unit is a joke."

Hazelnut checked the drawers, looked in all my shoes, then tried Roger's boot.

"Ha! Look!" He let out a huge exhale and sat back on the bed, then turned to me. "And you think Claymore is a good guy."

I ran forward. At that moment Bruce gave one of his squeaky snuffles. His bushy little tail waved out of the top of the boot for an instant, then disappeared.

"Oh God, Roger, you could have flattened him! Is he okay?"

"Traumatized, no doubt." Hazelnut and I watched as he shifted around and tried to resettle. This time, he put his tiny paws over his eyes while his tail limped down. I gasped and looked at Hazelnut. He shook his head.

"I didn't put anything in that boot. Is that the dormouse?" Roger moved towards us.

"Move away from the protected species," Hazelnut said, holding up his taser.

"Roger, don't hurt Bruce!"

"Cyd? You were in on this? I can't believe you lied to me. How could you collude with this unhinged human horseshoe?"

Hazelnut tried to pull his legs together. "She can do whatever she wants. She doesn't belong to you. She's not your personal property."

I whipped my head around and stared at him. "Correct. I am no one's personal property, including yours!"

"Why would you be his?"

"Lay off her," Hazelnut said. "As much as I hate to admit it, it's not her fault. I slipped him into that cavern of a purse because someone was after me. And she's just been trying to keep him alive."

Roger shook his head.

"What exactly are you actually doing to solve this case, Special Agent? She's not the problem and neither am I. If you and Scotland Yard were doing their job, none of this would have happened. This is not about dormice, it's about economics. You have the resources, go back and see who's funding the hormonal disruption and genetic modification program at the zoo. It's a development company. They're moving the dormice out because they want the land. You can read all about it on my website."

Then he walked out, with Roger's boot and Bruce.

We both heard a moan.

Roger went over to help his law enforcement girlfriend up.

She looked around the room. "Did he get away? Was it Hazelnut? What happened?" Roger looked at me, then at her. "You don't remember anything?"

"No." Roger hesitated. Closed his eyes for a minute. "He zapped all of us. I think since you were first, you got the strongest charge. We just woke up, too."

"What about the mouse?"

"He must have had it with him. He was in the hotel and spotted you."

"Are you sure? This sounds very strange."

Roger took her arm. "He was probably trying to get your tracker."

She felt for it. "God, it's gone. And my baton. The Guv is going to be furious." I stared at Roger, who put his arm around her to help her towards the door.

She glared at me as she passed. "Apologies for disturbing you, Miss Redundo."

"No problem, Mother Hubbard."

Roger propped her up against the splintered door, came toward the bed, and leaned down. At least he was going to kiss me goodbye, even if it was for the last time, I thought.

Instead, he shoved his foot into his remaining boot and straightened up.

"This was a mistake," he said, and limped out the door.

Chapter Forty

I didn't wake up until ten. I had to be out of the room by eleven. I couldn't avoid getting up, or dealing with my life, anymore.

In order not to think about Roger, I made a list on the Savoy stationery of all the things I could do in the meantime. In an ideal world, the first thing would be to terminate Hazelnut, with extreme prejudice. Not only had he lost me Roger forever, he'd totally reneged on his promise to help me with Shep. I didn't even know how to get in touch with him—he'd always found me—save going on one of his walks. And there was no guarantee he'd be there anyway. So that particular homicide was going to have to wait.

The one place I hadn't checked for Shep's laptop was his office at the university, so I needed to go there. Once it was morning in Brooklyn, I'd check in with Sister Ellery about all my clients. I had two snowbird trips that left today. One was for a couple whose bones were too brittle to ski, but who loved to ride up and down the lift. I had special arrangements at Sugarbush with the lift operator. I needed to remind him they were coming.

In terms of people who might help me here, the only friends I had, such as they were, were Shelagh, the staff at the Savoy, and the embassy.

I took the time to make some calls while I packed, happy for the speaker function on my new cell phone. I left a message for Shelagh that I was taking her up on her offer of staying at Shep's paid-up flat, provided the police were done with it. Then I called the coroner's office and was on hold long enough to take a shower and fix my face. They were patronizing, polite, and gave me no information.

I also called the airline, explained the situation, and was able to postpone our return—and Shep's—until I could find out when we could fly back. It always paid off to send a gift basket to your airline contacts. And fix them up with cute firemen, in the case of Melinda at British Airways. I'd call Heep International too, just in case they had connections who could help out. At least that might placate Dean Dean.

I looked out the window at the Thames and wished I had been here on a real vacation. I was completely in love with the city. At least I'd be able to talk to my clients about it now, for real. If I still had any clients.

I nabbed the rest of the stationery, the pens, the lotions and shampoos, the digestive biscuits, and the coasters, and put them in my carry-on.

Then, I put on my embassy outfit, swapping out my white silk blouse for a cropped cashmere V-neck that someone had left in the dressing room at Loehmann's. With my pencil skirt and peplum jacket, and at least partially broken-in LK Bennett shoes, I felt a bit better. I checked the room multiple times, including under the bed, which made me nauseous. Even more so when I found Martin Thompson had left a copy of his self-published *Victor Victorian: The True Ripper Story* there. There was another one in a drawer. He took the idea of self-promotion to a new low.

I thought about what to do with Shep's stuff. Leaving it here, even in the safe, seemed risky. There'd already been two people in my room and I still didn't know how they'd gotten in. Shep's place definitely wasn't secure. Then I remembered Jeremy's offer. Surely it would be safe in the British Museum. I would go there first.

My favorite receptionist, Polly, was on the desk and said they were very sorry to lose me. When she started the checkout process, she got a little worry line between her eyes. She tried again. She typed more furiously.

"Polly?"

"I'm not sure what's happening. The bulk of your stay was authorized on a Dean McAfferty's Visa card, correct?"

"Yes, that's right. Did I not allocate enough miles?"

"It's not that. Mr. McAfferty seems to have canceled the authorization. There's a note here that says he has put a stop on this card and you should contact him."

"That's really weird, give me a second?" I tried his number. It just rang. That bastard. "So what's the total I need to pay now?"

It was lucky I was holding on to the counter or I would have done a Jemima when I heard the total. I guess the Dom Perignon, the room service, the drinks in the bar, and the three bottles of water required to rehydrate me this morning had been a mistake.

Polly looked at me. "I'm having a review at the moment, or I would give you some time to sort it out. You were so lovely to give me those coupons for the Eurostar, I feel horrible."

"Don't. No, I wouldn't want you to get in any trouble. It's no problem." My mind was racing. I didn't have enough room on my card to cover all of it and I couldn't use it all, anyway, in case there was yet another disaster, since they seemed to come about twice daily. I wasn't going to ruin my reputation with a string of luxury hotels because of fricking Dean Dean. What could I do?

This was the time I would have, in the past, called my Uncle Ray to bail me out. But that wasn't going to work this time, and Uncle Leon was always borrowing money from me. He'd be no help. There was my mutual fund. My life savings, never to be touched until I was sixty-five, without extreme penalties. But it was tied in to my debit card. I would have to worry about the repercussions later.

"Put fifteen hundred pounds on this card, and the rest on this." I handed Polly my future.

It didn't matter. It wasn't like I was going to have kids, since I was never having sex again and was probably going to throw myself in the Thames in the next three days, anyway.

I said goodbye to the fabulous Savoy. No matter what, it had been worth it. I stopped at the concierge desk on the way out to leave all of my remaining cash for Kent and thank him for last night.

"Not at all, Ms. Redondo. I very much look forward to your next stay. Are you going back to America now?"

"I'm staying on for a few days with friends."

"Well, if it's not too presumptuous, here is my beeper number. This is, after all, a city of eccentrics, and some of my professional contacts might come in handy."

"I'm not going to propose again, Kent. I do have my pride."

"I will strive to be worthy of the offer." I felt like crying. "May I call you a cab?"

"My friends are picking me up. Thank you, Kent."

"It would be a farewell gift from me."

Concierges were the shamans of the travel industry. I thanked him, as I knew the shoulder bag would be safer in a cab. As it pulled away, Kent tipped his hat.

Once I was in the taxi, I called Uncle Leon's friend Jeremy from the British Museum. He told me to pull up at the rear entrance. For the first time, I was relieved the cabbie wasn't expecting a tip. I gave him a smile instead. I could see Jeremy with his wild white hair waiting for me.

After everything was secured in his personal curator locker in the basement, I asked if I could buy him a cup of tea. We sat down in the atrium, underneath the Easter Island heads.

He stirred his tea. "You in some kind of trouble?"

"Maybe. I'm just being on the safe side. I'm more worried about Uncle Leon."

"He's always been pretty resourceful."

"Lately his resources have been pretty much confined to me. Unless there's something I don't know about. He was with a woman at Shep's funeral. Thin, white hair, hip glasses. He said she's his boss. Is that true?"

"I couldn't discuss it without his permission."

He was loyal, which was good. And I knew why, anyway. "Well, in that case, could you tell me what Uncle Leon was like when you knew him? He was already forty-three when I was born. I'd love to know about him when he was young."

Jeremy laughed. "Ah, you want me to tell tales out of school."

"Well, maybe a few." I took a sip of my cappuccino. Why did cappuccinos always go cold in forty-five seconds?

He laughed. "He was always a hard worker, better with eyes than anyone I've ever seen, and fast. His skins never dried out. The best of the bunch, really. The Natural History Museum here wanted him to stay, you know?"

"I didn't. Why didn't he?"

Jeremy shrugged. "Girl trouble. That's what you really want to hear, isn't it?"

"Kind of yes, kind of no. I love my aunt."

"As you should. And so does he. There's not too much to tell. We worked hard, but we did get to the theatre and down to Soho on occasion and Americans were still exotic at that point. He was always dapper, a great dresser. So he broke a few hearts. And got his broken at least once. I think that's why he decided to go home. Then, he saw your aunt going the other way on an escalator in Grand Central Station and the rest is history."

"Is she still here, the one who broke his heart?"

"No, she was Australian. She went back there. Died a few years ago. So your Aunt Helen doesn't need to worry about that, not a bit." Jeremy took my hand. "Can I give you a bit of advice? Don't coddle him. We're all tougher than we look."

"I actually know that. I just forget it sometimes."

"Got to get back to work, we've a shipment coming in. You'll let me know when you want your contraband?" He took out a notepad and wrote down some numbers. "And, in case I'm not here for any reason, here's the locker number and combination."

As he walked me out, Jeremy introduced me to Solomon the security guard, then sent me on my way. As I got to the museum gates, I looked back to see his hunched figure waving and blew him a kiss.

My phone buzzed with a text from Shelagh saying no problem about the flat and asking if I wanted to meet for a drink. I said I would call her later. At least I had somewhere to stow my luggage before I started tramping around town. I was grateful for my carry-on and Shep's request to be so near the museum.

I rolled my luggage up to the apartment building, hoping there wouldn't be crime scene tape across the door. There wasn't. The flat was still a mess. I put my carry-on in the armoire, where I caught a tear-inducing whiff of Shep's Acqua di Parma. If the police did a search, they were welcome to rummage through it, since everything incriminating was in the British Museum, or in various compartments in my purse. I left Inspector Blethly a note saying I was staying there, to cover my fingerprints.

Next, I needed the extra death certificates I'd asked Harley for. I traveled via Tube this time, grateful I had put fifty pounds on my Oyster card when I bought it. I jostled against commuters and looked at ads on the wall to avoid making too much eye contact. One was for a weekend getaway in Paris. After my conversation with Hildy, I needed to have Sister Ellery look up Shep's Paris reservations. After all, this whole thing had started with his asking Jimmy to add the trip.

The embassy security guard let me past and I made it to the elevator without drama. Just as it was closing, the one opposite me opened and I swear, Chip Jessup walked out. I tried to hit the Open button but was too late, and even the attempt elicited a very nasty look from what looked like a woman wrestler in tweed chintz. What kind of childhood trauma would make her wear that? And what on earth would Chip Jessup be doing here instead of Bay Ridge? Especially if I hadn't made his travel arrangements.

Delores wasn't there. Harley was staring into an empty coffee cup. There was another one on his desk. He didn't seem to notice me come in. I knocked, loudly.

"Harley? Did Chip Jessup just leave here?"

He raised his head, pushed his hair back and grinned. "Ms. Redondo, nice to see you. Yeah, he did. I guess he's over for some wedding or something, stopped by to say hi. I told him you were here."

"Thanks. Look, the police won't tell me anything. I can't afford to stay here indefinitely. Can you, or someone here, make a call? Please?"

He looked toward the outer office and yelled, "Delores? Coffee?"

"She's not out there." I sighed. "I'll do it." Women making the coffee was the kind of sexist malarkey I normally didn't participate in, but it seemed like the only way Harley was going to be any help. I made it triple strong and practically poured it down his throat.

I was shocked at his jovial, semiprofessional demeanor on the phone. I guess his old boy network included the Coroner of the City of London, who knew everyone, and by the end of the call, he had an answer. It wasn't the one I wanted.

"They're suspending the ruling on cause of death, pending tox screen results. He suspects Shep might have ingested something that triggered his heart attack. That other guide—Babcock—same thing."

"So they think the same killer, for sure?" Harley shrugged. "And I still can't claim the body?"

"Apparently not. Sorry. I've got your death certificates, though." He handed me a large stack. Definitely at least twenty.

"Thanks. Do I have to reregister everything if they change cause of death?"

"I don't think so. Actually no idea. Hey, if you're stuck here, Chip and I are going out tonight, you could come along. We're hitting Boodles."

"I beg your pardon?"

"It's a gentlemen's club. It's been around since the eighteenth century. They have an amazing wine cellar. And they allow female visitors. I'll vouch for you."

Great. Wasn't having ten male cousins enough? Was I fated to spend my entire life surrounded by men with a mental age of fifteen? Who else would let something be named Boodles for four hundred years?

"Can I call you about it later?"

Well, at least that gave me more time to find the laptop, the rest of Shep's research, and, of course, his murderer. It was time to try his office.

Chapter Forty-one

Because the whole city looked like an Ivy League campus, it was hard to distinguish Shep's university from everything else, but I finally found the institution I needed, tucked up behind the British Museum. A student directed me to the right building, which appeared to be circa Boodles.

As I headed down the hallway, I found cigar smoke seeping out of a door near the end of the hall. Shep's name was still on the door, which gave me a little gasp of sadness. I knocked.

"Enter at your peril!" That must be encouraging to the students, I thought. I had always been intimidated by my City College professors, so, after an anxiety flashback, I eased the door open and stuck my head in.

There was my pal from Shep's service, Sir Rod, drinker of absinthe, behind the far desk, reading a book, his flask and an elaborate standing ashtray by his side. The walls were hung with antique and polished hatchets, muskets, swords, pistols, sabers, and a dagger or two. This did not decrease my anxiety.

Then he looked up and smiled. "Ah, I cannot tell you the joy with which I see that you are not one of my sniveling charges. Please, Miss Redondo, is it? Come in!" He held up his flask. "Snifter?"

I grinned. "No, thank you, Sir Rod."

"Well then, have a seat." He gestured to the chair behind what I guessed was Shep's desk. On it sat another copy of the wedding picture I'd seen in Shep's apartment.

"You have the honor of being the first and probably last person who'll sit in that chair, as I am getting a new office mate—horrors—who has no doubt insisted on something ergonomic." He gestured at the walls. "I daresay these will come in handy. How may I assist you?"

"Well, a few things, if you don't mind. First, if the embassy hasn't already been by, I'm here to collect Shep's things. His research, and if it's here, his laptop? Have you seen it?"

He leaned back in his chair and took a puff. "Do you have any paperwork confirming you as his executor?"

I pulled the papers out. He sifted through them, then handed them back.

"Right. You should know you are not the only supplicant who has applied for these items."

"The embassy was here?"

"No, that silly Goldilocks girl and one of his Ripperologist lunatics."

"Do you remember which one?"

"He was wearing some kind of flowing outerwear."

"I wish that narrowed it down."

"Yes. Ludicrous haircut as I recall."

"Martin Thompson?"

"I believe that was his name. He said Shep had asked him to keep all his research safe. I told him to bugger off."

"Thank you. Thank you. Jemima, too?"

"Well, I might have given them to her if she'd agreed to dinner, but as she did not, I tossed her out as well." He grinned.

"I can't have dinner with you tonight, but I am going to kiss you on the cheek right now," I said, and did.

"His files are in the bottom drawer, here's the key."

I unlocked the drawer and took out more reams of papers. I'd have to look through them later. Dean Dean would be pleased. "I guess the laptop would be too much to ask for?"

He balanced his cigar on the ashtray, moved to a bookcase, pressed a book, and the bookcase swung out, revealing a safe. "The monks had a safe hole. We just improved upon it." He twirled the combination lock back and forth and took out a MacBook covered in a red "Keep Calm and Carry On" case. "He said if anything happened to him, only to give it to your uncle, or his representative." He handed it to me. I kissed him again.

"People will say we're in love." He took a long puff of his cigar.

"Sometimes a cigar is just a cigar," I said. "A million thanks, Sir Rod. He must have trusted you a great deal."

"And you," he said.

I took out the laptop and hit the power button. It came on and asked me for a password. I looked up. "I suppose 'From Hell' would be too obvious?"

He shook his head. "Try Elena65."

It worked. The screen saver was the same wedding photo I'd found at Shep's flat.

"Do you know when he got married?"

"When he was twenty. She was killed on their honeymoon. Stabbed. Here in London. Never solved."

"Oh my God. I had no idea. He never told me. How awful." My eyes filled up again. I really was going to have to get a grip on myself.

"He only talked about it once. When he'd had a lot of absinthe."

I sat back. Suddenly, the trips to England, the Jack the Ripper stuff, it all made sense.

"Jemima said he'd gotten threats. The Met thinks he might have been murdered. Do you agree?"

"It's possible." An alarm went off, giving me a flashback of the dormouse beeper. He turned it off. "I've a class to teach. Where are you staying?"

"At Shep's flat."

"Is it safe?"

"It's been broken into twice."

"You're welcome to stay here for a bit. I'll be back in an hour. Lock the door."

I woke up the laptop. Where did I start? He was a Jack the Ripper expert, it's not like there was one JTR file. I figured I would look to see if he had parts of the new book. Maybe that would have a clue as to what his discovery might have been. I found a file labeled *All Jacked Up!* but it was just snippets of a note that made no sense, and a few photographs of what looked like a vintage handkerchief with embroidered initials that looked like an *A* and a *K*, but they were so faded, I wasn't sure.

Shep used the same password for his email accounts, but they were little help. I checked in the trash and found a few between him and the dean, but they were just about his teaching schedule for the spring. The only others were confirmation of his registration for the Jack the Ripper: Tintypes to Texts conference in Paris.

I forwarded the emails, the file with the book notes, and photos to my account. It seemed smarter to leave the laptop here and, once Sir Rod returned, he agreed. I took the papers, though, as I hadn't had time to go through them.

"I can't thank you enough. Truly."

"Where are you off to, now?"

"Back to the flat, if the police aren't there."

"Well, just in case they are, I'll accompany you. Shep would want me to."

Then he went back to the safe and took out a jewelry box that was about three by four inches. "Will this fit in your purse?"

"You'd be surprised what will fit in my purse."

"Well, you need some protection and I don't have any daggers I can spare. This, however, might prove useful in a pinch."

He opened the box and pulled out a tripod of iron with hooks on each end that resembled a medieval frog gig. "It's a caltrop. No matter how it lands, or how you hold it, there's a spike at the top. It will blow a tire, or an ankle, and it will definitely take out an eye, if necessary. It's a bit heavy, but you look fit."

"But isn't this a museum piece?"

"Yes, but it's from my own personal collection, so consider it a gift. I'll feel better if you have it, all things considered."

We checked that the coast was clear and Sir Rod hailed a black cab, which I really hoped he was paying for. When we got to the flat, he offered to accompany me in.

"No need. If anyone comes near me, I'll caltrop them. Thank you so, so much. If you ever need an all-expenses-paid vacation to Monte Carlo, I'm your girl."

Today just reinforced my belief that, when you were really in trouble in the modern world, senior citizens were the only ones you could count on to save your ass.

As I didn't know whether Martin Thompson had actually been arrested, I took the stairs and kept my eyes peeled for anyone in a cape, one hand in my Balenciaga, the other around the caltrop box.

There was no sign of the police. I made a triple espresso, then sat down at the desk. It was finally morning in Brooklyn, and I had some screaming to do.

Chapter Forty-two

I was torn about calling Heep International, as I wasn't in the mood to help Dean Dean, but I still hoped he'd cover Shep's repatriation. Maybe I could hold his research hostage until he sent the funds. Keeping in mind what Ginger from Air Trays Galore had said about their dubious policies, I took out Heep's number and made the call.

"Andrew Heep, Heep International."

For the second time I thought how odd it was that the owner of an international mortuary service would answer the phone.

"Mr. Heep, Cyd Redondo, Redondo Travel. We spoke last week. I'm working with Dean McAfferty to get his colleague back home."

"Yes, I remember. In fact, we've been distressed that we haven't heard from you. Have you obtained the death certificate and registered the death?"

"Yes."

"And obtained the Burial or Cremation certificate?"

"Yes."

"Then explain."

Obviously patronizing jerks stuck together. I went through it as quickly as I could.

"So you are telling me there's been an autopsy already?"

"Yes."

"That is completely unacceptable."

"Well, in theory I agree, but it's a little late to object."

"You should have called me immediately. I see Dean McAfferty's trust has been misplaced. I will sort this out. Is this the best number on which to reach you?"

"Yes." Before I could say anything else, he hung up.

What the hell? I mean, the idea of an autopsy is always upsetting, especially if you know the person. But as far as I knew, Heep didn't know Shep personally. An autopsy probably created more work for a mortuary, but his voice didn't sound inconvenienced. It sounded furious.

Before I called Brooklyn College, I put in a call to Evelyn at the British Library, told her Heep International was handling Shep's body, and could she please gather up any information she could about them? She said she would do it right away, "the average daily rainfall in Upton Snodsbury" could wait. I told her I would stop by later, since I still had the claim check for the cloakroom.

"Brooklyn College. Department of History."

"Dean McAfferty, please."

"May I tell him who's calling?"

"Cyd Redondo, Redondo Travel."

Click. Unbelievable. He really had just left me high and dry. Maybe I should get me and Uncle Leon on the plane today (at least those tickets were prepaid), go home, and work towards a law degree or some other profession that overcharges—not from Brooklyn College, obviously.

I figured I'd try Dean Dean one more time, since I was legendary for mimicking my brousin Eddie's Brooklyn drawl. I switched over to my burner phone and a lower register.

"May I tell him who's calling?"

I said the first name that popped into my head. "Tell him it's Chip Jessup."

She put me on hold. In about thirty seconds Dean Dean came on the line. "Jessup? You know you can't call me here! I've got it under control." He hung up.

What the hell? I just sat there for a moment, stunned. First of all, did everyone in the fricking world know Chip Jessup? And why couldn't he call the college? Did "it" have to do with Shep? I was completely confused. So I made one more call.

"Redondo Travel, Ellery Malcomb, honorary Redondo speaking."

"Honorary Redondo?"

"Well, are they going to speak to me, otherwise?"

"Well, certainly not if they were in your eighth-grade class."

"I've had a few hang-ups."

"Great."

"You don't really want any cowardly clients, do you?"

"If they pay in advance, yes. Look, I'm trying to save data on my phone, could you look up a few things for me? First find the Helnikov file and find his arrangements for Paris? Jimmy made them."

"Well, it's probably good he's not going to need them, then."

"Sister Ellery!"

"Sorry, not funny. True, but not funny."

I sighed.

"Anything else?"

I was not looking forward to this one. "I need to know every particle of info and gossip you can round up on Chip Jessup."

"Ha! I knew it. Background check, huh? Smart."

"It's not for me. I mean, it is for me, but I'm not dating him, as I've said before. He has something to do with one of the weird things that's happening in London. It's too complicated to explain. While you're at it, see if you find any connection between him and Dean McAfferty."

"The dickhead who sent you on this suicide mission?"

"The very one. Please, no more jokes, this is for real."

"Are you all right?"

"I've been better."

"Well, there are a few things that might cheer you up. First, I've booked six Key West Conched Out tours."

"That's fantastic. I've been pushing those since Christmas."

"I made an appearance at Bingo. Took a ruler with me."

I snorted. "I guess that's what I needed. An enforcer. Are the Hampshires in Saint Martin yet?"

"Arrived and already sunburned."

"Did you include the SPF 50 in their packet?"

"Of course. You can lead a horse to sunscreen . . ."

"Well, at least there's some aloe vera in there too."

"There's also a surprise coming your way."

"Come on, I've had enough surprises for one trip. What is it?"

"Sworn to secrecy. Ah, here we go. Shep's file. Actually there are tickets for the Eurostar, Waterloo to the Gare du Nord, leaving Thursday night and back Monday. There's a hotel reservation here too. Are his credit cards still good?"

"God, I'm not sure. Good question. Can you email me all the stuff, including the tickets?"

"You got it."

"Any family members lurking around?"

"Your mom's been by. I think she's lonely."

"Okay, twist the knife again."

"The truth hurts."

"I'm hanging up."

"Don't do anything I wouldn't do."

Well, at least that didn't limit me.

I sat for a minute, looking at that wedding picture. I still couldn't believe Shep hadn't told me about his wife. I felt nervous, suddenly. It was too quiet. No snuffling. I missed Bruce. I hoped Hazelnut had found a place to keep him safe and that Mother Hubbard hadn't gotten her grubby hands on him. I looked at my watch. Evelyn might have the Heep information by now.

I made sure I had Shep's British Library cloakroom ticket. I debated not taking my purse, as it caused me so much anxiety to leave it in those lockers, plus I might have purse snatchers following me. But with at least one key to the flat unaccounted for, I couldn't leave it here. I took out one of the color-coordinated bungee cords I had in my carry-on (just in case my luggage wouldn't zip) and hooked it through the purse strap and around my waist. As Kent said, it was a city of eccentrics. I could be one for a day.

Chapter Forty-three

As soon as my Balenciaga was safe in the locker room, I went straight to the Information Desk. Evelyn said she couldn't take a break, but we could go over it while she worked. Fine with me. After last night, I was on the wagon.

She set down a stack of printouts. "Everything's in here, but I'll just go over it quickly so you know what you're looking at. As far as I can see, Heep International was formed about five years ago by the brothers Heep." She gave me a significant look. "They were interviewed in *The Economist* saying with the rise of terrorism and crime, there was a need in the market for firms that specialized in dealing with the death of foreigners—and their pets—abroad. They handle not only the undertaking aspects, but the paperwork and shipping as well, for an additional fee. They have offices in most international airports around the globe and have formed relationships with a few travel and travel insurance companies."

"Really? Because I'm a travel agent and I'd never heard of them until last week. How do they make enough money? Not that many tourists actually die abroad every year. I check."

"You're right." Evelyn looked at her notepad. "Only an average of 827 out of 69 million travelers die abroad, of accidents or unnatural causes."

"That doesn't really seem like enough to finance a multimillion-dollar business, does it?"

"As it happens, they seem to be having a bit of a cash flow problem at the moment."

Maybe that's why they were so anxious to get Shep into the cargo hold and get paid. "Is that in the paperwork?"

"No, just a bit of gossip I got from a source." She grinned.

"How's their reputation? Any complaints about them?"

"A few. I've included the letters in the file. Not enough to put them out of business, but not great. I gather from the comments the Heep brothers lack charm."

"I can verify that."

She gave me another paper. "The interesting thing is that they're part of a larger conglomerate—that may be how they survive. I've given you a list of all their subsidiaries, just in case you need it. Anything else?"

I asked if I could print something—Sister Ellery had sent me a ton of attachments—as I needed to plan out the rest of my questions.

She gave me her key card and a code for one of the Reading Room computers. I printed the travel documents and returned the card.

"Evelyn? I didn't realize you went to drama school with Jemima and Luke."

"Snakes! Both of them. Jemima went after my drama school boyfriend, too. She was just using both of them." Evelyn was now getting librarian looks herself. "I have to get back to my average rainfall search."

"Of course. Thank you so much for this help. Just one more question. Did Shep ever talk to you about his new discovery? I assume you were helping him with whatever it was?"

She let out a huge wail and gestured for me to help her out. I shrugged my shoulders at the guards, who waved me through. I was going to have to send a muffin basket to the British Library or they were going to ban me.

As soon as we were outside, she stopped crying and shoved me into a nearby restroom. She checked the stalls, locked us into one. "Do you have the handkerchief?"

Now the pictures on the laptop made sense. "No."

"Do you know about it?"

"There were pictures on Shep's computer."

She lowered her voice. "Have you found the doctor's notes from the asylum?"

"No, but he left a lot of papers I haven't gone through. Anything else?"

"He had one other piece of evidence he wouldn't tell me about. I do know he was keeping everything separate until the conference. He said it would take all three to prove it."

"Prove what?"

"The identity of Jack the Ripper. I'm sure that's why he was killed."

Chapter Forty-four

"So he knew who the Ripper was? For sure?" She nodded. "Well? Who is it?"

"He wouldn't tell me. He didn't want to put me at risk. And some of the evidence wasn't from the library, it was from some lost police files he found in a warehouse. I've got to get back."

"Can I call you if I have more questions?"

"Yes, but be careful." She hugged me, then started to walk away.

"Hey, Evelyn?"

"Yes?

"Shep's screen saver? It was a picture of you." Then I ran down the stairs as fast as I could to outrun the salty waterfall that was coming. It was going to be awhile before the Reading Room security guys were going to let me in again.

I got into the line at the cloakroom. It would have been smart for Shep to hide the evidence here. Now that I really knew what I might be carrying around, I hesitated when the woman asked for the ticket. I didn't have any loyalty to Dean Dean anymore, but I did owe it to Shep to bring his things home.

The woman handed me a satchel. I returned to the Discovery of Bruce Memorial Restroom, went into a stall, and opened it. It was his magic kit. I didn't see any papers or handkerchiefs. I would look closer once I got it out of here.

The security guard ignored my Balenciaga but opened the magic kit, revealing a wand, flattened top hat, two decks of cards, a sequined waistcoat, and some scarves. He looked at me.

"No doves? Off you go, David Copperfield," he said and waved me through.

Was it safe to take these things back to the flat? I couldn't bother Jeremy again so soon. I decided to risk it, since it was an easy walk. I rehooked my bungee cord through the strap and around my waist, then passed it through the satchel and made for Red Lion Square.

The caltrop was more complicated than the "lipstick pepper spray" I employed in Brooklyn. When it was in its box, it didn't shred everything in my purse, but when it was out of the box, there was almost no way to hold it where I didn't stab myself. So I waited to pull it out until I entered the building, hoping I wouldn't trip on some uneven carpet and perform an accidental hysterectomy.

I made it up the stairs and into the flat. After checking all hiding places, I moved the kitchen table in front of the locked door, put the caltrop on the desk as a temporary paperweight and started going through my huge stack of papers. My cell phone rang.

"Cyd Redondo, Redondo Travel."

"Cut it out. I have the scoop on Mr. Jessup. Where are you, anyway?"

"Shep's flat. For now."

"Okay. First, the important stuff. He is six-foot-one, weighs one eighty, and works out at a gym four times a week. He also plays pickup basketball with your cousin Eddie on Saturday mornings. However, his ex-fiancée, Pam Owens, is back in the institution, so you still can't date him. We don't want her put on suicide watch. Plus, rumor has it he has stamina issues, so not as big a loss as we thought."

"Tell me you have more than this?"

"He's got a law degree and an MBA and is the in-house counsel for TRIFEX Investments. Handles their foreign accounts. He just bought a five-million-dollar condo on Long Island and some folks think he's making more money than an in-house counsel would. He still keeps his old apartment on 5th Ave. Do you want me to break in?"

"No!"

"Didn't find any connection with Brooklyn College or Dean McAfferty, though. Not a neighborhood or a school thing. Our subscription to Ancestry.com has expired. Do you want me to renew? They're running a Two Family Trees for the Price of One special."

"No. Could he invest with TRIFEX?"

"Don't know, I'll keep digging."

"Thanks."

"By the way, just out of curiosity, what's the easiest way for someone to get into London from Heathrow?"

"The Heathrow Express, then a cab from Paddington. Why?"

"Is that the easiest, or cheapest?"

"Cheapest."

"A cab then?"

"Why do you need to know? We don't have anyone scheduled to fly in."

"Just trying to up my skills."

"Okay. Thanks. Call me if you need me."

The paperwork Evelyn had given me was on the top, so I started there. Two particular company names stood out: TRIFEX and my nemesis Peggy Newsome's parent company, Patriot Travel International. This made me even more interested in figuring these Dickensian degenerates out. They were connected to Chip Jessup via their parent company. But what connected them to Dean Dean? Well, if it took going to a gentlemen's club to find out, that's what I was going to do. I called Harley and he said to meet them there at eight and they'd accompany me in. Whatever that meant. As I was royally hungover, I decided on a nap.

I set the alarm, crawled under the orange coverlet, and dreamed of lemmings that looked like Bruce Springsteen.

The alarm woke me. I took a shower and doused myself in Shep's Acqua di Parma, for courage. How did you dress for a four-hundred-year-old gentlemen's club? It wasn't a problem in America, as most women just wore a G-string, if that. Was pole dancing around in the seventeenth century, or just beheading?

The fanciest thing I had was my little black, backless dress. It hadn't lost too many sequins at Shep's memorial service and was still adequately sparkly. And the peplum jacket would work again for back coverage outdoors. It would have been nice to top it off with a fascinator like Fergie's little princesses wore, but I wasn't sure where to find one.

My phone buzzed with a text from Shelagh: *Just leaving work, time for a drink?*

I didn't really feel like a drink, but she was doing me a huge favor. *Quick one nearby? Have to be somewhere at eight.*

She texted me an address. I dragged the kitchen table away from the door and put the caltrop box back in my purse. I threw on my patent leather Charles David Mary Jane stilettos—as surely they spoke the international language of gentlemen's clubs—and walked to the Museum Tavern, a place Shep had called his local.

Shelagh was wearing another pin-striped suit, obviously bespoke, with a lovely pink blouse underneath, but again with the court shoes.

I air-kissed her and sat down on a stool. "Drinks are on me this time."

"Nonsense, you brought us that lovely champagne. In fact, let's have some champers now, to celebrate your being here and my sale today." She gestured to the bartender, who came back, as the English would say, quick smart, with a silver champagne bucket and two glasses.

"So you made a big sale?"

"Huge. Something I've been working on for months. Of course, there will still be negotiations and paperwork to get through, but you have to celebrate when you can, don't you?"

"Agreed. To your sale. And to Shep." We raised our glasses and drank.

"It's such a shame about him." She looked around the pub. "We used to meet here for drinks. I'm going to miss that."

"He was very good company." I wasn't sure how her affair had fit into her relationship with Derek.

"Please thank Derek again for me. It was so kind of him to help me on a Sunday."

"Oh, I will."

"He seemed quite the mover and shaker."

"He is. Certainly in business matters."

"How long have you been together?"

"Oh, ages. Since university." So she had cheated on him with Shep.

"Is he a solicitor or a barrister?" I knew the difference from reading *Bleak House* in eleventh grade.

"Barrister. He advises on financial matters in the City."

"Interesting. The friend from Bay Ridge I'm meeting tonight is the in-house counsel for an investment firm. His name is Chip Jessup. Small world."

"Indeed. So where is it you're going tonight?"

"Boodles."

"Well, you'll be up to your neck in barristers and financiers there." She clinked my glass and swallowed her drink in almost one gulp, then poured a refill. "You've been warned they aren't always welcoming to female guests."

"I'm familiar with the setup. I told you I'm the only female of the eleven cousins, right? I'm used to being outnumbered."

She emptied the rest of the bottle into our glasses. "So, what's happening with getting Shep home?"

I gave her the short version.

"I hear his death is Ripper-related?"

I took another sip of champagne. "I'm not sure."

"Well, surely that's it. What else could it be, with two of them?"

"I just want it figured out."

"Absolutely. Another bottle?"

"No, thanks. Best keep my wits about me, I think."

"Right. Well, lovely to see you. Keep me posted. Oh, Cyd? I might need to show the flat at some point?"

At least I didn't have Bruce to hide anymore. "Of course. Give me a fifteen-minute warning?"

I kissed her on both cheeks and asked which Tube stop would take me to 50 Pall Mall. Ground Zero for the Restoration.

Chapter Forty-five

Boodles was a far cry from Girls! Girls! Girls! on the Jersey Turnpike. It was a four-story red brick building, painted white on the ground floor, with curly columns and white trim around the three bay windows on the street level and around the floor-to-ceiling arched window in the center of the floor above. There was a portico over the entrance. I wasn't sure women were even allowed to knock, so I texted Harley, *Here.*

On our way, came back. Great. I felt a little like a streetwalker in my Brooklyn clothes, in a place where, if you squinted, was still pro-wigs for men and pre-toilets for all. A black Jaguar pulled up in front and was spirited away by a man who probably didn't wear that outfit anywhere else. Harley was in his standard work suit. Chip had on a double-breasted navy pin-striped suit and a pocket square right out of *Esquire.* He grinned and started to hug me. I saw an image of Pam, screaming in her straitjacket, and gave him the European "two air-kiss" treatment instead.

"You clean up well, Squid," he said. I silently cursed my brousins for inventing that nickname. The two of them gestured me through the door. They were welcomed. I was admitted. The cloakroom attendant asked for my coat. And my Balenciaga.

"Bags are not allowed in the club, madam."

"It's a handbag. Every woman has one."

"Only clutches are allowed in with our female visitors. We do not allow satchels, briefcases, bags of that size past this point." He pointed to my purse, which I had to admit looked as big as a chair in the cramped eighteenth-century space.

"I'm not comfortable parting with it. I'm sure you understand. Women don't have pockets for their valuables."

The man gave an insulted look to Harley. "I can assure you it will be perfectly safe."

I was absolutely not going to leave my purse in a den of strange men who made a practice of excluding women. There were too many vital items in it, including my lipstick, passport, and blowtorch. But I needed to get some answers out of Chip Jessup. I decided to rely on the oldest chestnut in the book, often used to keep my cousins out of my business.

"I'm sure it would be safe, of course. I'm sure you're not a thief. That's not the issue. There are just things inside, things that men wouldn't need, which a woman might need. Urgently. And I wouldn't want to interrupt anything or have to go through my bag on this counter, publicly, in case of any emergencies." He didn't have to know I meant my caltrop, which was the only weapon I had that was century-appropriate and would not be ideal as a sanitary product.

Every part of his face, except his red nose, had gone white, which was not flattering for someone in a white jacket. He shuddered and gestured me in.

Harley guffawed. "Bay Ridge girls. You were right about them, Chip."

"You two could have helped, you know."

"I think you handled it perfectly all on your own," Chip said. "Brandy?"

They ushered me into a world of burnished wood, shining leather, and flocked wallpaper peppered with paintings of men's faces, men's torsos, men in hats, men in chairs, men with dogs, men with horses, men with guns, and still lives with fish.

Everything seemed to be dark red, dark green, or dark brown, possibly to match the pool tables. The strong smell of furniture polish duked it out with stale cigar smoke, cognac, and aftershave expensive enough to cover a weekly VRBO rental.

As I followed Harley and Chip into the room full of laughing men, I felt as welcome as I did during my presentation of our "Pizza on the (Turn) Pike" day trips to the Daughters of the American Revolution. I accepted the snifter and sat down, tucking my bag next to my very bare legs. When I was seated, this dress hiked up to mid-thigh, no matter how much I tugged on it. The purse covered one side, at least.

"So, Chip, you didn't tell me you were coming over."

"Didn't I? Who remembers? All I remember is a lot of bourbon." He winked at me. "One of my associates at the firm is having one of those destination weddings. Country house, morning coats. Apparently his bride is the *Gosford Park* type. And I have clients here. You didn't mention your trip, either."

"I didn't have one yet. I came last-minute when one of my clients passed away."

"Condolences. It must be complicated, all the paperwork. Do you have someone sorting it out for you?"

I pointed to Harley. Chip looked mildly alarmed. "And I'm getting assistance with the repatriation from this place called Heep International." I detected a small twitch in his left eyebrow.

"Hey, Chip, didn't your parent company buy them?"

"Possibly. WOCAM is constantly acquiring and divesting companies. It's hard to keep up."

"I bet." That corporation name sounded familiar. "So they don't just deal in investments?"

"No," he said, a little too loudly, "that's the whole purpose of a conglomerate, you see, Cyd, diversification. If one sector experiences a slump, it's bolstered by the others. And it allows us the cash flow to move into new sectors, when the opportunity arises. And to support as many NPOs—nonprofit organizations—as we can." My stiletto itched.

The very discreet waiter interrupted this torrent of patronization to replace our drinks with fresh ones. I wondered if there would be a bill, or if these came gratis with the millions of pounds I assumed it cost for membership. I looked around.

"This looks like the kind of place you have to be born into. How did you wind up a member, Chip?"

"Harley helped me jump the line." Charming.

The waiter returned. "Miss Redondo? There's a call for you."

Chapter Forty-six

There was no way this could be good. Who knew I was here?

"You may follow me, miss." I reached for my purse.

"We'll keep it safe for you, Cyd." Chip grinned.

I followed the man, or manservant, into another small room, filled with books, newspapers, cigar smoke, a wall of wine bottles, and Sir Rod.

I breathed a sigh of relief. "Of course you're a member of Boodles. How could I not have expected that?"

He handed me yet another glass full of dark, expensive liquid.

"No absinthe?"

"The club considers it in poor taste to bring that out until the early morning hours."

"Schnapps too, probably."

He laughed. "I just thought I'd give you a break from those Ivy League Colonials and see whether the caltrop had been of use, yet."

"Only as a paperweight so far. I do have it with me." Although it had only been a minute, I was having separation anxiety about my bag. And I was dying to get home and look at that WOCAM paperwork. "Actually, I don't really want to spend the evening with them. Could you help me escape, politely? They're holding my purse hostage."

"Come with me." We passed a group of men in crisp shirtsleeves around a snooker table who all stopped, cues in the air, and stared at me. One of them looked like Shelagh's boyfriend Derek. I curtsied, then kept going. We found Harley and Chip, and my Balenciaga.

Sir Rod came forward to shake hands. "Gentlemen. Pleasure. Roderick Buckminster, OBE, at your service. I was wondering whether I might spirit the charming Ms. Redondo away. We have some business to conduct."

Chip's eyebrows went into overdrive. I wondered what "we have some business to conduct" was a euphemism for in a gentlemen's club?

"Would you mind terribly? It was so kind of you to invite me. I feel awful."

"No, of course not," Harley said. "You wouldn't want to be here when the Schnapps comes out, anyway."

"I know you understand, Chip, how complicated mixing business with pleasure can be." I air-kissed both of them, picked up my purse, which felt a fraction heavier—the caltrop must have shifted—and followed Sir Rod, who retrieved my coat, helped me into it, and held the door.

"Thank you for rescuing me twice in one day."

"You're quite welcome." A Rolls-Royce appeared out of nowhere. A valet opened the door for me and handed Sir Rod the keys.

"And I thought my Cinderella days were over. Why are you being so kind to me, if you don't mind my asking?"

"Initially, it was in Shep's honor. But when you took your absinthe like a trooper, I felt it was my duty to keep you out of the clutches of the Chip Jessups of the world."

"He has clutches?"

"Many. Here we are." He waited until I'd gotten inside and tooted the horn goodbye.

It wasn't until I put my purse down in the silent flat that I heard the snuffling.

I locked the door, put the table back in front of it, and eased my purse open. There was a mutilated Tupperware bowl inside. Beside it, chomping on one of my tissue packets, was Bruce. I was glad the caltrop was in its box and hadn't shish-kebabed him on the ride home.

He looked up at me and made a new sound, like a cross between a chirrup and mini-howl.

I was too tired to even try to figure out how Hazelnut had pulled this off. It didn't matter. I was so glad to see the dormouse. I got him settled in the armoire for the night, double-checked all the windows and doors, and fell into bed. I would do more research in the morning.

At six a.m. there was a violent banging from the street. I pulled my pillow over my head. It didn't help.

"Cyd!" Bang! "Cyd Elizabeth Madonna Redondo. Get down here this instant!"

I ran to the window. Aunt Helen stood on the steps, with three enormous suitcases, pummeling the front door with her cane.

Chapter Forty-seven

Oh brother. I threw on one of Shep's shirts and started the water boiling for coffee before I dragged the table away from the door. I opened it as quietly as I could and tiptoed down the stairs. The tenant below me was glaring on the landing.

"Americans, honestly," I said, in the best British accent I could muster without caffeine, and sped down the endless staircase. The banging was louder the closer I got. When I opened the front door, Aunt Helen came within a whisker of taking my eye out with her cane.

"Hey," I hissed. "Cool it! What are you doing here?"

"Your job," she said, hunching in and leaving her luggage, apparently for me to carry up. This time I was taking the elevator. Of course, it only fit two people or one ginormous suitcase. I sent Aunt Helen up, then the cases, one at a time.

By the time I had schlepped everything upstairs, she'd made the espresso.

"Okay," I said, dropping the last three-hundred-pound suitcase. "I'm hugging you and shooting one of those before we start fighting," and did just that.

She sat down at the table. "You look terrible. Wake up your uncle, please."

"I can't."

She crossed herself. "I knew it, he's dead."

"He's not dead, he's just not here."

"I knew it, he's with that woman."

"No, he's not with a woman. He's with a dog."

"Exactly! I'm glad we agree on that at least. A female dog."

"I mean a dog carcass." She stared at me. "He's working. On a dog."

"He's never stuffed dogs. That's where he draws the line. Plus, he's retired. He's just lying to you."

"No, he's really working at the Natural History Museum."

"All night?"

"He's got a skin he's worried will dry out. Seriously, he's working there."

"For a woman?"

I hesitated. "In a sense."

"I knew it! I gave you one simple task. One! Keep an eye on him. And you have totally failed me. Now, where is your bathroom?"

I pointed down the hall. I watched her hobble out. She looked exhausted, even more curved than usual. It can't have been easy for her on a red-eye, especially since she would have spent the whole flight in the "brace for impact" position. I had to stop myself from following her. She would just whack me with her cane again. The door slammed. The lock clicked.

I heard a scream, then a thud.

I sprinted to the bathroom and banged on the door. "Aunt Helen? Are you all right?"

No answer. I put my ear to the door. Nothing. According to her doctor, Aunt Helen was basically a breathing piece of peanut brittle. She could be in a million pieces in there.

I ran to my Balenciaga and grabbed my lock picks. My hands were shaking, but I kept remembering my brousin Frank's rule: one deep breath, wait ten seconds, then start. In another twenty, I had the door open.

Aunt Helen was curled on her side on the bathroom rug. She appeared intact. She gave a small moan that was as close as you could get to a harrumph.

"What happened? Are you okay? Did you hit your head?"

When I finally got her as straight up as she was going to get, she gestured to the sink. "Are you going to kill it or do I have to?"

I looked over. Bruce was curled up in the soap dish, his paws over his eyes.

"Kill it? That's Bruce! We're not killing him. He's endangered, for one thing."

"Rats are not endangered. At all."

"He's not a rat, he's a dormouse." She gave me one of her looks. "I'm kind of babysitting him."

"You really have lost it. Get married or something!"

I helped her to the bed and brought her some water. I was still terrified she'd fractured something.

"Are you sure nothing hurts?"

"Don't be stupid. Call your uncle."

I got my cell phone and tried him. In part to convince her of my story, I called Security at the Natural History Museum on speaker and they said he'd asked not to be disturbed, but they'd take a message for him. I also texted him with an SOS. Nothing.

I could tell she was trying to put on a brave face. As far as I knew, this was the first time she'd been out of the Manhattan area since the early seventies. She must really love him.

"Stay put," I said, and ran to the bathroom.

I didn't like to handle Bruce too much, especially when he was sleeping, but I also didn't want him killed in some Aunt Helenian "stand your ground" situation. I carried him, curled up on his side, into the bedroom.

"I'm sorry he startled you. But come on, look at him."

"You're not going to cheer me up with vermin."

Just then, he snorted, squeaked, flipped over in my hand and resumed his "tail through the legs" position. I stroked his little head. It almost looked like he smiled.

"Hmph. He doesn't look like a Bruce."

She rolled over and went to sleep.

I put Bruce in the Tupperware, lid on, armoire closed, then got to work.

First, I went through the magic kit again. I took apart the wand, but it was empty—no James Bond secret-message business inside. The scarves went on forever, but seemed to be actual scarves. I stuck them in my bag, as they were less bulky than the Yale one I'd been carrying. I went through every card in both decks. There were lots of doubles, but no little pieces of paper, and no handkerchief inside. I felt all around the lining of the top hat. Nothing. Fine. On to Chip Jessup. I picked up my phone for some Bay Ridge gossip via Debbie Pinkowski, who stayed up late. I accidentally hit her business number.

"Brows for Life is currently closed," Debbie snapped.

"Hey."

"Hey. Are you home?"

"Not yet, it's complicated. Look, can I ask you a strange question? Do you think Chip Jessup has the makings of a criminal mastermind?"

"Well, he did run numbers for the Tooleys when he was high school."

"What? I never knew that."

"Of course you didn't. You were in the Redondo cocoon. Did your uncles ever let you go out with him?"

"No."

"I rest my case."

"What exactly did he do?"

"I think he specialized in local colleges. He was such a preppie, good-looking guy, he was perfect for reeling in undergraduate morons."

"Brooklyn College?"

"Yeah. Students and teachers. I guess a couple of the professors there have gambling problems going back to the eighties." Could Dean Dean be a gambler? Could this be the connection to Chip?

"And have you ever seen him with Peggy Newsome. I mean, in public?"

"Well, if you call the Manhole public."

"No!"

"That's what melted Pam's brain to begin with."

"That bastard."

"When will you be back?"

"After the tox screen." I hung up.

I tried to remember my conversation with Chip Jessup in Queens. We did drink a lot of bourbon. Had I let it slip that Redondo Travel was in trouble? Or talked about Shep? I honestly couldn't remember. I'd been trying too hard not to be attracted to him, for Pam's sake.

I guess it was in the realm, if he was in cahoots with Peggy fricking Newsome, he might have sent Dean Dean my way to make me the patsy. But for what? Shep's death? Or was something going on with the repatriation? It was still murky. Chip and the Heeps might be dodgy, but I couldn't see how they'd be involved in his murder. It still made more sense that Shep's death had something to do with his Ripper discovery.

I pulled out the documents I'd gotten from his university office, looking for the items Evelyn had mentioned. There were lists of lunatic asylums, voting rolls, notes on a couple of Whitechapel butchers. Then I found a faded, crumbling letter, protected by a small folder, addressed to the Metropolitan Police and dated January, 1889.

It was from some sergeant, name unintelligible, who'd been there the night of the Double Event—the night the Ripper had left a bloody apron and a chalk message on the wall. He said he'd picked up a handkerchief on the way to the scene in Mitre Square, put it in his pocket, and forgotten it. It was only later, when his wife, the jealous type, asked about the blood spots and the faded ink monogram that he realized it might be evidence. If Scotland Yard were interested, it had now been logged with the City Police.

Wow. If Shep had this handkerchief, it might have the DNA of both the victim and the killer, provided the psycho actually used it to blow his nose. No wonder he was being careful. This must be the evidence he hadn't told Evelyn about and something the Ripper cult would definitely kill for. It put Martin Thompson back in first position for Shep and Babcock.

Then I came across a few documents dated 2006. They had a series of account numbers for various international bank accounts, with some totals circled in red. The part-time accounting major in me perked up, especially because one of the accounts belonged to London's Afoot! Incorporated. Why were they in the pile with the Ripper documents? Had I mixed them up? I called Evelyn. They weren't part of her research.

Why would Shep have financial documents for London's Afoot!, Nature Free, and something called SHO Enterprises? Where were Hazelnut's forensic accounting skills when I needed them? That made me wonder how the hell Hazelnut knew where I was last night? Was he following me? Who knew? I wanted these papers in a safe place, and now that I knew what I was looking for, I wanted to go back through all of Shep's things in Jeremy's locker.

I checked on Aunt Helen. She and Bruce were snorting in harmony. I left her a note and went downstairs. Nigel and Madge were on the front steps. With keys.

Chapter Forty-eight

I don't know which one of us was more alarmed. Madge stood there in another bizarrely stretched cardigan. Nigel's burgundy down jacket, over a shirt and dull brown tie, did not flatter him, either.

I kept the front door partly closed. "Yes? How can I help you?"

Nigel tried to smile. It was painful to watch. "Miss Redondo. What are you doing here?"

"I'm staying in Shep's apartment while I sort out his affairs."

Madge moved in front of her husband. "On whose authority?"

"Shelagh Gulhogan, the real estate agent." They looked at each other. "Oh, she hadn't mentioned it."

Why would she? I thought. "What are you doing here?"

Nigel tried to smile again. "We own the building."

Madge started to push her way in. I couldn't let them get upstairs to Aunt Helen or Bruce.

"Oh, then you must be here to assess the damage."

That stopped Madge.

"Oh, I guess Shelagh hasn't told you about the two break-ins? I'm assuming you have insurance?" I pointed to the dents in the door and the lock Aunt Helen's cane had made two hours ago. "Clearly the building isn't secure."

Nigel looked pale. "So the money is gone?"

"What money?"

Madge started to edge forward again. "The proceeds from his walks. It's money contractually due to us. I assume as his executor we apply to you for that."

"If you can give me proof of the debt, of course."

Nigel took over. "It's more of a moral debt, a gentlemen's agreement."

Madge sighed. "He did three walks on the Tuesday and didn't bring the ticket money back to the office."

"That's probably because he was dead," I said, staring at her. "And you came to look for it in his flat? Well, as executor I've gone through everything that's here and there wasn't any cash. Perhaps it's still with his things at the coroner's office. Or perhaps Jemima Comstock has it? She was in his apartment when I arrived."

They exchanged another look. Was this enough to warn them off?

Then I noticed a welcome distraction walking across the square. I waved. "Shelagh!"

Nigel and Madge turned. Shelagh smiled as she came up the steps. "Cyd. Just making sure you survived Boodles." She looked at Madge and Nigel. "Hello."

Nigel moved back a step. "Well, hello."

"The Hammersmithsons just told me they own this building. I had no idea. I assume you all know each other?"

"Oh. Yes. In fact, I was just walking towards Tottenham Court Road. Nigel, Madge, shall we go together?"

I mouthed "thank you" to Shelagh and she grinned, then mouthed "no worries."

Madge turned back to me. "We'll be in touch."

"Of course." I was already trying to figure out what kind of *Home Alone* traps I could set in case they came back. Maybe I could hang the caltrop like mistletoe, just inside the door. My need to get all these documents safely to the British Museum and get back here quickly seemed more urgent.

Jeremy was not in his office, but Solomon the security guard let me downstairs and I got Shep's satchel and papers out of the locker. For what felt like the fifteenth time, I went back through the pieces of paper tucked into the "stolen" pamphlet. The first one was somewhat unintelligible, but the second was a patient evaluation with an unreadable signature—I guess doctors hadn't changed—stamped Colney Hatch Asylum and dated 1889. Did I now have two of the three crucial pieces of evidence?

I couldn't stay, so I took pictures of the document, put everything back in the locker, and walked to the exit. As I was saying goodbye to Solomon, I noticed a man watching us from the courtyard. He was *sans* cape, but I would recognize that haircut anywhere. Martin Thompson. The police must have let him go. I explained the situation to Solomon. He took me to an employees' exit on the other side of the building. Did this mean the items weren't even safe in the British Museum?

I climbed the stairs to the flat, in dire need of a rest and time to think.

Aunt Helen was at the kitchen table, purse out and hair up in a half-lopsided French twist. She was wearing a vintage navy suit with ballet flats and tapping her walking cane on the floor. "Let's go."

She allowed me a quick espresso before I hailed a cab, which I wasn't sure I could pay for. I got her, her cane, Bruce in his Tupperware, and the Balenciaga all inside the vehicle and made a quick visual sweep for

Thompson before I gave the cabbie our destination.

On the way, I tried to point out a few famous bits of the city to Aunt Helen, but she seemed distracted. Or maybe scared. The only time I had ever seen her scared was when my brousin Frank, the cop, got shot in the shoulder. She had exactly the same look on her face.

We made it to the Natural History Museum for a tip-free fare that left me with a whopping two pounds. As we pulled up, Aunt Helen took off her shoes, put them in her purse, and pulled out a pair of polka-dot kitten heels. Once they were on, she let me help her out.

She didn't say a word until we made it to the entrance. Then she touched my arm. "How do I look?"

"Gorgeous." She let me squeeze her hand.

A guard helped us down into the bowels of the museum, where we stopped in a hallway filled with crates, clay figures, a bag full of various feathers, and something covered with a bright yellow rain slicker. We knocked on the door to the workroom.

The woman Uncle Leon had brought to the memorial service opened the door.

"Hello," I said. "Cyd Redondo, Redondo Travel. This is Helen Redondo." The two women assessed each other while I shook her hand.

"Emma Park Hastings, how do you do? I'm the curator of the department."

Aunt Helen looked confused. "You're not the Heep woman?"

Heep woman? How did Aunt Helen know about the Heeps?

Emma smiled. "No. She left some years ago." She shook Aunt Helen's hand. "Your husband has been doing us a great service, thank you for letting him come."

Oh God, not another catfight. "May we see him?"

"We were hoping he was with you."

Chapter Forty-nine

Aunt Helen grabbed my arm. "One thing. One thing I asked you to do!" She turned to Emma. "How dare you wrench my husband out of retirement and then lose him!"

"I apologize. We are very concerned as well." Emma turned to me. "Anywhere you can think of he might have gone?"

"Well, had he finished the, um, piece?" If he hadn't, I knew nothing but a kidnapping at gunpoint would have dragged him away.

"Yes." Oh thank God. "Well, except for the eyes. Mrs. Redondo, I'm sure you're aware of how picky he is about his eyes."

Aunt Helen harrumphed. "Picky? He's psychotic."

Emma smiled. "Exactly. So do you think he might have just taken a walk? To have a break? He has time, the unveiling isn't until Thursday."

Aunt Helen stared at me. "The unveiling?"

"Uncle Leon said it's a surprise," I said. I didn't want Emma knowing I knew what he'd been doing.

A voice from down the hall said, "What's a surprise?" I stiffened. Roger. How many blindsides could one girl take in a day? Of course, I had Bruce. Dammit.

Aunt Helen peered up at him. "You're that only child, aren't you?"

"I am, Mrs. Redondo. I'm flattered you remembered. Hello, Cyd." He didn't put out his hand.

"What are you doing here?"

"I have a meeting with your uncle." He turned to Emma. "Roger Claymore, Special Agent U.S. Fish and Wildlife. I'm seconded to Scotland Yard at the moment."

Emma went white. "Emma Park Hastings. Have we committed some kind of violation? You're not here to take Algernon back, are you?" We all looked at her. "He's a California condor, kind of our Elgin Marbles," she said.

"Oh no, of course not. I just wanted to speak to him about another matter. Is he around?"

I explained the situation. Roger ignored me, but patted Aunt Helen's shoulder and said he would make calls to the police, hospitals, etc., just to be safe.

"Try the racetracks, too," Aunt Helen said as he walked down the hall.

I helped Aunt Helen into Uncle Leon's office. We passed the curtain that I assumed still shielded the royal item. I was dying to see it, but restrained myself.

Roger came back. "No accidents or injuries reported. It's not racing season, but I called the nearest OTB and there aren't any bets under his name."

I asked if I could speak to him alone. He frowned, but followed me back into the hallway.

"Can we just get this out of the way? I'm so sorry. I know how disappointed you are in me. But I really need your help, so I hope you won't hold the sins of the niece against Uncle Leon."

"Of course not."

"Thank you. Do you think someone's taken him? Could it have anything to do with drugs in the dog?"

"I think they were just a distraction, something to throw us off. I think it might be the air tray. That's why I'm here. He was saving it for me. If I could get a quick look at it, it might give us some answers. Did he tell you where he put it?"

"No, but Emma might know."

Five minutes later, we were lifting the yellow rain slicker off of the used air tray with the dog silhouette. Roger reached into his coat and pulled out rubber gloves and a box cutter. Then he made a fine cut in the middle of the fiberboard side. A few inches down, he was able to pull it into three thin layers. Inside each one were scores of hundred-euro bills. The whole air tray was reinforced with layers of them.

We went back to the office and Roger gave the bad news to Emma.

She gasped. "They had the nerve to send that here? To implicate us? Who dared do that?"

"If Mr. Redondo located the waybill we might have an idea."

She dug around his desk and came up with a pink slip of paper. Roger looked at it, frowned.

I looked up at him. "Let me guess? Heep International?"

"How did you know that?"

Aunt Helen hit her cane against a crate. "Those no-good Heeps! They're everywhere!"

"I need coffee," I said.

Minutes later, we all had caffeine plus sugar for the shock. Emma had let Roger lock the air tray away in their vault for now.

Roger turned to the curator. "Perhaps Cyd and I should confer about this?"

"Yes. Special Agent, I do have some arrangements to make for tomorrow. I'll be back. Very nice to meet you, Helen," she said and disappeared. We looked at Aunt Helen.

"You're going to be the endangered ones if you don't tell me every single thing that is going on with my Leon."

We gave her a bit of background, minus the royal connection. Then I turned to Roger. "So you think someone might have him because they want the air tray?"

"Well, he did say that he picked up the whole thing. Is that the normal process?"

"No. Usually it's removed and discarded once the coffin or cremains reach their destination. So there was probably someone waiting there to pick it up. They might have followed him. And you think the drugs have nothing to do with it?"

"I think they're irrelevant. It was under the weight for a serious conviction, and if anyone checked or X-rayed the shipment, they'd think that was the only contraband and ignore the five hundred grand in cash that's probably in that box."

"It must be them. It must be the Heeps. They must have him. What do I do?"

Just then my phone buzzed. Oh God, I thought.

The text read *If you want to find your uncle alive, bring all of Helnikov's Ripper research, including the three relevant items—you know what they are—to Buck's Row at four o'clock.* Buck's Row. The site of the first Ripper murder.

"It's got to be Martin Thompson."

"That jerk under the bed? He has your uncle? I'm going to let him know what a real disembowelment feels like!"

Aunt Helen grinned at him. "Are you sure you're an only child?"

Chapter Fifty

Aunt Helen grabbed for my Balenciaga. "Where are the relevant items? Are they in your purse?"

I lifted it out of her reach. "Careful! No!" Roger couldn't find out I had Bruce—again. "They're safe. They're locked in the bottom of the British Museum."

Emma returned. "What's locked in the British Museum?" We told her about the text. "So I'm with your aunt. What are we waiting for?"

Aunt Helen banged her purse on the table. "What? Cyd Elizabeth Madonna Redondo!"

Roger snorted.

"I'm missing one of the relevant items." I looked down. "The most important one."

I saw their horrified faces. I couldn't let Aunt Helen or Uncle Leon (not to mention Queen Elizabeth II) down. I looked around the room and had an idea. The handkerchief might be the most important piece of evidence, but it was also the easiest to fake.

The taxidermy workroom had almost everything we needed. Emma called the fashion curator at the Victoria and Albert Museum across the street, while I alerted Jeremy that we might need some Whitechapel cobblestones. I learned a few things I didn't know, like really old blood on fabric turns gray instead of brown, and the glue Uncle Leon used to attach bird eyes dried into the same crusty feel of Victorian snot.

I ducked away to call Evelyn, since I figured if anyone had an idea where Thompson might stash someone, it would be his ex-wife. No answer. When I went back to work on the handkerchief, Roger moved away and made his own call. Luckily, it was echo-y in there.

"Detective Hubbard? Special Agent Claymore. Yes, it's what we suspected. I have the evidence secured for the moment and I'm in the process of locating Mr. Redondo for a statement. In the meantime, could you please get a warrant for Heep International? We need to search their premises as soon as possible. Thank you, I'll keep you abreast of my progress."

Aunt Helen leaned in and whispered, "Abreast? What's wrong with him?"

"They're dating."

"I hate her already," Aunt Helen said.

"Yeah, she's pretty awful."

Roger caught us listening, turned too fast, tripped over a pair of water buffalo horns, and almost took down the royal corgi curtain.

"Coffee coming up," he offered, and made a quick exit.

By the time he returned, we just needed to fake the faded half monogram. Happily, Aunt Helen had taken the Calligraphy for the Housebound course at the Y. She managed to etch out a good facsimile from the picture on my phone and Emma used a "fade fast" solution that almost obliterated it. Perfect.

Fifteen minutes later, we were in a town car with Uncle Leon's driver, headed to pick up Shep's research at the British Museum. I tried to convince Aunt Helen to stay with Emma, but she insisted she was coming with me if she "had to roll all the way."

Apparently, my favorite aunt still had her charms. When Jeremy met us at the rear entrance to the British Museum, he froze the same way I froze the first time I saw Roger. He rushed to help her out of the cab, leaving Roger with me.

"I know you have other things to do," I said. "I'd understand."

"I need your uncle to be safe as much as you do. Well, almost. I can delegate the rest."

To your leggy law enforcement hussy, I thought. I looked around to make sure we weren't being watched, then followed Jeremy and Aunt Helen into the museum.

If it weren't for my having Bruce in my purse, I would've been grateful to have Roger along. I needed all the help I could get. Martin Thompson was, at best, a delusional narcissist, and at worst, a serial killer.

Solomon the security guard kept an eye on the employee elevator while we laid the handkerchief on top of a slab of Victorian cobblestones and stomped on it with a Victorian work boot borrowed from the V&A basement. It was ready.

Then I went through all of Shep's papers, putting the three relevant items—the policeman's statement, the asylum doctor's note, and the fake handkerchief—at the top of the shoulder bag.

I separated out the mysterious financial documents, as I wanted to ask Hazelnut about them. If I ever saw him again. I considered leaving Bruce in the locker, but what if he got out? We'd never find him. Roger and Aunt Helen, though, might be easier to ditch.

I told them I'd be right back and went into a stall in the ladies' room to check on Bruce. When I opened the lid, he eased his tiny eyes open and made a new, loud chirping noise. I leaned in closer. "Bruce, what is up with you?" He just got louder.

I made sure the top was on properly this time, so he wouldn't get out and chew the Responsible Raisin I'd just reapplied. The more I thought about it, the more I thought I should go alone. Aunt Helen had just gotten here this morning. She'd been so brave to come and must be exhausted. And every minute I spent with Roger made it more likely he'd discover Bruce and truly hate me forever. If I went on my own, they'd be mad, but they'd get over it.

I moved my personal alarm to my pocket, then walked out and turned right toward the exit. Aunt Helen and Roger, both in their coats, were blocking the door.

"What'd I tell you?" Aunt Helen raised her eyebrow at Roger. "And you! You made your fire escape face. Don't even think about going without me."

"Me either," Roger said.

"Thompson said no police."

"I'm not police. I'm Fish and Wildlife."

I shook my head.

"I'm going too," Jeremy said.

I went over and kissed him on the cheek. "I need someone I can call if we get in trouble."

He gave Aunt Helen a lovesick look. "You'll take care of your aunt?"

"I can take care of myself," she said, blushing.

Cripes, had everyone forgotten Uncle Leon was missing? "We have to go!"

Jeremy waved as we walked to the car. The sky was a dark purple, with a few pink streaks. By the time we got to the East End, it was black. I made the driver stop a few blocks away from the site and looked at Roger. "You're in charge of her."

"I beg your pardon, missy," my aunt said.

"I'm serious. And if he spots either one of you and you screw this up, I swear, I will never arrange travel for either one of you, ever again. I mean it." This was an empty threat, but it was all I had. They made me promise to keep my personal alarm in my hand. I agreed. It was more practical than the caltrop.

I took off down the block, my Balenciaga on one side and Shep's shoulder bag on the other. I got to the sparse streetlights by the murder site and looked around—nothing but construction cranes and a creepy Victorian school building. Then I saw a lump of clothes on the sidewalk. Oh God. Uncle Leon.

I hurried forward, then stood, eyes closed. Finally, I looked down.

It was Martin Thompson. The Ripper guide.

Chapter Fifty-one

There was blood on the cobblestones around his head. Was he dead? I dropped to my knees and put down the shoulder bag to reach for his wrist. The instant I landed, a hand snatched the bag. I whipped around to grab it back and got socked in the eye. A black figure jumped on a scooter and was out of sight before I could even scramble up. I couldn't see the license plate. Dammit.

I dropped back down to Martin and located a faint pulse, called 999, and started CPR. Given my clientele and relatives, I renewed my certificate annually and had the "Stayin' Alive" rhythm down. If I couldn't save him, I had no way to find Uncle Leon.

"Cyd!" Roger rounded the corner and ran to me.

In between breaths, I managed an "Aunt Helen?"

"Fine. In the car," he said. "Let me do the compressions for you."

We worked in rhythm for a minute. Thompson's eyes fluttered. He took a breath. Now I could kill him. Except a beat policeman was headed our way.

I leaned in close. "Where's my uncle? Where's Leon Redondo?"

"Who?" Thompson said and looked up. "You! You're the one who set me up."

"I most certainly did not. You set me up."

"Bloody Yanks!" He passed out again.

The policeman arrived. "Is he breathing, ma'am?"

"Yes. I've called an ambulance."

"I have as well. I was watching from that window—he pointed to the seventies monstrosity across the street. "Inspector Blethly's had someone watching all the murder sites."

"Did you see the attacker?"

"Not clearly, but I've asked them to call up the CCTV."

"Great. Cyd Redondo, Redondo Travel."

"Yes, I know. You're the CCTV pinup girl of the week."

Roger stared at me. I explained the situation to the officer as we handed Martin Thompson off to the paramedics. They asked if we had an emergency contact for the patient. I knew she might kill me, but I gave them Evelyn's number, as former next of kin.

I wrangled an ice pack from the emergency staff and said Detective

Blethly knew how to reach me, then Roger and I bolted before he could object and ran to the town car.

Roger helped me in. Aunt Helen stared at my face.

"It's just a shiner," I said.

"Enh. Lean back." She took the pack and put it on my eye.

"Where to?" the driver asked.

"Tottenham Court Road," I said. "I've been thinking about this. London's Afoot! is the one who stands to gain the most by not only having the Ripper evidence, but by having their guides killed on the walk. The story is going international, and if Martin Thompson had died too, it would have only brought more crowds. The walking tour company is the one thing that links the deaths. And if it were a crazed Ripper copycat, I think the murders would have been more violent. Don't you, Roger?"

"Probably."

"The heads of the tour company, Nigel and Madge, tried to sneak in and search Shep's flat this morning. I had to threaten them with legal action to keep them out."

"Why didn't you just lock the door?"

"They had keys. They own the building. Apparently they've been investing in real estate. Hazelnut—if I can mention Hazelnut—said they'd invested in the company that's building near the dormouse sanctuary."

"How does he know that?"

"He broke into their computer."

Roger threw up his hands. "The guy is a menace."

"That's why he's been working as a guide. The other thing I've been thinking about that might interest you? This business runs completely on cash."

We stopped in front of the walking tour office. Aunt Helen put her purse on her shoulder.

"You stay here."

"I didn't fly across the Atlantic to make small talk with a limo driver, no offense."

"None taken," said the driver.

"If he's there, I'll call. But I need lookouts." I gave her both my phone numbers.

"Well, I'm coming with you," Roger said. "You might have a concussion."

"It's a shiner, for pity's sake," Aunt Helen said. "Haven't you ever had one?"

"No," he said.

"Only child," we said in unison. I kissed Aunt Helen. "Call us if you see anyone come in or out the front door?"

We were on the third landing when Roger got a call. He held up his finger. "Okay, good."

"Her?"

"Yes. How many more floors?"

We climbed two more to arrive at a closed door. We could hear voices. Roger turned to me. "Are we knocking?"

"Hell no." I turned away and pulled out my nesting shot glasses. "Here." I handed him one and put mine up to the door and listened. Roger stared at me, then positioned his, too.

A woman's voice inside hissed, "Nigel, do something!"

A man cleared his throat. "It should have been with his things." Silence. "We haven't had a chance to search it again." Something hit a table. "We'll find it."

"You'd better. I need proof!" I got a bad feeling about this voice. It sounded like it had bowlegs.

Roger leaned in. "Is he talking about the handkerchief?"

I wished he wouldn't do that, as it made me dizzy. "Maybe."

My phone vibrated—or was that Bruce? I took a chance on the phone. Aunt Helen barked that a blonde woman in a beret was headed our way. Jemima.

I turned to Roger. "Kick it in or get caught out here?"

Roger tried the knob. It opened.

Inside, his taser aimed at Madge and Nigel, was Hazelnut, in full swinging sixties ensemble. The safe was open, and there was cash everywhere.

Chapter Fifty-two

Just as Hazelnut noticed us, Jemima came swaying in.

She looked confused, but that didn't stop her from striking a pose. "As the bard would say, 'What fresh hell is this?'"

Was I going to have to punch her? "That's not Shakespeare, you nitwit."

"Of course it is."

"No, it's Dorothy Parker."

Hazelnut waved his taser. "She's right. Hello, AntiChristine. Get the door, Claymore, I think this might interest you."

"Wait, first I need to know if they have my Uncle Leon?"

"Why would they have your uncle?"

"I was supposed to trade him for the Ripper evidence, but the guy just took it and left. I think these two are involved."

I pointed at Madge and Nigel, trussed up in separate chairs like Cornish hens. Nigel strained his stained ascot around. "He really had the evidence? Jemima, did you know that? Why didn't you tell us?"

Roger stepped forward. "Let Cyd ask the questions."

"Thank you. Keep that taser on them. Again, where is he? He's seventy-five, for God's sake. Do you really want another murder indictment on top of the two you're already getting for Shep and Babcock? Roger and I saved Martin Thompson, by the way, so we messed up your little trifecta."

Madge stamped her foot. "We don't know what you're talking about. We didn't even know you had an uncle. And why would we kill our best guides?"

"Then why were you so anxious to get into Shep's apartment this morning?"

Madge wriggled around, stretching her cardigan further. "That's Jemima's fault."

"I am only your part-time accountant. Why is this my responsibility?"

"Losing documents is the responsibility of whoever has them when they're lost. We only keep you on for the accounting, princess, your tours are appalling," Madge said.

That was Jemima's cue to do her stage faint into the nearest chair.

I leaned forward. "What documents?"

"The documents that prove London's Afoot! is a front for money launderers and eco-destroyers," Hazelnut said, waving the taser. "I told you this already."

Madge gave an exaggerated sigh, but looked nervous. "We run a cash business, which is perfectly legal, and we use our profits to invest, like any other business would. We are respected members of the British Tourism Association and the darling of Fodor's. You're delusional."

Hazelnut walked toward Jemima and smiled down at her. "Am I delusional, Jemima?"

He helped her up. Jemima smiled at Madge. "Only if it's delusional to notice that every single tour every single week is reporting income from a hundred walkers."

"A hundred walkers?" Hazelnut laughed. "We're lucky if we get thirty. Even on the Ripper walks, that's a huge night."

Jemima sighed dramatically. "That's what Shep said. I accidentally left some paperwork in his flat. He saw it and was furious. He thought Madge and Nigel were risking the reputations of all the guides. It would look like we were all in on it, that we were the ones overreporting. I hadn't really thought about it that way. But he was so passionate about it that one thing led to another. And I guess I forgot the paperwork again." She turned to me. "It's what I was looking for when we met."

You could tell Hazelnut was about an inch away from socking her. "Well, where is it?"

"In the British Museum," I said. Nigel fainted dead away.

Chapter Fifty-three

"Well done, AntiChristine. Let's go get them."

"We don't have to. They're on my phone."

Hazelnut tossed the taser to Roger, who fumbled then caught it. "Keep an eye on her," he said, pointing to Jemima. Hazelnut dragged me into the hallway. Once we closed the door, he asked where Bruce was. I pointed to my purse.

"Does Claymore know?"

"Not yet, but Bruce has been particularly vocal, so he's going to figure it out. Look." I opened the purse, then took the top off the Tupperware. Bruce was awake, and tried to scrabble up the side of the bowl, chirping in his new vibrato.

"I knew it. They've done more damage than I thought."

"What?"

"He's trilling. That's his mating call. He's courting you."

Poor thing. I figured I could do a lot worse than Bruce, but it was definitely a Montague and Capulet situation for him. I petted his tiny head, which set him off again. I put the top back on the bowl. "What do I do?"

"Don't open it."

"Besides that."

"I'll figure it out. Give me your phone." He started to scroll through the document photos. It seemed to take forever.

I tugged on his arm. "Hurry! This is not my priority right now."

"The planet is everyone's priority."

"Shut up, Earth Day. I'm actually dealing with an endangered species too—the only cool Redondo brother—so stop it. Are they what you're looking for?"

"Yes. Together with the records I found in their safe, it's pretty much proof they've been padding their numbers. London's not going to be Afoot for long. This is outstanding. Very clever of you to grab these."

"I didn't do it on purpose. They were stuck in the middle of Shep's research. There are two more." I brought them up on the screen. "Can you make any sense out of these?"

He zoomed in. "It looks like whoever was feeding the cash through here was doing it with other walking tours too. Laundromats, hot chestnut vendors."

"Chestnut vendors? Come on."

"Now we just need to know the source of the cash so we can stop the land sale. Let's ask Sarah Bernhardt." Hazelnut went back in the office to get Jemima. Roger followed them out and closed the door.

I showed Jemima all the documents. "Are these the ones you left at Shep's?"

"The first three. I don't recognize the other two." She looked again. "No, these definitely aren't ours. It looks like one of the accounts is listed as SHO Enterprises."

"Right," said Hazelnut. "Theirs don't add up, either. Someone up the chain is skimming." Hazelnut handed the phone to Roger. Jemima leaned in.

I took the phone back and looked at the numbers. "So, the liaison is skimming part of the cash? That would make this a dangerous document for Shep, or anyone, to have, right?" I looked at Roger. "The person who took my uncle asked for all of Shep's papers. Do you think there's any chance they were actually trying to get these, not the Ripper evidence?"

Roger thought for a minute. "Maybe. They're pretty specific. And damning."

"Damning enough to have killed Shep for them? Jemima! Whoever is doing this could be his murderer. Don't you owe him more loyalty than you do some money launderers?"

Jemima shook her head. "I don't know the direct contact, only Madge and Nigel do, but there might be a connection to a conglomerate called WOCAM."

The Heeps. Chip Jessup. Nature Free. Patriot fricking Travel. Bastards Incorporated.

I took out the subsidiaries list that Evelyn had given me and showed it to Roger. His eyes got wider and wider as he went down the list.

"I can't just stand around. Why don't you try to get the name out of Madge while I track down Chip Jessup? He's connected to WOCAM and he's from the neighborhood, so Uncle Leon might have gone with him willingly."

Hazelnut took Jemima back into the office, while I called the embassy from the landing. Delores put me right through to Harley.

I didn't waste time on small talk. "Hey. Do you have a number for Chip? Or know where he is? Just wanted to check in with him before he heads back to New York."

"He might be at his office, he works out of Gordon, Gordon, Gordon, and Lancaster when he's here." He gave me the number. "If not, he's probably at Boodles."

"Thanks, Harley, I really appreciate it."

"No problem, I was about to call you anyway. I have good news. They've released that guy's body. Your funeral home picked him up about an hour ago."

I grabbed Roger's hand so hard he actually yelped. "Thank you, Harley, really."

Roger shook his hand loose. "What?"

"Heep International. They've picked up Shep's body without my permission. Or my paperwork. If they're that anxious to get an air tray to New York, I'm guessing Shep's not going to be the only thing in it. Did your 'associate' get her warrant?"

He called the detective while I tried Chip's London office. No joy.

Roger had better luck. "She's on her way."

"Do you trust her?"

"I didn't tell her it was for you, so yes."

"Okay, you handle that while I go to Boodles."

"While you go where?"

"It's a gentlemen's club in Pall Mall. It's a long story."

"I don't want you going anywhere alone."

"I'm perfectly fine."

"You can only see out of one eye." He had a point.

"I won't be going alone."

Chapter Fifty-four

Sir Rod, lifetime Boodles member, picked us up in his Rolls. I hadn't planned on a threesome, but Aunt Helen had insisted, and to be honest, in Boodles, there was probably safety in numbers. We asked the museum driver to follow us there. By the time we turned onto Pall Mall, I'd given my aunt the background on the gentlemen's club and Chip Jessup.

"Those Jessups were always on the take," she said. "Chip's the worst. He just trades on his looks. You know he flunked algebra. What financial advisor does that?" Aunt Helen had been a substitute math teacher. "That Pam Owens dodged a bullet there."

But not a straitjacket, I thought.

"Nipper before we begin?" Sir Rod raised his absinthe flask.

Aunt Helen took a significant snort. "Good Lord, what is that?" she asked, taking another. Sir Rod laughed and accompanied us in.

We encountered the same cloakroom attendant, so I didn't have to go through the defense of my purse again. Since I was hiding Aunt Helen's handbag behind me, she didn't either. As we entered the club, she gave a harrumph possibly not heard in this room in four hundred years. "Who takes away your handbag? Savages," she said.

Sir Rod got us drinks, to help us look as if we belonged while we snooped, but my black eye, still swollen shut, wasn't helping me blend in. I remembered I'd used the only dry ice pack in my purse on Roger, whom I hoped was keeping Shep's body from becoming the conduit for an international conspiracy. I took my whiskey on the rocks to the ladies' room, put the rocks in a baggie, and held it on my eye for three minutes.

By the time I'd checked on Bruce, reapplied my makeup, and emerged, Sir Rod and Aunt Helen were nowhere in sight. I was just heading for the snooker room when my phone rang. I got about fifty outraged looks. Clearly phones were not allowed. I ran back into the restroom and ducked inside a stall. It was Roger.

It was hard to keep the relief out of my voice. "Where have you been?"

"Unconscious."

"What?"

"When we went back into the office, Madge and Nigel had disappeared and someone bashed me and Hazelnut on the head. I think Jemima just fake fainted. But by the time we came to, they were all gone. Along with the cash."

"How did Madge and Nigel get past you?"

"Fire escape, but someone untied them. So be careful."

"What about the Heeps?"

"I'm on my way there now." My purse was bouncing around my lap. Bruce must be excited. I didn't want to think about that. He gave an extra-loud trill.

"What was that?"

"Some opera singer is here. Attention whore. What happened with the Heeps?"

"She served the warrant and found your body. The strange thing is, it had all the correct paperwork."

"That's impossible." I checked my purse. "I still have it. It's right here."

"Well, who is Derek Lancaster? He's listed as temporary executor."

"Wow. That's Shelagh Gulhogan's boyfriend. He offered to officiate on all the paperwork. He must have made Uncle Leon sign something extra. Unbelievable."

"Who's Shelagh Gulhogan?"

"She's my real estate agent. Wait, wasn't Gordon, Gordon, Gordon, and Lancaster on the list of WOCAM subsidiaries?"

"Yeah, I think so."

"That means Chip and Derek are working together with the Heeps. I have to go."

"Wait. Felicity can search and hold the air trays and coffins, but she doesn't actually have jurisdiction over the body, especially if they've got the paperwork."

"Well, you better find some euros before they start the embalming process. I don't want those sons of bitches touching Shep. He deserves better."

Just as I hung up, I heard the door open and close in a man slam. Of course. The entitled members used the ladies' room. I put my Balenciaga on my shoulder, took my whiskey off the top of the dispenser, and walked out of my stall. A man in suspenders and overpriced shirtsleeves was urinating into one of the sinks. He froze. As I got to the door, Aunt Helen lurched in, took one look at the man and burst out laughing. "That thing makes a toothpick look like Moby Dick," she said. "Speaking of pricks, come on, we found Chip Jessup."

She'd left Sir Rod guarding the door of the snooker room. The three of us walked in to find Chip lining up a shot, while Derek gestured with a brandy. Sir Rod closed the door.

It only took one roundhouse kick to knock Derek's Waterford snifter out of his hand and a quick jab in the lower back to flatten Chip on the table and take his pool cue. I broke it against my knee, partly because I'd always wanted to do that, and partly because it gave both me and Aunt Helen a weapon with splinters. I threw hers underhand, obviously.

"What is the meaning of this?" Derek cowered against the wall of bookcases. I saw him try to sneak a pull on the service bell and gave him a snap on the wrist worthy of Sister Ellery. He sank to the floor. I took plastic zip ties out of my purse and threw one set to Sir Rod, who had Chip tied up in seconds. I did the honors on Derek, making sure I pulled them extra tight, after I took off his Vacheron Constantin watch, which was too precious to be on a cowardly con man's wrist. I would make sure he donated it to the British Museum clock room.

I told them Roger had confiscated half a million euros in one of the Heep air trays, was in the process of executing a warrant for their warehouse and facilities, and had handed Interpol the counterfeit paperwork Derek had passed on in my uncle's name. I said we'd found several laundering streams used by WOCAM and had turned that information over too. I hoped Roger had actually done that.

"So, if you don't want to have kidnapping and extortion added to the other charges, tell me where you're holding my uncle."

"Which uncle?"

Aunt Helen whacked Chip with her half cue stick. "Which one do you think?"

"Look, Cyd, you grew up in Bay Ridge. You know in business sometimes you do a favor for someone, a kind of *quid pro quo*," Chip said, trying to grin.

"I am going to *quid* your *quo* if you don't answer me. Where is he?"

"Ask Derek. Granted, I was involved in some of the financial stuff, but I had nothing to do with kidnapping anyone. I mean, he would have recognized me. Derek?"

Derek was shaking his head like he'd been electrocuted. Or maybe he was sitting on a sliver of Waterford. I hoped so. "I don't know anything about a kidnapping. I didn't need to, I'd already tricked him into signing the paperwork. Even if he'd objected, I'm an English barrister, I'd be the one they believed."

"Well, who's the one skimming from the London's Afoot! laundering operation? Shep Helnikov had proof. They might have wanted to trade my uncle for that."

Derek sat up. "That Jack the Ripper hack? Shelagh swore she wouldn't see him again!"

Suddenly, it all made sense. "Shelagh? Shelagh was the one laundering money?"

Chip perked up and grinned at Derek. "You are dead, man. Your girlfriend's skimming? There's no way they're not going to think you were in on it. I always told you she was flighty. I mean, she worked for a rock star, for Christ's sake."

"Which one?"

Derek was crying now. "Bono."

I wished someone had told me this a week ago.

Chapter Fifty-five

Over his strong objections, I left Sir Rod in charge of the Boodliens while Aunt Helen and I went to find Uncle Leon. Derek admitted that Shelagh usually kept a couple of properties empty for their operations, one in Mayfair, and one in Whitechapel. After I poked him with the splintered pool cue a few times, he gave us the addresses. Just before we left, I gave Chip a well-aimed kick in what the English would call his bollocks. "This is for Pam!"

We came out to wait under the portico while the valet alerted our museum driver, who pulled right up. The valet helped us in and the driver locked the doors and pulled away. I gave him the Whitechapel address.

"No problem, madam." The driver turned around. It was Shelagh.

Aunt Helen glared at me and pointed to the pool cue sticking out of my bag.

Shelagh smiled in the rearview mirror. "You're welcome to try something, but if you do, no one will ever find Mr. Redondo. He's already gone almost a day without food or water."

It was very tempting to shove the pool cue through her neck, but she was right. Derek could have lied to me. I needed to reason with her.

"Shelagh. We know everything. The laundering, the skimming, all of it. We don't care. We just want Uncle Leon back, we'll go home to Brooklyn, that's it."

"Well, if you'd given me the paperwork you were supposed to, instead of locking it up in the British Museum, you would have him back."

"It's not in the British Museum," I said, with as much indignation as I could muster.

"Perhaps if I hadn't bugged the London's Afoot! office, that lie might work. Besides, I've already retrieved the documents from the museum. Solomon the security guard was very anxious to help a friend of Cyd's."

I felt sick. She was right. Why hadn't I just put all the papers in the shoulder bag? Why had I tried to play detective? I was a moron.

Aunt Helen was fading. She'd only slept for an hour since her red-eye flight. She banged the back of Shelagh's seat with her head. "Where are we going?"

"I thought it would be lovely if you were all buried together."

"What kind of sinister, bad cop show dialogue is that? Seriously? I thought the English were supposed to be sophisticated."

"I'm Irish!"

"Sorry. Look, Derek and Chip are going to be arrested tonight. It's over. There's no need to kill anyone."

"It's not Derek and Chip I'm worried about. But with you and the evidence gone, no one has anything concrete against me. Plus, you hate Bono."

"Yes," I said, "yes, I do."

"He's a nasty shrimp!" Aunt Helen added. "And he can't sing!"

I let Shelagh cool down after that outburst, then put my pay-as-you-go phone in my pocket and hit record. "You did murder Shep, though, didn't you?"

"What did he expect? He was going to report me and the people I work for. I told him to forget it, but he was completely irrational. It's not like he was twenty or something. He was a walking time bomb. I used his own diabetes medication, for pity's sake. It's his fault if he didn't taste it in his pint."

I leaned forward, taking a chance. "So why kill Philip Babcock?"

"Again, his own fault. He hit on me at the Ten Bells that night, so he could place me there. Then he started telling people that Shep's body had been moved. That he really died in Mitre Square. It was perfect for me. All I needed was two guides dead in Whitechapel, and the police would have too many suspects to count, so two birds with one stone. Plus, it upped the intake for Madge and Nigel, which made the accounting easier. Everybody wins."

Not everybody, I thought. Shelagh turned left, heading away from Whitechapel. Dammit. Our only hope had been that we were bound for the addresses we'd left with Sir Rod.

Shelagh drove down several dark streets south of the Thames, then pulled up across from one of the few ancient buildings still there. Apparently not for long. There was a wrecking ball positioned on the side.

Shelagh got out and, despite strict gun laws in the UK, had a pistol. She gestured us into the crumbling place, with a staircase that didn't look stable.

I turned to her. "Stop! Do anything you want with me, but are you really going to make my aunt go up all these stairs?"

"Don't patronize me, missy. I'm fine." Aunt Helen did grip my arm, though, as we headed up. Bruce was trilling at an all-time high, probably in response to the scrabbling of his various female rodent cousins.

Shelagh finally opened a door on the fourth floor. The place smelled like rot, rats, and turpentine. It didn't stop Aunt Helen, who flew to the dusty but still dapper figure in the corner. His face lit up as he rose and crushed her to him. "Bella! Hella Bella, oh *ti amo*, my darling!" As Aunt Helen curled into Uncle Leon's chest, I realized she fit perfectly there.

"How touching," Shelagh said.

I was very tempted to try to knock out her teeth, along with the gun in her hand, but if it didn't work, who knows where a stray bullet might land. I looked around for any help in the room, but there was nothing but some trash and a sheet in the corner.

"Now I just need your phone, Cyd, the one with the document pictures."

At least I had swapped out my real phone and the pay as you go after her confession. She wouldn't expect me to have two and I had a locator and Acts of God insurance on the one she wanted. I held it out to her, hoping I could land a proper stiletto to her temple, but with a swollen eye, my aim was off. I only winged her shoulder pad and wound up on my ass instead.

"Aw, Cyd. It's been grand working with you. You did a fantastic job tracking down the Ripper items. They should finance my change of residence." She looked around. "Imagine what a place this was in its heyday. I could have gotten top price for it." She moved to the corner of the room. "They've already set the dynamite to implode it in the morning." She pointed to a small bundle of wired explosives near the pile of trash.

Suddenly the image of Atlantic City casinos tumbling into rubble ran through my mind. This was bad. "They're not using the wrecking ball?" With the wrecking ball we might have had a slim chance.

"It's just backup. They won't need it though. I'm giving the explosives a little assistance."

She flicked open her lighter and lit the pile of trash next to the dynamite on fire, then left, locking the door. We could hear her drag something in front of it.

I jerked off my peplum jacket and managed to stamp out the flames. Still, a twenty/forty wool-rayon blend wasn't going to work on dynamite. Was that smoke I smelled coming under the door? Had she lit another fuse?

Uncle Leon patted my shoulder. "Any ideas, Squid?"

I handed him a protein bar from my bag. "Maybe. If we could get that window open."

I tried a couple of jumps, but I still couldn't reach the sill of the only window in the room. It was just inches too high for me to grab the sill and pull myself up. And the latch was another two feet higher. I looked around. No furniture, nothing to stand on.

I opened my purse and Bruce did a few echoing trills. He was bopping the top of the Tupperware with his head. I took the bowl out. "Bruce! Cool it. You're going to hurt yourself."

"Have you been carrying him around this whole time?" Aunt Helen shook her head.

"What is it?" Uncle Leon perked up.

"Some endangered rat," Aunt Helen said. "She's its nanny."

"Good practice," Uncle Leon said.

"Very funny," I said, digging through my purse. I pulled out my pay-as-you-go phone, but recording Shelagh had run the battery all the way down. It was totally dead. I turned to my uncle. "Any chance you have yours?"

"On my desk at the museum. You know I hate the damn things."

After going through my bag, I put aside five things: the caltrop, two bungee cords, Shep's magic scarves, my foldable flats, and three panty liners.

I turned to Uncle Leon. "Did Shep happen to mention the magic scarves when he gave you the handcuffs? Are they going to disappear, or break apart when I'm halfway down?"

"Halfway down? You have to reach that window if you're going down."

"I'm aware of that. One problem at a time." Keeping an eye on the smoldering pile of paper, I enlisted the two of them to help me double-tie the scarves to each other. The three prongs of the caltrop were so sharp, we had to be sure the scarves went between them, or they would rip. I triple-tied them on. None of us mentioned the smoke sneaking in around the door, which was getting thicker, but I'd saved two scarves, which I handed them to hold over their faces.

"Hold your horses, missy. You're not the only one with a handbag, you know." Aunt Helen reached into hers and pulled out a thick metal object about a foot long, with an oversized trigger at one end and royal blue pincers at the other. Was it a mutant water pistol?

She held it up and hit the trigger. When it expanded to three times its size I recognized it—her collapsible pincher, reacher, grabber. I'd seen her use it to get boxes of rigatoni and cans of crushed tomatoes down from the top shelf in our pantry.

"How the hell did you get that through airport security?"

"Why do you think I brought a cane? They see the cane and suddenly everything in your suitcase is medical." Aunt Helen winked at Uncle Leon. "Sister Ellery suggested it."

"Okay. You're the pincher reacher grabber expert. Do you need a leg up?"

"Don't be ridiculous. You could help hold my hand, though." Aunt Helen lifted the device, and I held on to her wrist and forearm as she aimed it for the window latch. We all held our breath. Even if it reached, the lock could be painted shut.

"Don't worry. This thing once opened a jar of olives from the Great War."

After three tries, the latch wrenched open. She handed the device over to me. "You're taller. Just hook it right on the latch and push."

"Whoa," I yelled as the pincher reacher grabber instantly fell to the ground.

"Don't be a quitter."

"When was I a quitter?"

"Barry Manzoni."

"Uncle Leon? Can you control her?"

"Fat chance. Here."

He held it until he pinched the top of the bottom window, and we pushed together to jerk it up, just far enough for me to get through.

Then I picked up the caltrop. I hooked two of my bungee cords around it, on top of the scarf knot. This was insane. We all knew it. But what were our options? Smoke was seeping through the door and who knew how close it was to the dynamite. I invoked my dad's hero, Mets pitcher Tom Seaver, grabbed the bungee cords and used them to toss the caltrop toward the wall beside the window.

It took three tries to penetrate the ancient plaster wall. I had one more thing to do. Not only would my stilettos rip the silk rope, the spiked hooks in the caltrop would go right through the delicate leather. I put my stilettos in my bag, then filled the flats with the panty liners, in hopes the "extra protection" they offered would be enough to keep the caltrop from going through my foot.

"I love you two crazy kids," I said. "At least if we go down, we go down traveling. Internationally. Keep those scarves over your faces," I said to both of them, then to my aunt, "There is one thing I want to know before I potentially die. How did you pay for your plane ticket?"

"Sister Ellery helped me cash in the Boston trip. We put the rest on your credit card."

Oh God, with the penalties and new twenty-nine percent interest I would pay for going over my limit, I actually needed to die. My life insurance might just cover the costs. It gave me courage.

I tied the end of the scarves around my waist, then pulled myself up, hand over hand, to the windowsill. This was the second time rope climbing in Catholic school had come in handy in real life. Silk was a bit harder to grip than the rope I'd used to rappel down onto a cruise ship a month before, but the principles were the same. Sadly, this time I lacked ballast. I'd left my Balenciaga, and Bruce, with my aunt.

I found the medieval frog gig with my foot and shoved off it up into the open window. Somehow I managed to swing around so I could lower myself facing the building. I was glad I'd done that four-day, post-holiday juice cleanse with Debbie, as well as the wall climbing day to find her a rebound boyfriend with good pecs.

I pulled one more time on the caltrop, which held, then started lowering myself out the window, hoping there'd be architectural "features"—i.e., footholds—on the building. There was a gust of frosty wind and I swung out, then swung back hard into the brick. I stifled a yell. I didn't want my aunt and uncle to worry. The moon was bright, so I focused on the scarves. The fact that they kept changing colors didn't really reduce my vertigo.

I could see smoke coming from the third floor, but if I went any faster, I could tear the scarves. I inched down and was able to put my foot on a scowling cupid's head. With a new appreciation for cat burglars, I swung down to a window sash, repeated this on the next floor, then jerked to the end of my rope. I was about ten feet from the ground. I could break something, but probably not my neck, so what the hell. I wished I were wearing heels for balance. I tried to swing towards some dead shrubbery on the ground and prepared to let go.

"Cyd!"

I guess my life was passing before me, as it sounded like Roger.

"Cyd, hang on. I've got you."

I looked down to see the real Roger below me, grabbing my calves.

"Just slide down me," he said—the most poetic sentence in the English language.

The instant I hit the ground, I ran for the front of the building, forgetting I was still tied to the caltrop upstairs. I stopped still, then jerked back and up, almost knocking Roger down. "Untie me! Aunt Helen and Uncle Leon are trapped on the fourth floor!"

He unwound the scarves and followed me toward the front, jogging around a strange, squat vehicle in the middle of the lawn. We got to the front door, ready to break it down, but someone had gotten there already. It was open. Smoke was pouring out. I noticed bundles of dynamite scattered on the ground floor. I dashed for the stairs. One flight up, I saw movement. Bowlegged movement. Hazelnut had my aunt, and my Balenciaga, in his arms. My uncle was right behind him. Roger and I rushed up to help and in a minute or two, got them outside.

"We have to get across the street!" I took Uncle Leon's arm, Roger assumed Aunt Helen duty, and we took cover in an alley. I turned to find Uncle Leon and Aunt Helen holding on to each other. They seemed okay. Hazelnut was gone.

Roger pointed. "He's gone to save his EV1. We would have gotten here faster if we hadn't had to stop to charge it." The vehicle backed off the lawn and down the curb and parked a block away.

"How did you find us?"

Roger grinned and looked at Hazelnut, who'd returned with bottles of water for Aunt Helen and Uncle Leon. "The tracker he put in your purse."

"What!" I couldn't believe he had violated the sanctity of the Balenciaga twice.

Hazelnut handed me a water, too. "You don't think I'd leave the future of the hazel dormouse with someone I wasn't monitoring every minute of every day, do you? What kind of ecoterrorist would I be?"

"Bastard. Thank you."

He looked at my aunt and uncle. "Preserving endangered species wherever I go. That includes you, AntiChristine," he said, and ran back to his car. We watched it drive off.

I turned to Roger. "I thought it might be your dormouse tracker."

"I left it in the hotel. I was too afraid it would keep going off."

He'd known I'd had Bruce all along. And hadn't said a word.

I gave him the phone with the recording of Shelagh and the tracker info for the phone she'd taken. The confession wouldn't be admissible in court, but maybe it would help them find some evidence that was. He'd already called Inspector Blethly and, apparently, Uncle Leon's driver, the real one.

I found my aunt and uncle drinking pH-balanced water and laughing. Aunt Helen handed me my bag and actually kissed me, meaning she was more jet-lagged than I thought. "Your uncle's got to go to work."

"It's nine o'clock at night."

"Eyes wait for no man," he said. Yet another town car appeared. "Want a ride, Squid?"

"Please." It was time to figure out how to get Shep home, Dean Dean be damned.

Chapter Fifty-six

I made Roger check the driver's I.D. before he helped us in, then asked about Shep's body. "It won't be evidence again, will it?"

"Just the coffin, probably, but I'll find out," he said and squeezed my hand.

Was this the last time I was going to see him? I tried not to think about it. As we drove off, there was a loud rumble, a bang, and the house behind us collapsed into a pile of dust.

Oh no, I thought. Sir Rod's caltrop.

On the drive back, to avoid thinking about Roger, I focused on Uncle Leon's news about the royal unveiling. The piece was going into the museum at the Sandringham Estate. "The Queen winters there," Uncle Leon added.

"I need a fascinator," Aunt Helen said.

"Don't we all?"

On the way to the flat, I made them stop and let me buy another burner phone, then they went on to the museum. Once I got upstairs, I proceeded to wash off the three-hundred-year-old dust, put on one of Shep's old Brooks Brothers shirts, and dug his last bottle of vodka out of the freezer. I let Bruce out of his prison of #4 plastic so he could run around. He leapt back and forth on the chair backs, blasting his mating call. It was five o'clock in Brooklyn. Time to face the music.

"Brooklyn College Department of History." A different voice answered this time, so I took a chance with my real name. She didn't hang up. "May I ask what this is regarding?"

"I'm Professor Helnikov's executor and am in the process of collecting his research in London for the dean."

"Oh," she said. "Shep was our favorite. It's never going to be the same here without him."

"Yes, he was a very special person."

"You're in London now? So you don't know about the dean?"

"What about him?"

"He's on administrative leave." She lowered her voice. "Possibly permanent."

"What happened?"

"Stress is the official word, but we found racing forms in his desk, some kind of debt collector keeps calling and the department canceled all his university credit cards."

Great. "He had promised to cover my expenses. Is there a way to reach him?"

"Not for at least twenty-eight days. I think that's the rule at the facility."

Perfect. I finally had the chance to bring Shep home and now it was going to be the last thing I ever did as a travel agent. After trying so hard to save the business and do right by Shep, I was back at square one. Well, actually below square one, since I'd dipped heavily into my retirement savings. And I still needed thirty grand.

I checked on my clients, then pulled up my emails. There was one with attachments from an attorney's office I didn't recognize. It was an offer to purchase Redondo Travel.

"Ms. Redondo. We are expanding our holdings and are keen to add your small business to our travel family. Please find our offer enclosed." The email was signed by some attorney for PTII. Patriot Travel and Insurance International.

Peggy fricking Newsome. She'd been trying to run me out of business ever since she'd opened the Patriot Travel office in Bay Ridge two years ago. Why did this come today? And then I got it. Chip Jessup. Dean Dean was never going to cover my costs. It was all a mutually beneficial transaction between Chip and Peggy. They'd set me up.

It was a fair, if not generous, offer, but one I would never have considered while we were even barely solvent. After the last week, we wouldn't be. When things had gotten tough before, I had used some of my savings to cover, but they had dwindled to Christmas fund levels. I closed the email. I would deal with it later.

There was at least one thing I could do while I was still a paying member of the Travel Agents Association of America—do a ticket/voucher/ticket swap and send Hildy Hyde, Ripperologist, to Paris.

Growing up the way I did, I had a weak spot for anyone in an extreme male/female ratio situation: female astronauts, hockey players, and now Jack the Ripper guides. Hildy was the Cyd Redondo of Ripperologists. I got refunds for Shep's train tickets, hotel deposit, and conference fees, then rebooked them all in Hildy's name. Maybe it would make up for the evidence that had disappeared with Shelagh.

Bruce jumped into my lap, trilled, and then keeled over in one of his narcoleptic states, into his "tail through the legs" position. He started to snuffle. There was a knock on the door. It might be Hazelnut. I didn't want to be accused of leading Bruce on, so I put him back in his Tupperware and shoved the bowl in my purse.

It was Roger. He had Shep's shoulder bag in one hand and a bottle of Jack Daniel's in the other.

Maybe it was because we'd been interrupted before, or maybe it was because we knew it might just be another in our string of one-night stands, but this time we were shy with each other.

I poured us glasses of whiskey while he explained that he'd been able to track my phone, and Shelagh, back to her apartment and grabbed these before they were taken in evidence. "And of course, Detective Blethly has your 'phone' already," he said, handing me my real phone. I was sure it was happy to be back, after hours in the vicinity of court shoes.

I opened Shep's shoulder bag, took out the two real pieces of evidence and put them in my purse, so I wouldn't forget to give them to Hildy.

We took our drinks into the bedroom. Shep's magic kit was still on the bed. Roger picked up the wand and shook it at me, then picked up the black silk disk underneath it. "What's this?"

I figured I'd surprise him with the collapsible top hat, so I channeled my inner Shirley MacLaine from *Sweet Charity* and hit it hard, three times, on my derriere. I heard it pop open, took a bow and put it on my head.

"Whoa!" Roger sat up.

"Pretty funny, right?"

"Something flew out."

"Of where?" Oh God, I thought, my ass?

"Of the hat." He pointed to something white on the floor by the bed. We walked over. It was a dead ringer for the handkerchief we'd faked in the museum—Jack the Ripper's handkerchief. The real one.

"We have it. We have proof!" I burst out laughing. So did Roger, and then we were kissing. Though we still laughed on and off for the next few hours, that wasn't all we did. Intermittently, I heard Bruce trilling. I guess he was jealous. And to be honest, he should have been.

Finally, happy and exhausted, we curled around each other and slept for a bit. I woke up just before dawn and got up to secure the handkerchief in a proper evidence bag. When I went to put it in my Balenciaga, I saw Bruce had knocked off the top of the Tupperware. For once, he was silent, but he had gotten his revenge—the doctor's report from the asylum lay underneath him in a pile of confetti. Oh Shep, I thought. Your legacy. I'm so sorry. I felt like crying, but it was hard to be mad at Bruce for very long.

I sat on the edge of the bed and looked down at Roger the way I had the first night we'd spent together in Atlantic City. Finally, he opened his eyes, grabbed my hand and kissed it. I told him what Bruce had done.

He kissed my hand again. "The truth is, no one really wants to know who Jack the Ripper was. It's too late to do anything about it, and it would take all the fun out of it for everyone. Some things should stay a mystery." He pulled me down beside him. "They're sending me to China. Today."

We held on to each other for a minute. Then I got up to check with the airline. Sadly, his plane was scheduled on time, but I did wrangle an upgrade to surprise him when he checked in.

I made espresso while he was getting dressed. "Where's Shep?"

"Detective Hubbard has sent his body back to the coroner's office. He's ready to be picked up by whatever funeral home you choose."

"Thanks, Roger."

"Are you going to see Hazelnut again?"

"I'm not seeing him. For heaven's sake. He just shows up."

"Well, if he shows up, tell him the Wildlife Crime Unit has frozen Nature Free's assets and halted the land sale. But someone else will try again. We sent the dormice from the breeding program to the Isle of Wight. Bruce would be better off there."

He kissed me goodbye. This time, he didn't ask me to come with him.

I couldn't have anyway. I had an appointment with the Queen.

Chapter Fifty-seven

We had a three-hour drive to catch up on our etiquette and practice our poker faces. I needed both when I saw Queen Elizabeth's private weekend getaway, which made Biltmore House—the biggest residence in America and a client favorite—look like a time-share.

We arrived wearing our fascinators. My clients were always deciding to go to Ascot, or some other hat-requiring occasion, at the last minute, so I had a relationship with Hasty Hat Hire, who helped us avoid the two-thousand-dollar price tag for what was, essentially, a headband. I convinced Aunt Helen not to choose the one with a swan on top, as her curtsy was going to be top-heavy enough. We definitely stood out, since everyone else at the event was wearing the royal equivalent of L.L.Bean.

The museum featured classic cars alongside a room with so many royal endangered animal trophy skins that Hazelnut would have had a coronary. Uncle Leon, however, pointed out what he thought was a particularly lifelike grouse.

And then, there was the unveiling. Despite the time pressure, my uncle had completely brought the family pet to life, his head cocked to the side, his tail high, his eyes bright. We could see the delight on the family's face.

The Queen, purse behind her back even in riding boots, held out her hand and Uncle Leon kissed it. "Anything for you, Bitsy," he said. Aunt Helen threw her palm over my mouth, cutting my guffaw off at the pass.

I waited until we were back in the car. "Bitsy?"

He just grinned. "Cyd, I have something very important to tell you and it would be a lot easier if you took that ridiculous produce bag off your head."

"With pleasure. What is it?"

"You can't take Shep's body home."

"What? That's the whole reason I'm here, to bring him home."

"He didn't want to go back. It's in his will."

"I don't understand."

"He wanted to be cremated. And have his ashes thrown in the Thames."

I should have let my uncle suffer, but I kissed him instead. He'd at least partially saved my ass. Cremation was far from free, but it would be twenty grand less than shipping Shep home.

Happily, I had the Cremation Certificate I needed and a recommendation from the world's best concierge, Kent from the Savoy, for a local mortuary with a quick turnaround. Kent also arranged for special access to the lower level of the Tower Bridge for the scattering of the ashes, since if we threw from the top, half of him might wind up in Southwark.

• • •

The next morning, Uncle Leon, Aunt Helen, Emma from the Natural History Museum, Hildy, Evelyn, Martin Thompson, Sir Rod, and I gathered to say goodbye to our friend.

Uncle Leon told the group about Shep's wife and how she'd been killed on their honeymoon. He said his old student had only been twenty and couldn't afford the repatriation fees either. He'd scattered his bride in the river, in sight of his beloved Tower Hill, so he could visit her every winter. Now he'd be with her always.

This evoked a strangled cry from Evelyn, her first of the day. Apparently Martin Thompson's brush with death had effected their reconciliation. He gave her his handkerchief. Maybe he wasn't all bad.

Sir Rod provided the absinthe and Dixie cups and, since I had forbidden any quotations from Shakespeare, Shaw, or *Inspector Morse*, we raised our glasses and merely cheered, "To Shep!"

Hildy was thrilled beyond words with her paid trip to Paris. I gave her all of Shep's research I had left, without explanation. She'd figure it out.

"Hand him over."

I turned to see Hazelnut, this time in a very sharp James Bond–level suit and a Wall Street haircut. I took out the Tupperware bowl and lifted the top. "Goodbye, Bruce. We'll always have the Savoy." I gave him one last stroke on the head. I'd given Hazelnut Roger's message and Bruce was headed for a nesting box in a dormouse preserve on the Isle of Wight.

"Claymore isn't good enough for you, AntiChristine," he said, before he disappeared.

• • •

The next morning, we were just about to board our plane to New York when Detective Blethly stopped us. What did he want?

"Ms. Redondo, I've been charged to give this to you in person." He handed me a box with a toy knife sticking out of it. "There's something inside. It's the reward offered by the Edwardian Order of the Ripper for information leading to the arrest of the killer."

"Holy crap," I said. "Are you kidding me?"

"No, you've earned it. Safe travels."

I looked in the box. It was a check for thirty grand. Redondo Travel lived. I tucked it in my Balenciaga.

I'm coming for you, Peggy fricking Newsome, I'm coming for you. I picked up my carry-on and followed Uncle Leon's skinny suit onto the plane.

About the Author

Wendall Thomas teaches in the Graduate Film School at UCLA, lectures internationally on screenwriting, and has worked as a film and television writer. Her first Cyd Redondo mystery, *Lost Luggage*, garnered Lefty and Macavity nominations for Best Debut, and *Drowned Under* was nominated for a Lefty for Best Humorous Mystery and an Anthony for Best Paperback Original. Her short fiction appears in *LAdies Night*, *Last Resort*, and *Murder A-Go-Go's*.